Bumping

to Ruth

Frank

1

Two minutes out of Newcastle, the train judders. I grab the hand-rail, I spread my feet, but it's no good. Yes, the train stops. But for one fateful moment, everything that is not the train continues its onward journey to York. Someone's tea, slopped over the floor of the buffet car, as they take it from the counter. I can't see it, of course I can't, not from where I'm standing, not from the toilet, but I know it's happening. A child's packet of crisps, too, held not quite tightly enough to prevent the unexpected accident, because they're not good at that, children: they're not good at protecting themselves against the unexpected. Yes, they too are on the floor, stared at, shortly to be cried over. And a score or more other mishaps, no doubt, for such is the nature of kinetic energy. What is there to do? And as for myself, well, I've pissed my trouser-leg.

Yes, indeed. What is there to do? The trousers are light grey, so the stain is obvious, a long, black, ragged streak from crotch to kneecap. I grab some toilet paper and try to wipe away the surface water from the material. This, however, serves only to spread the stain further. I think again. Perhaps it is raining in York. I don't mean to say I'm reflecting upon the weather per se. No, I'm thinking, perhaps there will be puddles, through which vans and lorries might splash, to furnish me with an alibi. I squint through the small segment of window which isn't frosted. But I know quite well that there has been no rain this morning and that, although it's mid-November, none is forecast. It is crisp and sunny. A fine day.

The train judders into motion again. I can, of course, simply zip up and go back to my seat, holding my jacket over the stain, and hope that it dries by the time we get to York. Visually, I've no doubt this is the best option. My accident will be beyond detection, at least to the naked eye. Alas, this is not enough. Because, although I am unaware of it at the moment, I know that the smell, that most treacherous of attributes, will endure. Worse, it will wax, even as the stain itself seems to wane. And to sit all day in close proximity to colleagues, watching out for every small sign of recoil, of avoidance, of disgust, would be unsustainable. The nose is so much more easily offended than the ear. And the merest twitch, the slightest wrinkling, would give the game away. Now if I were younger, a lot younger, a mere babe in arms, it would be different, natural even. Or older, of course. Yes, especially older. No less unpleasant, no, on the contrary, but to be expected. I am, however, neither young nor old. I am 49 years of age and should be in control of my bodily functions.

I have no alternative, therefore, but to tackle the problem at source. I am a careful and methodical person, not easily fazed by small adversities. In fact I pride myself in my ability to overcome even quite daunting challenges by breaking them down into manageable portions. And this is what I do. I draw down the toilet lid, sit on it, and carefully remove each shoe, all the while holding my stockinged feet well clear of the small pools of water dotted here and there across the floor. (These, I presume, are the residue of previous accidents.) I then take off my trousers. There is a crucial moment of instability when I must lift myself up and lean on one arm in order to draw the upper part of the trousers down over my backside but, with the aid of good fortune and a surge of adrenalin, I get through it without mishap. I put my shoes back on, to protect my socks, and then rinse the trouser leg, inch by inch, under the tap. I don't use soap as I feel that the meagre trickle of water available to me would be insufficient to wash it out afterwards. Replacing a urine stain with a soap stain would scarcely amount to success in an operation such as this.

After five minutes or so of rubbing and rinsing, rinsing and rubbing, I pull my trousers back on. The stain is bigger now, of course, and uncomfortably cold against my leg. But it is what you might call an innocent stain, a stain cleansed of malevolence. And my jacket, draped over my left fore-arm, covers it well enough. I return to my seat where, mercifully, the table provides more secure concealment. I busy myself. I check my diary, my watch, my mobile. I view the passing scenery, first on this side, then on that, with, I freely admit, a rather affected nonchalance. The trees are gloriously burnished in the late autumnal sun. I beam back at them, transported by their ineffable beauty. I study it all, as if to say to those around me, You see, I have the composure to consider such things, the leaves, their colour, the angle of light. Nothing else concerns me. Nothing. Yes, such a fine day.

And it is then, as Durham draws in to view, that I see him. He's sitting on the other side of the carriage and his face is partly silhouetted against the window. He leans forward to get a better view of the cathedral and for a moment I can look at him without fear of his catching my gaze. Well, well, I think, after all these years. He's put on weight, of course, but only a little: the neck is thicker, perhaps. The hair has greyed, too, and the features are more deeply lined, although this may in part be an effect of the light. But, all in all, it is still Fenwick, he's still there. I can see him in those busy eyes. In the way the mouth, slightly open, just showing the teeth, seems set always to break into speech. In the impatient fingers, tapping on the table. Eager. An eager boy, full of promise.

A few passengers get off, more get on. As the train pulls out of the station Fenwick sits back and I suddenly feel exposed. I shield my eyes, against the sun, against him. Presently a woman sits down opposite him, a stout woman in her fifties, out of breath. She's carrying two heavy Kwiksave bags, although it's not yet 8.30 in the morning. They exchange pleasantries, and I'm relieved at this, that he's occupied once more. I see now the slight tilt of his head, the raised eyebrows, the stratagems he employs, instinctively, no doubt, to tell his new companion, 'Your company is agreeable to me. I'm glad our paths have crossed.' And she responds, warmly. She's flattered, perhaps, and a bit embarrassed. She's a little too ready to laugh. I see no more than the back of her head, tightly bunned, bobbing from side to side as they chat about this and that, but I can imagine her blushes.

After everyone has settled down, I hear his voice clearly for the first time, a put-you-at-your-ease voice, confident of itself, and surprisingly sophisticated. Well modulated, I think they call it. That's something new, or something I don't remember. At least this is what I think, for a moment, before reminding myself that he is, of course, no longer a boy, that he cannot, therefore, have the voice of a boy. He's a doctor. Or a teacher. Or a loss adjuster. Or something, God knows what, but he's had thirty years to become it, whatever it is. And this thought, the thought of time passed, of unknown destinies, almost compels me, there and then, to get up from my seat, to walk to the other side of the carriage and say, in a breezy manner which would, of course, be a manner borrowed from himself, 'It's Fenwick, isn't it? Paul Fenwick…?' I inwardly rehearse the smile of recognition and surprise, the handshake

11

I would offer. 'Well, after all these years, Paul Fenwick.'

But this would be foolish. Because, although I am certain, in the instinctive part of me, that it is indeed Paul Fenwick who is sitting there, tapping his fingers on the table, my mind tells me that this may not be so, that my eyes may just as likely be deceiving me. Between the bright sunlight and my poor vision – even corrected by contact lenses, what they see is never more than an approximation of what is actually there – it is quite possible that I have made too much of a superficial resemblance. As we know only too well, since the advent of DNA identification and the like, the sworn testimonies of even the most insistent eye-witnesses are often found to be as insubstantial as fairy tales. Am I a reliable witness? I ask myself.

And then, of course, there's the stain. The impossibility of rising from my seat, of relinquishing the refuge of my table, of lunging forward to greet an old friend, an acquaintance at least, with its obscenity in full view. Yes, I know, I said it was now an innocent blemish, purified of all harm. But who else knows this? No, it is out of the question.

In any case, he hasn't seen me. Or at least, if he has seen me, he hasn't recognised me. And why should he? If I am not wholly sure of this man's identity, how much more reason has he to be uncertain of mine. I'm not saying I've worn especially badly. I've followed the path my genes have mapped out for me, that's all. Like my father before me, I was bald at thirty and by thirty-five my sluggish metabolism had rounded the belly and padded the jowls in such a particular way that, when I look in the mirror, I can say, with conviction, 'Hello, Dad.' My beard, which I've grown only in recent years, is my one badge of individuality although it, too, would make identification difficult under the present circumstances. And what would you say then, Fenwick, to the bearded stranger before you? How would you finesse that embarrassment? I dare not find out. That would be your way, not mine.

Yes, yes, it's come back to me now, the last time I saw you. Do you remember, Fenwick? At Jackie Milburn's funeral. Not at the funeral itself, of course, but the parade, or whatever they called it. Amongst the crowds in the Gallowgate, me on one side, you on the other, just as the hearse went by. Sixteen years ago that was. My God, sixteen years. Just think. But you turned down Stowell Street and I lost you. Perhaps you weren't there for the funeral, anyway. Indeed, I'm sure you weren't. Because, although you were certainly a social animal, you were not, I think, especially at home in crowds: that is, crowds properly understood, which are such impersonal entities. There was an older man with you, tall like yourself. A lot like you, in fact, except he had a pronounced limp. He could have been your father, your older brother, even. I did wave. And perhaps, Fenwick, you saw me but didn't realise that the wave was meant for you. In such a crowd, with so many people waving – at each other, at the cameras, at nothing in particular – you could be forgiven for that. In any case you'd disappeared into China Town before I could cross the road. A glancing recognition only. And that, too, may have been a case of mistaken identity. I remember it only because when I returned home, Jean – my wife – said that Mam had phoned. Dad had had a stroke. And before that? Well, before that, Fenwick, I'd not seen you since school.

But here you are again. Fenwick. How remarkable. How unexpected. But strange, too, and a little unnerving, the two of us thrown together like this, speeding off towards our different futures, two orbits touching for a brief second, only to be thrown apart again, off into the great beyond. And my mind is still adjusting itself to this apparition when it is brought to an abrupt and premature close. Yes, and I'm surprised that it is here you get off, here at Darlington, of all places. Surprised, and slightly disappointed. Now Darlington is a place I've passed through many times but have never, ever, had any reason to visit. In my ignorance, which I do not defend but simply state as a fact, I think it must be a failing, down-at-heel sort of town, like its football team. Like Hartlepool or Barrow or Workington in the old days. Childish associations, no doubt. I used to think West Bromwich exotic because it had an Albion. Stirling too. Perhaps even Burton, had I heard of Burton then.

And this, this residual association, may partly explain why, when you reach the platform, you look somehow reduced. You take on something of the drabness of the place, you become one of the crowd, a greying, middle-aged bank clerk or civil servant, and so small in this cavernous shed of a station. You set off without hesitation, as though this is a routine you are well used to. But perhaps not quite so briskly as I remember, because I can see now that you have certainly put on a few

13

pounds. And your body has a slight forward list. Perhaps it always did. But then, in youth, it signalled eagerness, it was the bearing of someone impatient to get things done. And now? Now, it has hardened into a stoop. So yes, I'm surprised. But at the same time I am also strangely and foolishly content.

2

I get back to Newcastle around eight and take the Metro downriver to Shields. Home is only a short walk from the station, in Lorraine Place. I whistle 'Cotton Tail' as I walk, because it's one of the Duke's best, and because I associate it with home. I like home. I like embarking from its harbour in the morning, I like returning to its sanctuary at evening. It's sweet. It's where the heart is. And although it's close to town, it's also tucked away. It's not town, but it's not suburb, either. An enclave, that's what I call it: a small, discrete enclave of Victorian houses which, though humble enough, are more spacious, more elegant, than the cramped terraces to south and west. (The bayed semis to the north were out of our price-range.) There is a small garden to the front so that the door, which has a pediment above it, does not open directly onto the street. Jean has hung baskets on either side, with fine trails of lobelia. Some of the houses, although not ours, have three stories. 'Come and see us in our little enclave.' That's what I say to our friends.

We bought No. 18 in 1990, when I first started working for Cowen Utilities, as it was then known. We had a bargain, by my reckoning. Being close to the town and the river kept the price down in those days. And Meadow Well too, of course. Meadow Well had just gone up in flames. 'You'll get the yobs over from the Ridges,' Dad used to growl. (He never called it Meadow Well.) But he'd been a policeman and was, for that reason, perhaps too preoccupied with such things. He'd have built a wall around the place, given half a chance. 'Broken glass on the top and no gate,' he'd bark. 'Keep the buggers in till they've learned how to behave.' But he was dead by then. Dead in his little bungalow in Whitley Bay, just two months before we moved in. Anyway, we're nowhere near the Ridges. Not really. So I still reckon we had a bargain. And if home is sweet, that makes it doubly sweet. Because we couldn't afford to buy such a place now.

Jean's out when I get back. She's left a note on the kitchen table. 'Gone to see Mam. Back soon. J.' I shout a hello to Veronica, our daughter, whose voice I now hear in the front room. There's no time on Jean's note so I don't know what 'soon' means. It's 9 o'clock, which strikes me as late already for her mother, who's in a home and retires early whether she wants to or not. But perhaps she's getting worked up again, like she does, when something knocks her off kilter. Molly. That's her mother's name. Although, for some reason, I can never bring myself to use it. Let alone 'Mam'. Dear God, no, not Mam. So I tend not to call her anything, at least not to her face. Jean's mother, that's who she is, but you can't call her that, can you? 'Hello, Jean's mother, and how are we today?' It wouldn't do. But the occasion seldom arises.

Jean's mother moved into The Quays last year. ('A home?' she'd said, incredulously. 'In Albert Edward Dock?') I'm sure she's content enough there, in so far as her infirmity will allow. Jean feels guilty, of course, being the devoted daughter that she is. Indeed, she would have moved her in with us if she'd had her way, if she'd succumbed to her first instincts. But I explained how impractical this would be and I'm glad to say that reason prevailed. She's as sharp as a razor, Jean's mother. She could go on for years.

I shout: 'When did your Mam go out, Vee?' but get no answer. I can still hear her voice, a little louder now, and for some reason I leave it at that. Steve, her fiancé, must be in there, although I can't hear him. Quietly spoken, Steve. You'd hardly know he was there. Fiancé. That's what Veronica calls him. This is my fiancé, she says. Sounds so old-fashioned. I suppose it must be making a comeback, the whole engagement business, weddings and the rest of it. Cash-cow for somebody, I suppose. But I wouldn't say it, of course. I wouldn't spoil their romance.

Am I selfish? Am I hard-hearted? 'We've got the room,' Jean said. And it was true, I can't deny it. When Christopher left, there was plenty of room. Too much room, you might say. 'She's not going to last forever, you know, Frank,' she said. And that's true, too, although,

15

at times, it's hard to believe. But all this is beside the point. Because, as I explained to Jean at the time, if her mother moved in, that wouldn't be the end of it. When the time comes – and it will come, quickly enough – my own mother will expect the same treatment, won't she? And after that, what of Hilda, her sister? Are we to become a full-time nursing home? And by then we'd both be just a dizzy spell away from dementia ourselves. Is that the life you want, Jean? 'You've let Steve live here,' she says. But we both know that's to help them save. The quicker they save, I say, the quicker they're out from under our feet. And in any case, he doesn't take up an extra bedroom. But as I say, I rarely see Jean's mother these days. I keep my head down.

I'm putting my supper together, still whistling 'Cotton Tail', because it's one of those pieces that stick in your mind, when I hear Vee's voice rising again. I would normally join them in the front room, to eat my sandwich, to share a Czech lager with Steve, or just to watch a bit of television. I get on well with Steve. He's an electrician, he's done his NVQs and served his apprenticeship, he's progressing well, as far as I can tell. And how could he fail? Just consider all the new houses, all the new flats, springing up around us, each requiring its full array of switches and sockets and circuits and junction boxes and ceiling roses and meters and so on. Reckons he'll have his own business soon. I wouldn't be surprised if he does.

So we get on, me and Steve. Which is odd, perhaps, given the difference in our ages, in our backgrounds. But what's oddest of all is that we share a taste for the same music. Or rather, I should say that our tastes overlap. I confess to deriving little pleasure from his other musical enthusiasms, in fact I don't even know how to describe them, being a bemused observer in the world of metal and acid and techno and God knows what other fads that are abroad these days. But he, I know, is equally puzzled by my partiality for tango. Carlos who? he asks. Astor Pia-what? But put on Howlin' Wolf or Muddy Waters or Sonny Boy Williamson or any of the old Chicago maestros and we are as one in our delight. What does it matter if we came to them by different routes? (I liked John Mayall, while Steve liked the Stones. The Stones were always too exhibitionist for my liking.) It matters nothing, because, you might say, we have both arrived home together, where it all began.

So we'd sit there, Steve and I, and perhaps we'd put on some classic collection, one of the Chess Boxes probably. (They're called Chess Boxes only because they were brought out by Chess Records in Chicago. They have nothing to do with chess.) And we'd chat about this and that, about the slide guitar in Elmore James's 'Dust My Broom', perhaps, or about how much we'd get for one of my old shellacs. (Steve has a goodish range of vinyls, but he can't get close to my 78 collection.) And there's a special pleasure to be had simply in holding those old records, in contemplating the picture of the black swan on the Black Swan label, the bluebird on the Bluebird label. Yes, even in wondering why they didn't bother to put a bird on the Grey Gull label.

That's what we might do, of an evening. Just Steve and me. Every now and again. Except that Vee's there now. So it would be different tonight. Tonight, we'd talk about the engagement party, no doubt, if we were to talk about anything. But, somehow, I don't think we will. I don't think we're going to talk at all, tonight, because something's wrong. Vee's asking, Why? Why? over and over again. Not loud now, just exasperated and, I think, a little tearful. And although I can't hear Steve's response, in fact because I can't hear his response, it's clear that this is more serious than usual. I get a beer from the fridge and I consider for a moment asking Steve if he fancies one, of going in there and breaking the ice. I stand, bottle in hand, weighing up the options.

If Jean were here, she'd mediate. That would be her style, that's what she's good at, and I love her for it. Yes, I do, and quite thoroughly so, in the way you come to love someone after twenty-five years of marriage, if you're lucky, if you get that far. And perhaps it's no exaggeration to say that it is this, this aptitude for mediation – for want of a less clinical phrase – that keeps us together. All of us. If you can't tell your brother, tell me, she'd say. If you can't tell your dad, tell me. If you can't tell Steve, tell me. And she'd sort it out.

Yes, that's her way. But, for good or ill, it's not mine, and I can't pretend that it is. So I sit down, by the kitchen table, to eat my sandwich, to drink my beer, to flick though my papers from York. I read and re-read the title on the top sheet. Utilities and the Law: guidelines relating to compulsory wayleaves and compensation. And I hope that Jean will come back soon. So that Steve and Veronica can be reconciled. So that I can tell her about Fenwick.

17

3

'I hate you,' he'd said.

I wake up at five, thinking of Fenwick, seeing him sitting there, on the paved terrace. I hear Jean's breathing from the other bed. She's a light sleeper, while I'm quite restless and prone to insomnia, so this is how we sleep, this is how it works for us. I would normally get up now, just to clear my head for a few minutes, to have a glass of water and try to chase away these distracting thoughts, but I'm anxious I'll disturb her. She had a hard night of it. She waited over an hour for a taxi to bring her home from The Quays and it still didn't turn up. So she rang home and I went and fetched her. It's only a two minute run in the car but you wouldn't want to walk that way, not on a Friday night. And then she'd had a session with Veronica. (Steve had gone out for a drink with his mates by the time we got back home.) Money problems, apparently. Which is no surprise. Who'd be young, these days?

So I close my eyes again.

'I hate you,' he'd said.

And I'm walking along the paved terrace again. On my right is the old part of the school, a single storey building constructed of some rough grey stone which skins the knuckles when you rub against it. Below me, on the left, is the school yard. Here, boys are playing football, not in regulation fives and elevens, of course, but in their beetling hundreds. Their games are at once both mutually exclusive and infinitely overlapping. It is no miracle of synchronisation, however: there are frequent collisions. It is, it was, it must have been a scene of deafening tumult. But I'm unable to recreate the noise in my mind's ear. I can see it all, but the memory is a poor keeper of sound.

I am also too big. Everyone on the terrace is smaller than me, as though I have walked onto a toy stage and have to crouch down to see things clearly. Even to see Fenwick, I must make myself smaller. But I know that if I'm walking on this terrace and he is sitting there, on one of the green wooden benches reserved for sixth formers, then I must, in reality, be small indeed, because he is five years older than me, because he'll have left school by the end of the summer term.

'I hate you,' he'd said, as I passed him.

But it's no good. My eyes dilate to swallow it all. I see too much. At twelve years of age I saw only through a pin-hole. If I am to become the right size, I must look at myself from the outside, I must choose a different camera angle. So this is what I do. I leave the terrace and descend to the school yard so that I can then look up at myself, set myself in context.

I take the vantage point of someone who's just scored a goal, threading the small plastic ball through the mêlée, striking it home between the two khaki haversacks which have been set down against the boundary wall for that purpose. The goal-scorer, whose eyes I'm borrowing, throws up his arms in jubilation and as he does so he catches sight of me, yes, it's me he notices first, above him on the terrace, at the top of the shallow grass bank, because he's surprised at the sudden change of expression on my face and he's wondering, What can possibly have done that? But he's too far to hear, especially in the middle of such a din. Such a din, Mam used to say. Do you have to create such a din, Francis? So he doesn't hear. And by then he's lost interest, of course he has. So he doesn't even notice Fenwick. No, it doesn't occur to him, in the brief moment he turns up his head in exultation, that Fenwick has anything to do with this event.

So I must recast the scene once more, shoot it from a more revealing position, secure mikes in strategic places, be bolder. I shall sit on the bench, next to Fenwick, even though this is not allowed, even though only those with black blazers may sit here. Here I am, then, sitting by him, because someone must be sitting here, he would not sit here by himself, surely, that is not his style. So I sit here, on my hands, kicking my feet, fingering the peeling paint under the seat, finding hardened chewing gum there. No, I shall miss nothing this time.

At this point it's possible that pink-cheeked, black-soutaned Father Dempsey ambles by, hands folded behind his back. No, not the hands, just the first two fingers. He is close enough for me to count the buttons, from top to bottom, all thirty-three of them. (The Jesuits, as you would expect, have hooks at the fly, not buttons. But this is not a Jesuit school. We see Jesuits only when we're on retreat.) Yes, it's without doubt Father Dempsey, gentle, beaming, full of grace, because otherwise I don't think Fenwick would dare, he just wouldn't risk it. Not if it were the Canon on patrol, for example, because the Canon has eyes and ears everywhere, he is the hawk man. So he walks by, Father Dempsey, and Fenwick relaxes. Yes, he's ready to chat with his young friend, with me, with whoever this is sat next to him, his ears cocked. And I'm listening, thinking, Go on, Fenwick. You can speak now. You must speak now. But what does he talk about? About girls? About football? About exams? About God? About what? What could possibly lead to this?

'I hate you,' he'd said.

And what could possibly follow it?

But there's no before, no after. Because I look at him and his face is blank, his own kind of blank, the lips slightly parted, so I can just see the teeth, as though he is ready to smile, as though the words have spoken themselves.

4

'This is your line, Frank, is it?'

Bill spreads the map out on the table and traces his finger along the blue line that runs from the site of the old antominy works by the river to the south-west corner of the retail park at Low Moor Farm, a distance of 1.6 kilometres. The line has two acute dog-legs, and a number of smaller kinks, where the original layers of the cable needed to evade old mine workings or awkward geological features, or where, perhaps, they merely failed to secure permissions and lacked the statutory powers to press ahead regardless. The map shows none of this. It shows only lines - blue, red, orange and green lines - a little like the London Underground map, except, of course, that these lines are precise, are real. The blue line is mine: the electricity line.

Yes, Bill, it is. My line.

'And here…? It's here we're having the site meeting tomorrow. Yes?'

Bill has drawn out another map of the same area. It is more recent than mine and, instead of lines, is divided into segments. These vary greatly in shape and size: some are as small as my finger nail; one, which resembles in outline a Wellington boot with a very pronounced instep (at Bewicke Dock) straddles almost the entire sheet. Taken together, the segments mark out the area of the proposed Hadrian Regeneration Initiative; individually, they show current ownership. Since 1998, the owner of the boot-shaped zone has been Lenco Holdings Ltd. Lenco Holdings Ltd is our client. In partnership with a well-known construction company, they intend building two hundred and sixty houses on this site and a medium-scale leisure and retail complex.

Yes, Bill. The site meeting. At Brewers' Bank.

'And the main issues so far…? What would you say, Frank…?'

Bill Pike is our Project Director and has worked for us here at Pierce Constant Solutions (formerly Cowen Utilities Ltd) for a little over a year, since we moved out to the new TecPark just north of Newcastle. He is my line manager and is amply qualified to be so, I'm sure. (His card says that he is a member of the Royal Institution of Chartered Surveyors.) However, given his recent arrival here, his youth and his ignorance of both the power industries and the area (he hails from Hartley Wintney in Hampshire), Bill is generally willing to defer to my depth of experience. I don't think I'm being immodest when I say that, amongst our staff generally – the majority of them, inevitably by now, younger than myself – I am known for my reliability, for my thoroughness, for having a safe pair of hands.

The main issues? I've listed these in the client file, Bill. You must know this. I emailed them to you last week. And I'm thinking, it's all well and good that you defer to my experience, perhaps even that you take me somewhat for granted at times, but surely this is not too much to expect, that you read my emails? Although I didn't call them issues, of course. This is your word, Bill. It's one of those weasely words people use these days. He has issues, they say, meaning he's barking, he's alcoholic, he's going to slit your throat. Do we have issues? Does Pierce Constant Solutions have issues?

Lenco has engaged Pierce Constant Solutions to manage wayleave matters on its Brewers' Bank site. The contract involves a wide range of entirely routine tasks, tasks too numerous and, I've no doubt, for the layman, too tedious to describe. Suffice it to say that much of my time is spent in negotiations with the utility companies about permissions (for pylons, poles, cables and the like) which have been inherited from the previous owners. No, there are no issues there, Bill. But no less important for all that, I'm sure you'll agree.

The contract also entails securing new wayleaves from owners of adjacent land, so that we can route a number of new lines, including fibre optic cables. This can be a more delicate business, for which skills of diplomacy and bargaining are essential prerequisites, skills which I believe I have acquired in some fair measure, over the years. For example, I am currently seeking compensation towards the cost of diverting a cluster of high voltage cables buried under one corner of the site. I am also busy establishing ways of evading an overhead substation in another corner. These are matters of complexity, it is true, but they are jobs to be done, and will be done, in time.

So I tell him this. These are the issues, Bill, as you call them. And there are others, many others. They are all listed in the file, the file I sent you last week.

'Can you explain this, Frank?'

And I know, from the tone of his voice, from the way he puts a quite unnecessary stress on the word 'this', that he is calling me to account.

It's the leisure park, I tell him. Which is what it says, under his finger. Lenco Leisure Park.

And I want to ask him, does he know that my schedule for this job precedes his arrival here by two years? Does he realise that some wayleaves take a decade or more to clear? That I've had to coordinate load assessments for the whole site and get civil engineers in to cost the rerouting of lines? That I've even had to bring the archaeologists on board, for God's sake, the archaeologists, just in case we disturb the Romans in their graves?

'All of it?' he says. 'It's all the Leisure Park?'

'All of it,' I say. 'Just as it says in the file.'

And if I sound a little impatient in my response, a little abrupt, and return to my desk rather pointedly, and start busying myself with other things, who can blame me?

5

It's half past nine before the band starts playing. I've been here since eight because Mam (that is, my mother, not Jean's) was anxious not to be late and anyway didn't intend staying long, what with the nights drawing in and all the trouble 'down that way', as she puts it. Veronica would have preferred a club in Newcastle, I've no doubt. She said one of her friends had her hen party in Prague. Good for her, I said. I'm forking out enough for this one as it is. But the Clipper's fine, good ale in fact, a CAMRA winner, and a nice piece of refurbishment. (It used to be a chandlers.) Not what you'd call cool, perhaps. Not what Vee would call cool. I don't think you can have cool with pictures of sailing ships on the walls and so much dark mahogany.

'Can't manage Newcastle these days, pet,' her Gran had said.

So that's how we ended up here. Yes, Vee's doing it for her Gran, she's chosen the Clipper so that her Gran can join in the family celebrations, and I think, isn't that nice? Doesn't that show that we've got something right between us, between Jean and me? To have such a considerate daughter? That, and the price, of course. You get better value here than in town and, as I say, I'm forking out quite enough even for this one, thank you very much.

I picked Mam up from Whitley Bay on my way home from work, so she could come over and see Veronica first, at our place, and 'pop a little note in her hand', as she put it. 'I'll not be stopping there long, Veronica,' she said, in that gloomy way she has. 'Just to drink your health.' And as an afterthought: 'The both of you.' Which perhaps would have been better left unsaid, because it poses the question then, doesn't it? And she wrapped Vee's hand around a twenty pound note.

'You remember Fenwick, Mam?' I asked her on the way over. Because of course Jean hadn't a clue. How would she? 'Yes,' she said, to my amazement. 'Of course I do. Stephen Fenwick. Little lad. He'd come to the house…' And in a way this was impressive. Indeed, I was quite moved that my mother should be able to recall one of my childhood playmates with such clarity. And it got me thinking how many of Veronica's school friends I could remember, or, indeed, Christopher's. With dismal results, I'm afraid. I comfort myself with the thought that perhaps this kind of memory comes with age. But it was Stephen Fishwick, of course, that my mother had in mind. She had no idea who Paul Fenwick was. 'Something to do with the shop, was he?'

And here she is, turned half past nine, out on the dance floor with Jean and her sister, Sally. Veronica's Aunt Sally – yes, the name has always brought a smile to my face – has come over from Prudhoe and will spend the night with us. And there's Des, too, the old chap from next door, showing off his new hip. And his wife Peg, and Steve's mam and dad, and one or two others I don't recognise, Steve's side probably. 'Two sherries and you're anyone's, Mam,' I joke. She doesn't hear.

The band is loud, but old-fashioned loud. You can still hear the tune, the riffs, and now and again some of the words, but we know them all, me and Steve. We know the words and we like their style. The lead guitarist, a short fist of a man with a grey crew-cut and a red face, stands rigid, feet wide apart, only the hands moving, and the head, punching out the beat. His posture makes him look smaller still, but this is the way he's done it for thirty years, and this is the only way he can do it. He wraps himself around his Fender as though it's gutting him, as though it might spin off into orbit if he doesn't pull it down, pull it down and keep it down. They're playing Chuck Berry. 'Johnny B. Goode'.

'Gone up with Voyager One,' says Steve, pointing to the ceiling.

'That right?' I say.

Steve's sitting next to me, so that I must look up when I speak to him because, for some reason, his small advantage in height seems accentuated when he is sitting down. And it occurs to me that we must make an odd-looking couple, me as I am, in the green jacket and tie which I wear at events like this, Steve as he is, pony-tailed, in his black silk shirt. But both of us brushed up for the occasion, yes, both quite presentable.

Then Vee comes over. To be honest, I don't see her for who she is right away. Her hair's pulled back from her face, clipped or tied somehow, and this seems to smooth out her features. Odd. Perhaps it's just an effect of the light. There's a bright spotlight which, from where I'm sitting, shines directly behind her head, haloing her, so that I need to shield my eyes as she approaches. She says something but I miss it. I cup my ear. She places her hand on my shoulder and bends down.

'Feel at home, Dad?' she asks.

'Good pint of Deuchars.' I raise my glass. 'Good blast of Chuck Berry.' I nod towards the band. 'It doesn't get better than this, Vee.'

And I hope I sound sincere, despite the cliché, but just in case, I put my hand on her arm.

'Glad you're both... you know... OK.'

I look to Steve for corroboration but he's downing his pint. Veronica makes her way back to her friends, unsteadily, because she's wearing stilettos, which is surely very unwise when dancing. And perhaps she's already had more to drink than she can really handle. I shall need to keep an eye on her. Except, of course, that it's Steve should be looking out for her tonight, it's his responsibility now. Yes. And I wonder why they aren't dancing together. I wonder why Steve's sitting here with me and not with Vee.

I ask him: 'You OK, Steve?'

'Aye, canny.'

'You and Vee not dancing?'

'Aye, mebbes, in a bit.'

But softly softly, I think. Leave it there for the moment.

'Might go and have a bit of a hop myself,' I say. 'With Jean. In a minute.'

'No problem,' he says.

But for the time being I sit there, watching. Mam is scarcely moving. She shuffles from foot to foot, her hands held slightly in front of her as though she's carrying an invisible tray. Her face is largely in shadow. 'Got to keep my hat on,' she'd said. 'For the glare... Else I'll get a migraine.' The hat is one of those glossy raffia affairs, blue with a large, turned up brim. She could be in church. She could be shuffling about in some happy-clappy church.

'What you think, Frank?'

Steve nods towards the band.

'Grand,' I say. 'Old fella deserves a distinguished service medal.'

Vee is now on the other side of the room with some of her workmates. One of them, a thick-set, red-headed girl with high heels and a short, tight skirt, is drawing on an inhaler. I'm surprised to see her do this every couple of minutes, without interrupting her dancing. Vee's laughing. That's where her party is, over there.

'Might as well… you know… while the band's still on,' I say. Steve nods.

'Pint?' he asks.

'Can't,' I say. 'Taxi duty.' I point towards Mam.

And I go out and dance. 'Make way for the main man,' I joke, and position myself between Jean and Mam. I sway gently from side to side. It's difficult, dancing with Mam. Do too much and you're saying, Look at me, bet you can't do this. Shuffle, and you're taking the piss. The music stops. Everyone claps.

'Say when you're ready to go, Mam.'

'Go?' she says, in that high little voice she lapses into when she's been drinking. 'Go? I'm just getting into the mood.'

So I sit down again and accept Steve's offer. Because we can always get a cab, if need be. Yes, Deuchars, please, Steve. Nothing but the best. And, of course, if that's the case, I needn't stop at a pint, need I? Because this is pleasant enough, keeping Steve company, talking about the band, about whether we prefer Dylan's 'Tambourine Man' to The Byrds', which they're playing now. Disputing whether the keyboard, let alone the keyboard player, is really up to 'Light My Fire'. Ha! But brave, yes, very brave. You can't fault them there. And I'm afraid we're already trespassing beyond my area of secure knowledge. Yes, where are we, 1966, 1967? And already well beyond my time. You sad git, Frank, he says. You sad git. And we laugh. And I ask him, I ask Steve, doesn't he think this mahogany's just stained pine, after all?

6

I've arranged to take the morning off and go straight to Brewers' Bank. I saw little point driving out to the office only to have to come back down river by two. In any case, I was glad of the lie-in. I have a headache. It scarcely merits being called a hangover, not after three pints, but I fear

I have something of a constitutional intolerance for alcohol. So that's how it manifests itself. A headache. And it seems a disproportionate penance to have to pay for such moderation.

But this is beside the point. I was glad of the lie-in because I couldn't sleep. Jean was up until God knows when last night, talking with Sally, whose husband has had a bad diagnosis. 'He's younger than me, Frank. He's younger than both of us.' I should sympathise, I know, and yet I have to admit to some irritation at this intrusion. No, not at her husband's predicament per se, of course not, but rather at their conversation. Because, hushed though it was, their talking nevertheless rose just sufficiently above the threshold of audibility, in the bedroom above, to make sleep impossible. Yes, it's unfair, I know it is. But there's something about hushed conversations, like the sound of mice behind the skirting board: they just can't be ignored. And the pent-up irritation kept me awake, even after Jean came to bed, even though the beer had made me sleepy enough, you'd think. Naturally I said nothing, not under the circumstances. Sally had already left by the time I got up, things at home being as they are. And that was a relief: it would have been unseemly to burden her with my ill temper.

But perhaps there's something there still, gnawing away inside me as I walk to the Metro, because, just before I turn the corner at the end of Russell Street, I almost collide with a cyclist. Maybe I'm just distracted – by the other pedestrians, by tiredness, by thinking about what Jean and Sally had been talking about last night. In any case, I hear the bike coming behind me, right in the middle of the pavement. I hear it clanking. It's got something loose, a mudguard, or a dodgy pedal crank. In fact, I half turn and prepare to get out of the way. And I almost do so, I am fully primed to step to one side, as I have done before, as people generally do, not wanting to make a fuss. But something stops me. I'm not sure I can give it a name, that something, but it's unusually powerful. I'm tempted to call it the 'Why should I?' instinct. Because I know I'm in the right. That's it. I'm in the right, and if those in the right give these anti-social yobs an inch they'll take a mile. Something along those lines. Although, as I say, I suspect, too, that this righteousness, whilst quite justified in its own terms, is also fed by some residue of last night's irritation. Be that as it may, at the last moment, and with a reckless disregard for my own safety, I step back into the cyclist's path. He brakes. (I assume it's a he, but the cyclist is wearing a hooded top and I can't be sure.) But the brakes clearly don't work too well, so he has to steer the bike suddenly sideways, making an emergency stop with his left foot. The front wheel turns too acutely. He comes off the saddle and staggers to a fall, hands still grasping the handlebars. He shouts some obscenity which I don't quite make out. Serves him right, I think. Won't do that again in a hurry.

I see the event in a split second, in a single frame. A brief, innocent, sideways glance is all that's needed, as I turn the corner into Nile Street, to capture the entire scene. And yet, as far as the world knows, I am in no way implicated in the matter. I am minding my own business. I do, however, through this snatched glance, see enough to be sure that the cyclist is not hurt. Bruised, probably, indignant, certainly, but not really hurt. In fact, it's possible I let my gaze, brief as it is, linger just a little too long, it's possible the boy (a young boy, I think: his voice is quite shrill) just catches my eye. That he sees concern in it. And yet this seems strangely fitting. He knows I've foiled him. He knows I'm the reason he's had his comeuppance. And he knows at the same time that I'm not indifferent to his welfare: and it's true, I'm not, nor do I take this to be a sign of weakness. And somehow this balances things out again, my passive resistance against his transgression, my solicitude against his profanity.

And as I turn the corner, it is by a happy coincidence that I come face-to-face with an elderly lady in a green hat, pushing one of those wheely walkers that double up as shopping trolleys. I stand back on the kerb so that she can pass, without having to divert her route. Of course I do. This is what one does. She smiles, and nods me a thank-you. So that, by the time I enter the station forecourt, I have regained my composure and feel in quite fine fettle again.

Brewers' Bank is only two stops and a short walk away. As I approach the site, a warm douche of nostalgia raises my spirits further. I'm surprised I didn't notice it at the first visit. It's on the side wall of a 1960s semi: the last in a row of similar houses squeezed between the riverside terraces and the old warehouse enclosure. It's unmistakable: a Rediffusion junction box, type JB166, of the once ubiquitous kind which I spent no small part of my early career installing and maintaining. Someone has scrawled ZIL over one corner – why, I have no idea – but otherwise it seems undamaged. This is surprising. The house itself is empty and there are the after-shadows of fire above the boarded-up windows at the back. Broken glass lies scattered widely over the ground, big jagged wedges of it, as though they've been throwing bottles against the wall. But the junction box is intact. Pehaps no-one knew how to break the seal. I crunch my way back over the gravel to the front of the house and make sure the coast is clear.

My watch says I still have ten minutes before we are due to rendezvous, so I take out my house keys and with some effort (I'd have used pliers in the old days) I turn the catch 90 degrees and ease the lid open. (This is heavy and opens at the top so that care is needed to avoid dropping it on my foot.) There are no surprises. The cable which originally led to the selection switch in the house has been clipped and bent back and the circuit board is covered in brick dust and cobwebs. Nevertheless, it is immensely satisfying to see this board again. The whole assembly is hand-made, each capacitor, resistor and inductor a splendid little piece of engineering, potted neatly in epoxy. Unfortunately, the plywood base has rotted through at one end. But then, the whole junction box has run its course, its brief life-span is quite spent. I sigh inwardly as I re-close the door.

No sooner have I resumed my position at the gate than Lenco's project manager reverses his silver Skoda onto the gravel. I wave exaggeratedly with both hands to divert him away from the broken glass. He winds down his window.

'You got an easement to do that, Frank?'

I've known Gavin since the beginning of the project and we're on good leg-pulling terms. Wayleave officers are used to such ribaldry at their own expense, yes, even to a degree of ridicule. I confess I have no idea why this should be the case. 'Best wellies today then, Frank?'

And perhaps he has a point. In our standard livery of suit, tie and wellington boots we do, it's true, make easy targets.

'Not sure about the hat, though.'

Yes, and the hat. A Christmas present to myself, a necessary measure to protect my balding pate from the chill easterlies. And the ears. Yes, to protect the ears as well.

'What's that, Gavin? What did you say, Gavin?' I quip, as I lift up the padded ear flaps.

Gavin hauls his bulk out of the car. He's wearing what seems to be full hiking gear: bright red anorak, baggy beige trousers and climbing boots.

'Which is it today, Gavin?' I ask him. 'Ben Nevis or the Cairngorms?'

Gavin's a Scot. He's the client and he's a builder, so he wears what he likes. We shake hands. I think of him as a big cuddly bear.

'This is Sanje.'

Gavin's companion is the Lenco surveyor.

'Hello, Sanje,' I say. 'Welcome to Hadrian's Fields. Or is it Brewers' Meadows this week? Eh, Gavin?'

'Hi,' says Sanje.

I can't help staring at his highly polished shoes.

'The wellies are in the boot,' he says. I chuckle acknowledgement. 'I know the place well,' he says, tapping the side of his nose with his index finger. Which is true, I suppose: he must have spent much of the last six months or so measuring up, doing the ground assessments, checking for toxic waste, what surveyors do.

Gavin and I have a catch-up conversation. He talks about Celtic's progress in Europe. I bemoan my own team's dismal performances under its new manager. We both gripe about the slowness of the planning department. When Bill's Porsche appears, ten minutes late, we are both in a state of bubbling mirth as Gavin tells the tale of a flat in Hebburn built, he claims, with the back door leading straight into the bathroom. 'Not my company,' he says. 'Ha!'

Bill apologises for his late arrival. I say, don't worry, we've been having a good crack, and I take it upon myself to introduce him to Sanje. I wonder whether to ask him if he's had trouble finding his way here but think better of it. It's sufficient that he sees the three of us together, talking, laughing, getting on, and is contrite. Gavin and I carry on constructing droll scenarios for the Hebburn cock-up.

We have about a month left before completion of the Brewers' Bank contract, that is, before our solicitors confirm the easements and other permissions. Not a trench has yet been dug, nor a brick laid, but these are not the concern of Pierce Constant Solutions. The purpose of today's site visit is to ensure that the deskwork and the mapping (which will accompany the solicitors' documentation) accurately reflect the situation on the ground, and in particular that the access routes for the cables are clear and cannot, by whatever oversight or unforeseen obstacle, impinge on adjacent properties which have not already assented to wayleaves. The task is straightforward enough, given thorough preparation and unstinting attention to detail, but it is by no means a formality.

We enter the southern end of the site through a high steel gate, a relic of this section's previous incarnation as an assemblage of warehouses, vehicle sheds and the like. Both the gate and the fence that extends from it in both directions are now redundant. The mesh has been breeched every fifty yards or so while the top end of the site, where it meets Low Moor Farm, is entirely open. And in any case, there's nothing left for them to protect: only a few small, abandoned sheds remain, the others having been demolished so that the youth of the parish are not tempted to break their necks. From here, I can see three cars of indeterminate identity which, I presume, have been driven through one or other of the gaps and left to rust on the concrete. But we still go through the ritual. Gavin has the key.

The tour takes almost three hours. Aware that his biggest construction project to date is about to take wing, Gavin is in ebullient mood. His view of the site is different from mine, of course: where I see power lines and access routes, he has a vision of houses, streets, pavements, kerbs, drains and the other detailings of human habitation. I must say, I find his enthusiasm infectious. It is uplifting, every so often, to realise that one has a part to play in the grander design of things. Bill and Sanje walk behind us, clearly engrossed in their mundane surveying preoccupations. We spend some time at the north-east corner, where the site abuts on the trading estate. This muddy patch, designated for the leisure centre, has required more complex negotiation because of live lines and wayleaves inherited from previous owners. But we are just ticking off today. The paperwork has all been done.

As we trace the perimeter back to our starting point we are followed, on the other side of the fence, by a knot of children of perhaps ten or eleven years of age. I try to ignore them, as I find encounters with groups of this kind invariably troublesome. But they are clearly intent on including us in their day's schedule of mischief.

'Ow, mister!' one shouts. 'You're not allowed in there.' And Gavin, who is in some ways no more than a child himself, responds in kind. 'Yes I am!' he shouts manically. 'It's mine. All mine!' He spreads his arms wide and looks about him, like a highland laird, you might say, surveying his estate. The children stare at him, open-mouthed, then look back at me.

'Ow, mister. Is he a nutter?'

And I surprise myself, I really do, by entering into the spirit of things. I don't know what comes over me but I feel quite light, elated even. And I shout back, with unforced gusto. 'He is!' I say. 'And we've just recaptured him.' And I laugh. We all laugh. Yes, even the children – they laugh too.

The site meeting breaks up around a quarter to four. The bright, horizontal light sends our shadows far across the concrete and the mud. Now, even the broken bricks and burnt-out cars and abandoned sheds seem cleanly cut, content to bare their fractures and fissures before the setting sun. Yes, even the tiny pieces of glass, the myriad fragments of smashed bottles and windscreens, even these catch the sun's fire, become shimmering diamonds. And I too am content. It's been a good day.

7

When possible, Jean and I do our weekly shopping together on a Monday evening, immediately after I finish work. It's quiet then and Jean will normally not be on duty until eight. If she's working the afternoon shift, there's little option but to battle it out with the weekend crowds. I might, otherwise, go by myself, but I rarely do. Together's better. This is our passeggiatta, you might say, our little Corpus Christi procession, if you'll forgive the sacrilegious overtones (I do mean it quite reverentially): a little pilgrimage in search of our daily bread. And our store, which is only a short drive away in Norham Road, is a thoroughly congenial place for this ritual. Indeed, it was recently named National Store of the Week by *The Grocer*.

I don't think I would have seen him on any other day, the busy days. Even on a Monday, it's possible I'd have missed him, the store being so big. Perhaps I've already missed him several times, over the weeks, the months: a thought which, as I reflect upon it now, causes me acute misgivings for which I cannot properly account. And in truth, I didn't notice him today until we were almost upon him. He was standing next to the dairy produce, pondering cheeses, whilst we made our way up the aisle in the direction of the breakfast cereals. In his casual clothes – a roll-neck black jumper, black leather jacket and jeans – he looked younger than on the train. The stoop was no longer evident. It was, no doubt, how shall I say, merely disguised by the posture one must adopt whilst pushing a trolley. But the effect was the same. His hair was longer, too. I recall it being quite closely cropped before, whereas now it curled over his collar, around his ears. Indeed, the impression he gave was no longer that of a businessman or a doctor at all, but of a much more bohemian type, not an artist, perhaps, more like a college lecturer.

Yes, I was surprised to see Fenwick there, at his leisure, in my home store. But no, surprised is too tame a word adequately to describe my response. I was affronted. And I use the word advisedly, without exaggeration. In fact, had I gone to the bathroom this morning and found Bill Pike doing his ablutions there I should scarcely have felt more put out. I showed nothing of this to Jean, of course, at least not deliberately. I could scarcely articulate these feelings to myself: how should I begin to justify them to my wife? I suspect, however, that I gripped the bar of my trolley a little more tightly and I certainly quickened my pace, because Jean asked, 'What's the hurry?' at which I smiled, not wishing to betray myself. And that is what I should certainly have done, had I spoken. In fact, I could feel an incipient tremble there, on the tongue, preparing itself to trip over the words, each one, as they emerged from my throat.

But the trolley. Yes, worst of all, he had a trolley. As though he were mimicking me, as though he were making fun of our domestic routine, our little ritual. And if this seems a fanciful conceit, I assure you that that is how I felt. Who had invited this man? Who had given him leave to use our store, on our shopping day, at our shopping hour? But that is not the point. No, the point is this. A casual shopper, passing through, in transit, seeking provisions only for the day, for the moment, will choose a basket over a trolley. The trolley is the vehicle of the strategic shopper, of the resident. That is the point. Fenwick had a trolley. Fenwick was living in our midst.

But Fenwick, by now, had disappeared from view. And as we walked around the store, moving from the tinned produce to the packets to the fresh fruit and veg, then the drinks, and finishing, naturally, with the frozen goods, I reflected that we were, in all probability, pursuing a course identical to that of Fenwick himself – for this is the logical way, in our store – and that we were therefore unlikely to encounter him again. My hypothesis proved correct. We had no further sighting of Fenwick until the check-out. By that point he was well ahead of us, laying his purchases on the conveyor belt as we joined the end of our queue.

From this vantage point, I became preoccupied, strangely enough, less with Fenwick than with the contents of his trolley. I tried to discern, for example, whether he was buying family sizes, or cooking only for one. Whether his tastes were sophisticated or plebeian. But the evidence was inconclusive. And there were puzzles, too. The single bottle of Coke, for example. What was I to make of that? Did it suggest not only that Fenwick was settled amongst us but that he was also a father? No, a grandfather, surely. Although that in itself, of course, presupposes fatherhood, children, the whole gallimaufry of family life. Yes, the Coke clinched it: there were three generations out there, and he, Paul, was their pater familias. I shivered.

'Seen somebody you know, Frank?' Jean asked.

'Don't think so,' I said. 'Just looks like somebody... somebody who couldn't be here.'

When we get back home, a little later than usual, Veronica is sitting by herself in the front room.

'Nothing on telly?' I ask. She shakes her head.

'You've been crying, Veronica,' says Jean. Not because Vee looks up, but because she fails to do so, because she merely stares at her hands. Jean is quick to read such signals. And I'm surprised by her lack of surprise. 'Where's Steve?' she asks, curtly and, I think, with a slightly accusatory edge to her voice. I'm perplexed. 'Will somebody please tell me what's going on?' I ask the question firmly, but without rancour, because I don't want to make matters worse.

'It's Steve you've got to talk to, Dad,' says Veronica.

And as she gets up, I see a letter lying on the coffee table. By the time I have retrieved my reading glasses, Veronica has put on her coat because, she says, she's going to see Keira. 'Keira?' I ask. 'At the party,' she says. 'Red hair.' 'Ah,' I say, not remembering. And Jean, of course, has gone to work, because her shift starts at eight. And she's gone without any further explanation, indeed without so much as a farewell. And me? I am left here, with the letter. With Steve's letter. As though Steve were my responsibility. As though he were my... My what? My son? And I remember. Yes, the girl with the red hair. The girl with the inhaler. 'Don't wait up for me,' says Veronica, as she closes the door behind her. I say, 'Alright, Vee, alright, take care.' And I kick myself for being so easily distracted.

The letter, which is headed Office of the Department of Work and Pensions, invites Mr Stephen Curran to attend an interview. The date and time of the interview would be agreed if he, Mr Curran, would please ring the Administrative Officer at his earliest convenience. The letter is dated 12 October. Almost two months ago.

Now these are clearly matters of deep significance, to have prompted such a reaction, both in Veronica and in her mother, but as to what that significance might be, I have not the slightest idea. Has Steve attended the interview? And if so, what was the outcome? Has he forgotten about it? Has he failed, perhaps, even to respond to the letter? And if so, what opportunity has been missed as a result? I toy with the idea of ringing him on his mobile, but think better of it. A father, still more a prospective father-in-law, is wise to exercise restraint in such matters.

8

I awake at five o'clock. I'm not sure whether I've been dreaming or the dream has slipped its moorings and drifted into my premature wakefulness. I'm sitting with my back to the school. I see the terrace at my feet and beyond it the school yard. To the right of me, ambling towards the end of the terrace, hands behind his back, the first two fingers of each hand interlocked, is Father Dempsey. To the left, at the other end of the terrace, is the priests' house, large, gothic, separate. A figure approaches, too small to identify. I try to bring him closer by an act of will but he blurs, recedes, dissolves. So I loosen my grip, I allow him to resume at his own pace. He walks towards me again, ever so slowly, hands in pockets. And although this is not allowed, although walking with your hands in your pockets is really quite unconscionable, I don't interfere, I let him approach. And as he does so, I begin to pick out the details, one at a time, because that is as much as your mind's eye permits. The thick glasses, the lank hair, the eyes squinting at the sun, the way the squint wrinkles the nose, lifts the upper lip. And I see that he is looking at me. I am looking at me.

And this is how it must be done, of course. How stupid I've been to think otherwise. The point isn't to see Fenwick: because this isn't really about Fenwick, is it? No, the point is to see myself, to see myself through Fenwick's eyes. It's the me drifting into Fenwick's gaze which I must capture, the me in his pupils, the me agitating the optic nerve, the me which, even before the word itself is formed, has lodged itself in the hate pathways of his brain.

I get up, put on my dressing gown and make my way down to the dining room. I do this quietly, even though I'm sure there's no-one else in the house. Jean's still on night-shift (she will return as I'm leaving for work) and Veronica, it appears, is still at her friend's: her bedroom door is open, the light which I left on in the passage, to welcome her home, is still on. As for Steve, I've no idea where he is. Quietly, and I'm sure a little furtively, for this is not something I would do if others were present, I open the sideboard and ease out a wodge of brown envelopes from behind the cups and plates. I place them on the table. It is cold, so I light the gas fire and go to the kitchen to make myself a cup of coffee. This is a task which cannot be rushed.

I have no photographs of my memory, of course. I have merely ancillary evidence, a dossier of snapshots. Of the half dozen items in the envelope marked 'St Aidan's 1967–73', the Form II photograph is closest, in time, to my schoolboy encounter with Fenwick. In time and, as it happens, in location. Because it was taken in the school yard, so that the terrace, even the bench where Fenwick sat, are clearly visible in the background. I recognise all of the faces and can still name many. Murphy, Finlay, Fishwick, Dodgson, the Barr twins, McGucken, Carr. I am sitting next to Carr in the front row: we have been placed here because we are slightly shorter than those in the middle and back rows. In this way, the sharp creases which Mam has ironed into my grey Terylene trousers are fully displayed, as are the polished black shoes, rounded like tugboats. My hands, all our hands, are clasped uniformly on our laps and our shoulders have a slightly hunched, folded-in look, probably because it is cold. March 1969 it says at the bottom. My head is tilted a little to the left and I have, I think, a generally amiable air about me, a genial half-smile, not too ingratiating, not too pleased with itself, yet not mischievous, either. I cannot see my eyes properly because of the reflection of the sunlight on my spectacle lenses. There is a fleshiness about the neck and something in the spread of the blazer which foreshadow later corpulence. But I'm not fat. There were three official fatties in Form II, and I was not one of them. Perhaps the hair is unkempt, but this is true of others: it was a cold, windy March day. I conform. I am anonymous. I am invisible.

I stand up and look in the mirror above the fireplace. I cannot stand too close because of the heat, but I can see that I'm no longer there. The boy has, quite literally, disappeared. The hair has gone, the mouth too: there is only a dark shadow between my beard and moustache. I scarcely recognise myself. And yet, does not this face, too, this stranger's face, also conform? Does it not invite you to walk by, incurious, indifferent? So why should you single me out, Fenwick? What did you see, what *do* you see, that I cannot see?

9

'It's a misunderstanding, Frank,' Steve said, yesterday, when he got back from Gateshead. So I took him down to the Vaults because Jean was too brittle and Veronica wasn't talking to him.

'Ah,' I said. 'And what is it exactly that's been misunderstood, Steve?'

And he didn't fidget. No, he didn't look up at the ceiling, either, or stumble over his words. He spoke calmly and deliberately, like someone who has, at last, resolved to unburden himself, to confide in those who, he realises, have his best interests at heart.

'I didn't think it mattered, Frank,' he said. 'The housing benefit. You know. I didn't think it mattered where I was living. I qualified.'

'But you don't pay us rent, Steve,' I tried to explain.

'Not as such, Frank, but…'

But I knew how they were fixed, he said, and how they needed the money to get their foot on the ladder and it was only £50 a week, and he did help Vee out with this and that, and the quicker they saved up the quicker they'd move out and we'd all be happier then, not happier, no, he didn't want to seem ungrateful, but how were people supposed to get themselves set up these days?

Steve drank from his pint and sat quietly for a moment. But as I took these to be rhetorical questions, I made no attempt to respond. So I sipped my own pint. In such circumstances, when one is slowly trying to build confidence, to tease out the truth as you would a little spelk from a tender finger tip, I believe it is more important to listen than to talk.

How were they supposed to start a family? he said, then, regaining his thread. And yes, he'd already fixed up a meeting with Fizz. I said I hadn't heard of Fizz. Which is true, I wasn't affecting ignorance just to put him on the spot, to catch him out. Down the dole, he said, as if I knew about such things. They'll get it switched, Frank, you'll see, he said. They'll get the money switched. No problem.

So I'm taken aback when I come home from work this evening and find a letter addressed to me and Jean which, to all intents and purposes, is the same letter that Steve had received, the letter which caused us all such consternation and puzzlement in the first place. We, that is Jean and I, are asked to attend an interview. And to that end we must contact the Administrative Officer at our earliest convenience. Indeed, because it is so similar to Steve's letter, I wonder for a moment whether this is a mistake, whether the letter has in fact been misdirected, I begin to suspect even that it could be a case of mistaken identity. Because they've misspelt our surname, they've typed Daly instead of Daley. Aha! I think. So that's it. An administrative error. A glitch. And I hold on to this life-line whilst searching for further errors that must be there somewhere, I think, lurking in the letter's curt prose, in the recesses of the envelope, somewhere in the system.

When Steve arrives home a little while later, I ask him, 'What is Fizz, exactly, Steve?' And I ask this more firmly, more insistently, than before, which is only reasonable, I think, under the circumstances.

'The dole office, Frank,' he tells me, again.

'Yes, I know, Steve,' I say. 'You told me that. But what does it mean? What does it stand for?'

But Steve says he doesn't know, it's the Job Centre, it's the dole office, the welfare, the social. And he starts to sound a little impatient. I can smell drink on him.

'I've got to get some grub inside me, Frank,' he says. 'Vee back yet?' And he goes on, seeming not to care whether I answer him or not. 'Lads on the box tonight, you know, Frank... Fancy a cuppa...? A beer...?' This is what he says. And I must suppress my growing irritation because few things test my patience more than evasiveness of this kind. This isn't helping your case, I want to tell him. This isn't winning you friends.

So I ask him straight out, 'Have you had your meeting yet, Steve?'

'It's sorted, Frank.'

'So what's this then, Steve?' I ask, and show him the letter.

'No idea, Frank,' he says, shrugging his shoulders. He looks me in the eye, shakes his head. 'No idea.'

So what am I to do? I leave Steve to get his tea ready, as I must, because he's quite determined to eat, and it is difficult to remonstrate with someone when they have their back turned to you, when they

39

are busying themselves with their chores. Difficult, yes, and somehow demeaning. As though the remonstrator were of less account than the slice of ham or the pickled onion or the piece of cheese being sliced on the counter-top. And for want of some other, more purposeful course of action, I go upstairs. We keep the computer in the back bedroom, Christopher's old room. And that is where I go, to search for Fiz, or Fizz, or Fis, because I don't even know how to spell it. And I pursue this, my quarry, in all the permutations I can muster, knowing it must be there somewhere, because everything is, isn't it? And indeed, at the outset I am buoyed up by the array of options available, from Fidelity Information Services to the Franconian International School, from the Federation of Infection Societies to Fizz Software, as though these bona fide institutions somehow lent a vicarious solidity to Steve's variant. It is only on the twenty-third page, where I find *Hello! I'm Fizz. I'm 7. Nearly 8. My favourite colour is pink* that, with a wry chuckle – because I believe I am something of a fatalist at heart – I acknowledge the futility of my task.

When I go downstairs, Veronica is back from college. I can see, from the way they look at me, and then at each other, that Steve has told her about the letter.

'Don't tell Jean,' I say. 'Not yet.'

10

We've had a site meeting today, a small contract out at Bywell. It went well enough. But Bill has arranged to take the client to lunch at some pub on the Stocksfield road. 'It's in Michelin this year,' he tells her. Bill is keen to promote better client relations, as he puts it. 'Your style up here is a bit impersonal,' he'd said, when he first came. 'No criticism,' he'd added, but I know it was a jab at my frugality. It all goes on the bill, I thought: it's good value the client wants, not a social life. Anyway, I suspect ulterior motives, whether commercial or carnal I'm not sure. Either way, I've got to stay put. I must help legitimise this item on Bill's expense claim. I must reflect the warmth of his bonhomie back at him, be a foil for his anecdotes.

'Heard the one about the farmer and the wayleave officer? It's a true story... Isn't it, Frank?'

My suspicions are borne out when I remind him, at half past one, that we have to sign off the LenCo job in an hour's time and he says, 'No sweat, Frank. You can do that, can't you? No need for the two of us to hang around here.' So I leave. And as I leave, I hear him add, in a phoney sotto voce, 'Been with the company man and boy, Frank. Very loyal.' Which might have been a compliment, had it been said by anyone else.

11

There is a complication in the Lenco deal. It is none of my doing. Dominic, our solicitor, a keep-fit zealot in his early thirties, says he cannot sign off because Lenco don't own all the land to which access is required. He has therefore postponed the meeting until such time as the parties have been through their land titles again.

'Tell Bill, will you.'

Dominic says this rather peevishly and I'm not sure that his irritation is not directed partly at me.

'Didn't we check?' he asks.

Perhaps I'm keeping him from some muscle-pumping session. I assure him that the Land Registry searches have been straightforward, that Lenco had bought the whole area, some sixteen segments in total, over six years ago, that all easements have been secured over adjacent land, that I can show him the paperwork if he wishes. I gesture towards the ranks of box files behind my desk. But it seems that Dominic is not to be placated this afternoon. He holds up his hands, as if to say, 'No more, no more,' and bids me a brusque farewell. 'Happy Christmas, Frank,' he says. 'See you next year.'

Yes, it is a complication. And i dislike complications. Not complexities, you understand. Complexities add variety and interest to a day's work. Complications, however, disrupt and delay. But as well as

41

being a complication, this is also a distraction. The Work and Pensions letter is burning a hole in my pocket. It pleads for my attention. And I had intended – yes, quite resolutely, I had intended – picking up the phone at some point today, perhaps now, before Bill gets back, to clarify matters, to point out that my name is not Daly at all, no, it's Daley, with an 'e', to enquire as to the purpose of the interview, and so on. And perhaps, in doing so, I could have the whole sorry business resolved at a single stroke. Yes, that is what I had intended.

But then, as I reflect upon these matters again, it occurs to me that they, too, if I'm not very careful, could become complications in their own right. Would I not, for example, on picking up the phone, wish to enquire about the nature and purpose of Fizz? And who knows what further questions might then ensue, with their own protracted explanations and qualifications? And would I not, thereby, lay bare my ignorance of these affairs, my naivety even, with perhaps damaging consequences for all concerned? So it's as well, yes, just as well, that a different imperative has arisen.

My task, then, is clear. I must cover my back before Bill returns. Even as the words form themselves in my mind, I realise that this is an unfortunate idiom, smacking as it does of concealment and evasion. But it is true. Bill will want answers; otherwise, like Dominic, he will lay blame at the nearest door. 'But Frank, it's been almost two years,' he'll say. 'We've looked at the plans together... I asked you, more than once...' Leaving me to fill in the gaps with fumbling acts of contrition.

So I ring Gavin. And he says, with a beery insouciance which makes me think that he, too, has been out to lunch today, 'Aye, a wee hiccup.' And he needs to ring his Regional Manager, which he hasn't had a chance to do yet, because of this and that, and I ask him, please, please, to ring him now. By half past four we have established the facts of the matter. We have established that our searches were impeccable. We have established also, however, that Lenco Leisure, a subsidiary of Lenco Holdings, have re-sold a small parcel of land previously allocated to them in the Low Moor Farm area, as it had been superfluous to requirements. 'And they got a good offer for it too,' says Gavin, who seems to think that this somehow ameliorates the problem. Yes, a good offer from one of the superstores, in fact, in the adjacent retail park. Because they need to build an extension. 'Desperate,' says Gavin, desperate to build their extension. And I'm tempted to reply, well, that's alright, then. I'll tell Bill that. I'll tell him they got a good price and that he needn't worry. But I am not given to sarcasm.

'Sorry about that, Frank,' says Gavin, in his bluff way, 'A wee breakdown in communication.'

Bill doesn't return to work this afternoon, and I am too agitated to ring anyone about the letter. I am left feeling frustrated. More than that, I feel not a little slighted, as though, despite my best intentions, my best efforts, circumstances are determined to get the better of me. I want to give those circumstances a name, a face, a silly man face with a bulbous nose and a leering grin, so I can look it in the eyes and accuse it accordingly. And I think, also, if it were possible, I would like to rewind the last twenty-four hours and approach each of my tasks differently, not so much to correct any errors of my own as to have more influence on the erratic, often unreasonable behaviour of others. I would ring Bill on his mobile and tell him, without rancour or smugness, but also without apology, that Lenco had ballsed up at the last minute and that I'd had to take swift remedial action etc. etc. What, you're still with the Prudhoe client, Bill? I'd say, unperturbed. Well, not to worry, my friend, have a shag on me, I'm in the office and everything's fine and dandy. Loyal, I am. Man and boy. Yes.

And as for Jean? I'd have been up front with Jean. For once, I'd have sacrificed Jean's feelings for the greater good, to get it all out into the open, about Steve, about the letter, about Fizz, to open the windows and let the fresh air in. These are the things I would do, if I could turn back the clock.

No, Bill doesn't return to work, but he rings, just as I'm about to leave. 'Been talking to Gavin,' he says. 'Think you took your eye off the ball there, Frank.'

12

When I leave the office at half past five, I am not yet in the mood for going home. It's a fine evening, crisp, with only a slight breeze. So I go for a stroll instead. Having crossed the Ouseburn footbridge, I don't turn right for the Regent Centre and my usual Metro station; instead, I press ahead for another half mile to South Gosforth. It is busy here, too, I grant you, with shoppers and commuters, but it's a busyness from which I can disengage. I do not swim through it; I surf it. And then, when I arrive and am already feeling revived by this break in my routine, I decide to extemporise further, by taking the coastal route. It is a little longer (what of it? I am in no hurry), but it doesn't require me to change and it keeps me out of the centre of the city. The next train, which is now approaching the platform, will get in to Shields at five past seven. Still a tadge early: I shall most likely run in to Jean just before she leaves for work. But I catch it nonetheless. After all, I can think about Jean, about what I shall say to her, quite as well in the comfort of a warm carriage as out here, on a bleak, windswept platform. (There is only a meagre shelter on this side of the tracks, quite inadequate for the evening rush.)

We are entering Whitley Bay (I can see the roof of Mam's bungalow from here) and I'm wondering how the journey can be protracted further, when he gets on the train. I see him first through the window and he is so close that I could touch him with my hand, were the window not in the way. He is so close that he would surely have seen me, too, were he not wholly occupied in tending to the needs of a little girl, perhaps seven or eight years of age, whose hand he is holding. The girl carries a package under her free arm, gripping it tightly with her hand. They enter the train and turn towards me, as I knew they would. Because, while their movements seem entirely random, indeed somewhat dithering (but ah! What cunning!), there is also about them a certain inevitability, as though every step and gesture, even every dither, were preordained. So that when, finally, they make for the seat opposite me I am appalled but not in the least surprised, as though we were tied by some invisible thread. And I brace myself for what must follow, for the greeting, for the acknowledgement that the game is up, that, hah! I had you going there, didn't I, Denman... or is it Deary...? Ah, yes, Daley, of course. Daley. Meet my granddaughter... my niece... my...

Fortunately, as I now become aware, previous travellers have left a trail of crisps and sweet wrappers over the seat and the floor below so that Fenwick changes his mind at the last moment. I say fortunately, but then reflect that this, too, might be no more than another teasing little twist of the knife. A 'now you see me, now you don't' moment. At any rate, they settle for facing seats on the other side of the carriage. Fenwick has had his hair cut since I saw him in the supermarket. And perhaps he has coloured it, too: it seems darker, except at the temple, where the grey remains. This may be a trick of the light, of course, but I'm not surprised to find evidence of vanity. He wears about him a rather exaggerated avuncular air. There are men who would be too self-conscious to engage an eight-year-old in conversation in such a public place. Not Fenwick. Oh, no, not Fenwick. Fenwick turns it into a performance art. Yes, he is quite full of it. Questions about school, questions about friends. And then, in a mock-plaintive voice, which he clearly believes to be a grandfather's prerogative, he simpers about how it's getting late for such a little girl, and so cold, too. The girl, who has a pleasant enough face, although too round to be really pretty, responds desultorily, in an adenoidal voice. I can tell that she is embarrassed. And I feel that we are allies in this respect. We sit there, squirming.

And then it happens. The girl catches my eye – that is, she becomes aware that I am watching her – and I smile, naturally, to assuage our mutual discomfort. This, in turn, and to my horror, draws Fenwick into our little act of recognition. He smiles, too, and says, 'She's been getting a present for her great grandfather.' So casually, as though this were the most natural thing in the world, as though he's known me all his life. (But again, I think, what guile!) And he turns to the girl. 'How old will Great Grandpa be tomorrow, Jemma?' So that Jemma must squirm a little more. She looks up at the ceiling and says 'Eighty-six,' then wipes the words from her mouth, the stain of the words, with the back of her hand. 'That's right, Jemma. Eighty-six.' He says this rather boastfully. Jemma kicks the seat with her heels.

As we pull in to Shields, it is still not ten past seven. I am not yet prepared to take on Jean or anyone else. So I have decided to have a pint in the Vaults on the way home, just to while away that spare half hour, and to steady my nerves. Anything would suffice, but the Vaults is handy and, besides, it's the sort of thing I might do anyway. I mean, it lies strictly within the bounds of the familiar and can, therefore, surely make no further demands on me. So that is what I have decided. But it is not what I do. Because although, as I say, I want this encounter to end, I have to admit that, having broken the ice a little, my curiosity is whetted. As though, the worst now being over, the taboo of silence having been roundly breached, there can be nothing more to fear. Look at me, I think, am I not still here, my person and faculties quite intact? And yes, emboldened in this way, part of me also wants to see how long Fenwick can keep this up, how long he can pretend he doesn't recognise me, that he has entered this carriage (that he shopped in my store) entirely by coincidence. Because, at last, I have decided to call his bluff.

Jemma is holding her package on her lap. It is wrapped in brown paper but around it someone has tied an incongruous blue ribbon.

'That your great grandpa's present, Jemma?' I ask.

She looks to Fenwick for permission to answer the strange man. She looks back at me and nods.

'And we had to go to Cullercoats for it, didn't we, Jemma?' he says. 'To the man with the sea clocks.'

Jemma pretends to cough, so she can cover her face with her hand, and looks out through the window.

So I don't get off at Shields. I sit tight, maintaining my dignity, testing Fenwick's mettle, giving as good as I'm getting. But scarcely have I begun to take stock of these new and unexpected developments, than Fenwick is gathering his things together – that is, Jemma's package, which is really rather big for her, and another package of his own – and they're making their way towards the exit. We are entering Meadow Well, an unlikely destination for Fenwick, I think, even more unlikely than Darlington. He makes Jemma wear her hat, which is a bright yellow ball of fur with big ear pieces.

'You keep your ears warm, pet,' I say, as I pull on my own hat. And I must say, I'm rather pleased with myself. I'm pleased that I can say such a thing so blithely, that I am, in fact, holding my own quite magnificently. I even wiggle my earflaps, as if to tell her, we're in this together, you and me.

'Bye now,' he says.

I alight just behind them, but linger a few seconds on the platform, allowing them to reach the exit, making sure they do not disappear entirely from sight. A minute later, they are heading down Bridge Road. They walk briskly, hand-in-hand, and it is all I can do to keep up with them. Even though Jemma is little, she is an energetic thing, and bounds through the cold air as though her life depends on it. And, to be honest, I am not in the best condition for exercise of this kind. Fenwick's stoop seems to have diminished, and I think, now, that it might have been the result of some temporary complaint. I think, even, that I might have imagined it.

Jemma is skipping ahead, which she can do freely, as Fenwick is carrying both packages. I see these things from the path which runs parallel with the road, first beside the allotments and then past the park. There are boys there, exercising their dogs. It is a little exposed, so I have to keep my distance. I must not dawdle, however, for to be seen skulking, spying, peeping, would arouse suspicion, yes, might even provoke the dog boys themselves who, I am sure, would be glad of the excuse to bait one such as myself. So I endeavour to look purposeful, to direct my eyes ahead of me, to adopt the demeanour of an ordinary man with a briefcase, going home after an ordinary day's work.

Fenwick and the girl cross Howden Road. On reaching the other side, Jemma looks back, perhaps at nothing in particular, as children do, perhaps merely to see the green man turn to red, the cars setting off again, but perhaps, as children also do, seeing things that adult eyes are too tired, too indifferent, to see, and for a moment, no more than the blinking of an eye, I think she catches me. And whether it's me, the strange man in the train, or whether it's just that man on the street, any man, in a dark coat, with a briefcase, with a hat, I cannot tell. But she tugs at Fenwick's sleeve. So I go down on one knee and pretend to fasten a shoelace. My hat, I'm sure, conceals my head and face. Does Fenwick himself look back? I don't know, because I stay like this, bent, genuflecting, perhaps for a whole minute, until my knees can take the strain no longer. But I will him not to, I will myself to be invisible.

When I look up again, they have already reached Chirton Way and are heading down, more steeply now, towards the river. I know Chirton Way because here, at the end of a row of new, three-storey town houses, is the home where Molly, Jean's mother lives. And I think, yes, that would be a good alibi, if the need arose, I'm visiting my mother-in-law. She's in The Quays, you know. So that, a moment later, when I hear a car alarm, when I might otherwise have felt the object of suspicion, I am unperturbed. No, officer, I can say, everything is in order, no thieves here. Just quiet, respectable folk minding their own business, visiting their in-laws, walking their dogs, taking their granddaughters, their nieces, back to their warm homes. They reach the bottom of the bank. Dock Road. And there is only one place left for them to go. They turn right and cross the road. A bus shelter stands a few yards down on my left. I stroll towards it, checking my watch, looking back over my shoulder. As I must do, of course, because my alibi has changed. I am no longer visiting my mother-in-law, I am now the man waiting for the bus. An innocent occupation, one which can arouse no suspicion. Surely the bus will come soon, that is what I make my body say, as I check my watch again, as I nod to the two women already huddled there, in the shelter.

And I watch. Because they can go no further now. I have pinned them down. Coble Court, it says. I repeat the name, aloud, under my breath, to pin that down too. Coble Court. Fenwick lifts Jemma up so that she can press the buttons, tap in the code. He pushes the gate open, the smaller of two gates. They walk through and it slams shut behind them. They disappear from view now, but I see them still, in my mind's eye, walking towards the condominium's main entrance. Soon, they will be inside, soonest of all if they are on the ground floor, but longer, of course, to get to the first, and so on. And there are, how many? Two, three, four. Four floors. And the lift. Perhaps quicker if they go by lift.

In my mind's eye I try to make a pattern of the lights. But it's too difficult, it has no symmetry. So I count them. Four lights on the ground floor. Two on the first. Two on the second. Five on the third. I repeat the sequence. Four. Two. Two. Five. Four equals two plus two. And five? How do I remember five? And that's no good, either. So I just keep my eyes open, unblinking, waiting for the next light, their light, to come on.

13

'So, Frank, if you can just tell them I was here, you know, pro tem...'

Steve wants me to tell the Fizz people that he still lives in Gateshead. Fraud Investigation Service, that's what Fizz is. F.I.S. When I asked the woman on the phone she said, 'You won't be under caution, it's just to ask you some questions.' And I must admit, when I heard these words, that I quite forgot about Steve and his benefit troubles. Instead, I started ransacking my memory for some misdemeanour which I might inadvertently have committed at work, some deed or circumstance which might give rise to suspicion. Or, if not a deed, if not an action, then an inaction, which is worse, much worse, because how can you file away all your inactions? How can you ever know?

It was the word 'fraud' that did it. It made me fear that, somehow, this business really did have something to do with me, after all. No, not that I'd ever defraud anyone, not culpably, as they say. But fraud happens. Perhaps some client had gone bankrupt, perhaps somebody had taken a backhander, or perhaps there'd been a delay in transferring an easement payment, and my name had cropped up, had been there in the files, on an e-mail. Is that possible? Because fraud happens. Because such things are out of my hands.

'Under caution?' I asked her then, the Fizz woman.

'No,' she said. 'Not under caution.'

'Ah, yes.'

I stuttered an apology. And she said, 'The interview concerns Mr Stephen Curran.'

Of course it does. Steve.

'Pro tem?'

'It's not like it's a lie, Frank,' Steve said. I've not seen him since

Christmas. He's been up in Gateshead, with his mates, till things blow over, he said. 'Tell them I just stopped over now and again,' he said. But you've been here for two years,' I said. And he reckons they won't know that. Because he thinks they can't keep tabs on him twenty-four hours a day. That's what he said. And I told him. 'Steve,' I said, 'they know everything. '

14

A month has gone by since I last saw Fenwick. Sometimes I am consoled by this fact. If he were intent on doing me harm, I tell myself, he would surely have sustained his pursuit, even intensified it, at a time of year when we are at our most vulnerable, when we have little defence against a determined predator. And at such times I wonder whether my three sightings of Fenwick were in fact no more than a rogue cluster of coincidences, the significance of which, the improbability of which, diminishes as time elapses, as they retreat into the dimly-lit back alleys of my memory. I think to myself, it's nothing more than a game of snap. You don't expect a match, not this time, not the next, and it's always a surprise, when it comes, yes, there's always that little squeal of surprise, and you know it's going to happen, if not next time, then the next, or the next. It's as simple as that. Fenwick was my match. It might have been Carr or Turnbull or Finlay or Fishwick or one of the others, because we all got shuffled together. But it had to be someone. And this time it was Fenwick. It happened. It will happen again. It's not important.

So that's how it feels, sometimes, it's just a game of snap, and I'm consoled. But tonight, with Jean at her sister's, and Veronica at her friend's, the one with the inhaler, and Steve still in Gateshead, and Herbie Hancock's 'Watermelon Man' there in the background, doing his best, but his best is not enough, I know it's all beside the point, it's nonsense, it's idle distraction. Because Fenwick is the whole pack, it's his face on every card, he's burrowed his way inside me and the Fenwick in the mind is worse even than the Fenwick in the supermarket or the train. Because at least the Fenwick in the shop will check out, sooner or later, the Fenwick on the train will get off. This Fenwick, the one that's taken up residence inside me, never alights, never checks out, but sits there, ever so patient, ever so casual, his lips slightly parted, as though on the brink of saying something.

And it's then I think, how stupid I've been, because this is what it's all about, this is the cruelest twist. The other Fenwicks, on the train, in the supermarket, on the quayside, they were just the first cuts, the little keyholes, the incisions he needed, to get in here, inside me.

15

There's slushy snow on the ground when I go to the Job Centre. Freezing water bites at my toes and I think, what are shoes for, yes, what are they for, if they can't keep my feet dry? I should have worn wellies, but it's not a wellies day, it's an office day. So perhaps I'll invest in a pair of galoshes, when I get the chance, tomorrow perhaps, not today, because today is already full. I make a mental note of it, but wonder, do they still make galoshes?

I've arranged a nine o'clock interview to minimise disruption to my day's work. Jean is in bed after a hard night-shift. Two fatal RTAs, she said. Ice on the roads. 'You look bushed, pet,' I said, when she came in this morning. Of course she did. And it's beside the point, I know, but Jean's exhaustion and the unspoken awfulness of her night assuaged my anxiety about the interview, put it in perspective. I am also pleased to see the woman with the green hat and the wheely walker approaching the chemist's. I venture a smile, a nod, and although she is bent over her frame and quite intent on controlling its wheels and brakes and what have you, she reciprocates, she offers me a gentle, slightly surprised smile in return, and a little tilt of the head.

So when I am ushered into the interview room by the Investigator (a grandiose title for such a slight, thin-lipped sliver of a man) I do so with a degree of equanimity which surprises even myself. In fact, I go so far as to instigate the conversation.

'I understand,' I say, 'that you need some clarification about Stephen. Stephen Curran.' And I apologise for my wife's absence. 'On duty at the hospital,' I say. 'Very difficult to get time off.' And that's all well and good, but it seems that there are (aren't there always?) various facts that need to be checked first, forms that must be completed and signed, before we can get to the meat of the matter. I do my best to respond, I really do, in the prevailing spirit of courtesy and cooperation, but I find myself having to say, repeatedly, 'I'm sorry…?' and 'Come again' and 'Could you speak up, please?' Because the little man is talking into his chest, he really is. Speak up, man, I want to tell him. Talk behind your teeth, as Mam used to say. Indeed, I feel that, if only he would allow me to take charge of the meeting, I should make a much better fist of it, and we'd be able to get away from here and resume our lives. But I must bite my tongue. He is, I remind myself, only doing his job.

I am not under caution, he says. I nod. But I may be called back for a further meeting – it is only a possibility, you understand, it may well not be necessary – and at that meeting I may be questioned under caution. I nod again, vigorously. Yes, yes, I say, I understand fully. Because I am here to help.

'And would you tell me, Mr Daley, who lives at this address?'

He is looking at his computer screen. And it is only now that I begin to suspect that he already knows the answers to his questions.

'Myself and my wife, Jean,' I say. 'And my daughter, Veronica. She's at college. Final year.'

'An expensive business,' he says, 'keeping…' But I miss the rest of it.

And for good measure, even though I'm impatient to move on, I tell him that she is studying graphics, that the prospects are good in that field. I even tell him about Christopher, our son. That he lived there, too. (But of course he did, where else would he live?) Yes, lived with us until five years ago. No, almost six. 'In the services,' I say. 'The armed services. Never got home much, though. Just Christmas, that sort of thing.'

And perhaps I ramble a little, about this and other matters, because I don't want my little Investigator to get the impression that I harbour any prejudice towards him because of what may, for all I know, be a speech impediment, even some kind of personality disorder. Or, of course, that I have anything to conceal. (The garrulous, I think, are generally regarded with less suspicion than the reticent.)

'No-one else?' he asks.

'How d'you mean?' I say. And I tell him we have visitors, of course we do. Jean's sister stays the occasional night, or used to, but not lately, no, not with things as they are, it's the other way round now, really, I say, it's Jean goes over there. And then there's my mother, but that's once in a blue moon. Yes. And of course Steve himself, Stephen Curran, who's Veronica's boyfriend. Ha! How things have changed, I quip. And I allow myself to anecdotalise for a moment about how my mother doesn't know to this day that I would often stay over at Jean's before we were married. Yes, when she was training to be a nurse. Staunch Catholic, I explain. My mother, I mean, not Jean. Yes, even in the seventies. In the free-and-easy seventies.

'So Mr Curran does not live at… 18 Lorraine Place?' he asks.

'Mr…?' And that's it. I've got it. The poor man cannot pronounce his 'r's. They're not 'w's, not quite like Roy Jenkins, no, or that other one, that Jonathan Ross fellow, they're more like 'v's, then the word just melts away, gives up the ghost. Mr Cuvva, that's what he's saying. Poor man. And what an unfortunate affliction, in a profession such as this.

Mr Curran? I say. No, no, Mr Curran's home is in Gateshead. And I'm sorry, I can't provide him with an address, no, he just comes for the odd weekend, that sort of thing. And here I begin to extemporise a little, to fill out the story, which I am starting to sense is a little thin on detail. I say that Veronica spends quite a lot of time at Steve's. That they go clubbing, and who knows where they end up? That they go off together – holidayed in Greece last year, I tell him. Yes, it's hard to keep track of your kids these days.

And then he asks me whether Mr Curran has a key. He asks whether, perhaps, Mr Curran could enter and leave the house without my knowing. Whether, indeed, he could even spend a whole night there and neither my wife nor I be any the wiser. For example, he says, referring to his screen again, take the week beginning Monday 6th November – 'Would you please try to cast your mind back, Mr

Daley?' – and he asks me, how many nights do I think he spent at the house that week? How many nights? I say. And shake my head. How can I possibly know? How can he be serious?

And he does, I'm sure, pose these questions in as civil a manner as he can muster, given his disability, yes, and given the inquisitorial nature of the proceedings. So I can have no complaints on that score. Except that even civility can become tiresome after a while. Because civility, strictly speaking, is for greetings and farewells and introductions and other such brief encounters. When it's done its business it should quit the room and give way to a less, how shall I say, less pernickety manner of engagement. When civility outstays its welcome, I find its edges become a little abrasive.

It is at this point that the Investigator brings out the photographs.

'Can you confirm that this is Mr Curran leaving your house…? And again, here…? And the following morning…? You see the dates, Mr Daley? And the times? And again, entering your house, that afternoon. Wednesday, 8th November.'

Tossing these questions at me, the Investigator has suddenly become more assertive, more articulate. Or perhaps it is my ear that has adjusted to his idiosyncrasies. He recites the dates as though they were accusations. Yes, I say, that's Steve. Although, of course, I would have been at work at these times, and Jean too, very likely. She works shifts, I remind him.

'And here…?'

Another photograph shows Steve walking down the front path, carrying a suitcase. A taxi is waiting. Vee's following him but has turned her head back toward the house so that I cannot see her face. She is waving. She is waving at Jean and me. We are standing, shadowed, in the doorway. We are all in our summer clothes.

'When was this taken?' I ask.

I know, of course, when it was taken. Because this is Steve and Veronica setting off for their holiday in Greece, back in June. I can see where it's been taken, too. The gate pillar outside the school down the road has been used to provide concealment: its edge is a blurred perpendicular line near the right margin of the picture. There's a child's forearm in the bottom left corner. And I say 'when', but what I mean is, who took it? And why?

'Perhaps you could tell me, Mr Daley,' he says, disregarding my question, 'whether this is Mr Curran's own suitcase?'

I say I'm not sure. And I'm not. And I really don't see what difference it makes. Not that I say this, of course, because such a response would, I'm sure, sound defensive, and even to sound defensive is, to the suspicious ear, in itself a kind of admission. But I fear that it may already be too late, that I may already have given something away, simply by confessing my ignorance. Steven's case? My case? How would I know? And if I don't know, doesn't that mean…?

'And here, I think, is Mr Curran's car… 7th September, and again, 9th September, 11th September…'

Steve's maroon Montego stands in front of the park railings at the end of our street.

'It was off the road for a while,' I tell him. 'It's an old car, you see. Difficult to get parts.'

I have nothing else to say, except to embellish this statement further, to tell him they don't make the Montego any more, it's the Sable now, and not the same thing at all. And although I don't know whether I'm answering wisely or not, I am still sure that words are less implicating than silence. But it is only my mouth that speaks. Inside, I am heavy with it, a dead, leaden silence.

'Yes,' he says. 'But your road, Mr Daley. It was off your road. It was nowhere near Gateshead.' He says, 'Your voad. It was off *your* voad.' And the words are all his now, mangled though they are. I have none of my own left. He looks at me, raises an eyebrow and, unaccountably, smiles.

'Perhaps,' he says, 'if you could have a word… Mr Curran might reflect… It would be in everyone's best… Be doing him a favour….'

16

Steve thinks Jean is the snoop.

'Who do you think took the photos, Steve?' I asked him. We were sat by the kitchen table. Jean was out visiting her mother at The Quays. She'd taken Veronica. It was Molly's birthday. 20th January.

He said: 'I don't give a toss about the photos, Frank. Who grassed us up?' And I didn't understand. He looked at me incredulously.

'You seriously think they've got somebody staked out there twenty-four hours a day, just on the off-chance?'

I said I supposed not. But what do I know of such things?

'Jean doesn't want me here,' he said. 'Never did.'

'Well,' I began, but the denial petered out.

And Steve's got a point. But I know it wasn't Jean. I knew it couldn't be Jean. Surely it couldn't be Jean.

17

'I hate you,' he'd said.

Not like Newton. Newton was a bully. Newton ran up behind me and knocked my glasses off because he could, and maybe because he had red hair and freckles and had been picked on himself. They're poor reasons, but they're still reasons. There was a balance of sorts. A Punch and Judy sort of balance.

'What did he do that for, Francis?' Mam asked.

'It wasn't just me, Mam,' I said. 'He hit Fishwick on the head. And he stuck sellotape over O'Farrell's mouth.' Which was worse than knocking my glasses off, to my way of thinking, and that meant I wasn't special, I wasn't being singled out. But Fenwick? I can't fathom Fenwick. I know I must have done something, something really awful, because why else would he bother?

Kirchhoff's law states that at any junction in a circuit through which a steady current is flowing, the sum of the currents flowing to that point is equal to the sum of the currents flowing away from it. That's how things are. What goes round comes round. But I can only see Fenwick's hate. There's no circuit, no exchange, no balance. So I never told Mam, about that day, about Fenwick.

18

Steve's changed his plea. I spoke to him, just like they asked me to. I'll help you out, I said. No witnesses, no photographs. It'll be like it never happened.

19

I have resolved to go and see Fenwick. Yes, I know I should have taken the opportunity when it presented itself. And I freely admit it, my nerve failed me, not once but three times. I was weak, indecisive, it was altogether a poor show. But regret is a futile indulgence. And in any case, the stakes are so much higher now, so many others are implicated, I couldn't play the spectator any longer, even if I wanted to.

Now some might say, indeed a voice within me does say, Leave well alone, Frank, you've not seen him for two months, what can be gained? But then, that's the point, you see. He doesn't need to reveal himself again because he's carrying on his campaign by proxy. He's getting at me through Steve, through my family, through the legal system. His capacity for manipulation knows no bounds. And now that he has set the wheels in motion, he can sit back and admire his handiwork.

And I wonder, fancifully perhaps, whether he, too, has some surveillance mechanism at his disposal. It need not be very elaborate. I even wonder whether this may, in fact, be his profession. Was it Fenwick, I think? Was he the photographer at the school gates, keeping his daily vigil? He could, for all I know, be observing me now, here in the office, as I receive the news from Gavin, which is not really news at all, is merely confirmation of what I have long known. That following the sale, in error, of the small parcel of land near Low Moor Farm, Lenco have been unable to secure access to the main part of the development site. That, while negotiations continue, power lines may have to be re-routed. That this process will, in turn, require reopening the easement file, thereby delaying completion for another two months. That's barring further complications, you understand, says Gavin. Of course, I say.

So I have resolved to go and see him. The time has come. To ask him why.

20

It's a fine day, so the three of us – Steve, Veronica and myself – make our way over to the magistrates' court on foot. We arrive half an hour early. (I am, I know, overly anxious about good time-keeping.) The court is a bright, airy building of glass and red brick, too anonymous and too new to be intimidating. And we have, in reality, little to fear, leaving aside some unaccountable aberration on the part of the magistrates. Our solicitor – I mean, Steve's solicitor – assures us that a custodial sentence is unlikely. Nevertheless, we are eager to get it over with, to restore some normality to our lives.

Jean's gone to Prudhoe for a few days to give her sister a hand. It's also her way of detaching herself from events, of keeping out of Steve's way, of not having to appeal to Veronica, exasperatedly, yet again, to kick that waster into touch, as she puts it. And perhaps to keep out of my way, too, because when I said we should accept that people make mistakes, that we had to consider the circumstances, that we had to help get them back on their feet, she said I was worse than either of them. You're a fool, Frank, she said. A weak, misguided fool. It's as well she's not here. I shall need to do some bridge-mending there, I think. But all in good time.

Some of the other defendants have arrived early, too: a few with their families but most, I think, by themselves. No-one speaks, so it's difficult to tell. We line the corridor either side of the courtroom door.

I am glad to see that everyone has made an effort, irrespective of their plea. Indeed, there is something rather touching in the delicate decorum of it all. The men have put on their ties and smart jackets, the women their sober shoes and trouser suits. And although we have never met, we know we are in this together, and we have, I think, some primal respect for one another.

It does strike me as odd, however, as we sit here, silently, and the minutes pass, as the first half hour passes, then the first hour, it does strike me as odd that we have all turned up so early, that there has been so little progress. I had expected that some fixed, immutable block of law time had been allocated to us, the Daley family, free from trespass by others, untarnished by such – and, to my shame, I catch myself saying it inwardly – untarnished by such ne'r-do-wells, by such hopeless cases, as those arrayed around us. And I notice, in this surplus time, that one of the smart jackets I'd observed earlier has frayed cuffs. I notice a twitch here, a shuffle there. I notice a woman's face – no, don't look too intently, I caution myself, don't make eye contact – her pouched, thumbed, wax mask of a face, ridiculous above that yellow blouse. And that one, strutting up and down the corridor, in his leather jacket? Who does he think he's going to impress with that? Corner-enders, Dad's voice says in my head. Yes, one's best is often not good enough, not good enough at all.

So, strange as it may seem, I am relieved when our turn comes and we are ushered into the courtroom. I breathe deeply as I enter and am surprised at how relaxed I feel. The room is carpeted, the seats cushioned and I sense that there are people here who belong: the gowned usher, the clerk, head down over his papers, the solicitors huddled at the back, conferring, attending to their files, their schedules. Due process, I think. Efficient, dependable. So when the magistrates enter and we stand and the proceedings begin, the incense of absolution is already beginning to permeate the air.

I sit with Veronica at the back of the room. Steve stands at the side and confirms his details. The chief magistrate is a man in his fifties with a tan and a rather splendid, leonine head of silver hair. He has an authoritative but courteous manner. He is perhaps a little hesitant, too, a little uncertain – he refers regularly to his clerk and chooses his words carefully – which makes me think he must be new to the bench. I feel sympathy for him and indeed a degree of admiration. Here is a person of the same age as myself, of no special status – his accent suggests he hails from Sunderland or thereabouts – who has dedicated himself to a new and onerous responsibility, and that for no reward except the knowledge that he is serving the public good. And I wonder, idly, whether this is a role to which I might myself aspire. In fact, I do believe that, with regard to temperament, and the ability to tackle problems in a methodical, detached manner, I would be well suited.

It is the clerk, however, who has the main speaking role. This he executes rather mechanically, as befits one who must recite the same litany of instructions and explanations day-in, day-out. And yet, even these mumblings, like a well-worn jumper, baggy and covered in bobbles, induces a feeling of ease. Steve says he understands, that he pleads guilty. He knows what he needs to say. Mr Nugent, the prosecuting lawyer, a fresh-faced, fair-haired young man, relates Steve's indiscretions briefly, accurately, with a proper detachment and, I'm pleased to say, a complete absence of bombast or self-satisfaction. Yes, a debt of £5,598 has accumulated. Yes, Housing Benefit payments to this value have been fraudulently obtained. However, he adds, similar payments were quite properly applied for and received in connection with the defendant's previous place of residence. Oh, yes. There is no question that the original application was a fraudulent one. How generous, I think, for you to clarify this point. Because it is important we realise that this is a sin of omission, not of commission. And the line between culpable omission and mere carelessness is surely, at some point, a fine and shifting one.

'As my friend will describe in greater detail...' he says, referring to our own counsel. What a fine institution indeed, I think, in which such generosity of spirit is allowed full flight. As for the man himself, however, that is, our solicitor – I mean, Steve's solicitor – I fear that he is altogether a less appealing man, stout, bibulous, with puffy eyes and a shuffling stance. He is also, to my mind, much given to over-egging the pudding. The mitigating circumstances are real enough, God knows they are, but it would have been better to present them unadorned, stated modestly, with humility.

'Mr Curran is otherwise a man of unblemished character... Mr Curran has not indulged in a luxurious lifestyle. On the contrary, Mr Curran has been planning his future with great prudence... Mr Curran has been a tower of strength to his new family following the tragic loss of their son on active service... ' And so on. Mr Nugent, I'm sure, would have made a more dignified show of it. Our man also has the irritating habit of clicking the button of his ballpoint pen, in and out, in and out, over and over again, as others are talking. It's very off-putting. 'His prospective father-in-law has already paid off half the outstanding amount and set up a monthly standing order for payment of the remainder.'

And that is that. I pay the money, Steve works his hundred hours community service and we resume life on an even keel. Restitution has been made. So where has the money gone, Steve? Why have I had to bail you out? I don't have the heart to ask these questions. Perhaps I don't want to know the answers. This is simply what I have to do, to balance things out.

21

'Hello, Mr Rutherford. Frank Daley here. If you don't mind, I'd like to speak to you and your wife about access to your roof... yes, to your roof... to carry out maintenance work.'

Google delivered two Paul Fenwicks in the area: an elderly minister of religion and a builder in Shiremoor, who was really Paul H Fenwick and who interested me briefly only because, by a strange coincidence, he is one of the contractors working on the Hadrian Park site. I know this because his wife told me that's where he was, at the new Tesco extension, when I rang. There was a baby crying in the background. She was a young mother; he, presumably, a young father. She said, sorry, but he doesn't do loft conversions. Because that was my pretext for ringing.

To my surprise, the Northumberland telephone directory also

contains only two P. Fenwicks, neither in plausible locations. I have checked the electoral register, too, and found that there are no Fenwicks at all in Coble Court. But this is not as significant, as absurd, as it might at first appear. Coble Court is a recent refurbishment. The register is almost a year out-of-date. And even if Fenwick has registered, he may have kept his name out of the edited version, the only version to which someone like myself, a humble member of the public, has access.

I have discovered, by process of elimination, that there are in fact five such gaps in the electoral register for Coble Court. This, I think, lends weight to my conviction, growing by the day, that mere documentation proves nothing, it only flatters to deceive. However, only two of these unnamed, unnamable dwellings are on the second floor: that is, the significant floor, the floor on which the light went on, as I stood at the bus stop on that evening of our last encounter. They are numbers 14 and 17. (I am certain that these are on the second floor because there are only 24 apartments in all.) So I am almost there, the quest is almost at an end. But the website of Peterson's, the Estate Agent, informs me that number 14 is vacant, for sale. I ring to check. ('Would you like to view it, sir?' 'Perhaps, perhaps. I'll be in touch.') And there we have it. No, it may not be cast-iron proof, there's no neon light in the window declaring to the world, 'Fenwick lives here', of course there's not. But it is, I think, a fairly sound deduction. Number 17 it is. I have tracked him down. Surely I have tracked him down.

So here I am, standing outside Coble Court, shivering slightly, although I think this is caused as much by my state of heightened expectation as by the chill in the air. Now, having reached this conclusion, having tracked down Fenwick and, indeed, having expended some considerable effort in doing so, you might think that I would simply ring the buzzer marked 17. And there is, indeed, a voice inside me that says, Go on, man, you're here, get on with it, just do it. But I've considered this course of action at length and, ultimately, decided against it. No, not because I'm afraid of being in error. It is easy enough, after all, to say, 'I'm sorry, sir,' or 'Forgive me, madam, I've made a mistake, good evening to you.' No, it's because to do so would put me at a disadvantage. Because down here, outside these locked gates, this tawdry little gatehouse, from which the attendant eyes me with increasing suspicion, I am Fenwick's inferior, I am nothing but a pathetic supplicant. And if I said, 'Fenwick, it's Daley, Frank Daley here, I'd like to talk to you, I want to put things right between us...' or, perhaps, 'I need to understand why you came back, Paul, why you are...' or, better still, and somewhat more directly, 'There is something from way back, Paul, back at St Aidan's, that I'd like to sit down and discuss with you...' – yes, if I say any of these things, even if I say it calmly and soberly, is it likely he will let me in? Will he reply, 'Of course, Frank, good to hear your voice, come on in. Fancy a beer?' Of course he will not. And he wouldn't do so for one of two reasons:

1. He is, indeed, conspiring against me and my family, for God knows what reason, as obscure now as it was thirty-five years ago. He pretended not to recognise me on three occasions, whilst ensuring all the while that I saw him, that I realised he was on to me. He will say, 'I've no idea who you are' and replace his entry-phone handset and then ring the attendant to warn him that there is a suspicious visitor at the main gate.

2. He doesn't remember a thing about me, he is merely the Paul Fenwick of coincidence, the match in the pack. (I played snap with myself last night and produced two matches in a single session.) And he will say, 'I've no idea who you are' and replace his entry-phone handset and then ring the attendant, even the police, to warn them that there is a suspicious visitor at the main gate, that he is being stalked.

So I'm afraid there's no choice in the matter. I must confront Fenwick on equal terms. We must see each other, face-to-face. No, confront is the wrong word. This need not be an adversarial encounter. nevertheless, I need him to see my eyes when I look at him and ask the question I should have asked then, at the time, on the terrace, 'Why, Fenwick?' And maybe, then, if I get an answer, 'How can I make amends?'

And to this end, I have devised a plan. I have noticed that there is a mobile phone antenna, a small microcell base station, in the eaves of Coble Court. It has been manufactured in the same colour as the surrounding brick so that it does not obtrude, but my trained eye is attuned to such subterfuge. Now I have no certain knowledge of this, but it is highly likely that there is, buried away somewhere in the title deeds of the occupiers of the third floor apartments, that is, the apartments on the top floor, an easement which affords access to the telecommunications company in question, for the purpose of maintaining or modifying its equipment, located on or about their roof space. (I assume, on the evidence of the flat currently for sale, that these occupiers own the freehold on their properties, but I must be cautious: some, at least, will surely be buy-to-let investments.) There will, in addition, be a clause requiring the said company to inform the occupier precisely when this access will be required, and why. And if additional equipment is to be installed at a number of sites, over a wide area, it is not inconceivable that a firm such as Pierce Constant Solutions would be contracted to carry out the wayleave negotiations. A firm, for example, like its predecessor, Cowen Utilities Ltd. My old Cowen identity card will do fine as my warrant of authority.

According to the electoral register, flat number 24 is occupied by a Mr George and Mrs Florence Rutherford. Common sense tells me that their flat is on the top floor. I'm fairly certain, too, that they are an elderly couple: I know no Georges under seventy and I haven't met a Florence since my Auntie Florrie died over twenty years ago. So they are likely to be polite, compliant, and ill-informed about wayleave matters, telecommunications and the like. They are also, almost certainly, the owners of their property: this, after all, is their last retreat, they have chosen to end their days looking at these views, eastwards, down the Tyne and out, out between the piers to the wide ocean. Such retreats are not to be rented. They are paid for with cash, with a life's savings.

I press the bell. Mr Rutherford answers. And while I am speaking to him, reassuring him, saying I have full ID, apologising for calling so late (it is half-past five), but I need to make sure that residents are at home and won't keep them more than ten minutes, and then affecting surprise when he says they've had no notification through the post – 'I'll make enquiries,' I say – I see a figure appear in the furthest window above me, and a hand drawing apart the curtains. Mr Rutherford pauses. The head in the window turns. I hear a muffled exchange. And then the golden words: 'You'd better come up, Mr Daley.'

In the event, I spend half an hour with the Rutherfords. During this time, I drink two cups of tea, commiserate with Mr Rutherford, whose eyesight is failing ('cataracts, you see, but not ripe enough yet, they say') and try to explain the precise nature of the microcell on their roof, its frequency range, its transmitter power, that it is UMTS, not GSM, and so on. Because it transpires that Mr Rutherford is a retired British Telecom engineer and (I can scarcely believe it) maintains a lively interest in the sector, despite his infirmity. So I need to hold my own. They are both wary of strangers and I must prove my credentials.

'The Fort,' says Mr Rutherford, with pride. 'That's what they call this place.'

I nod appreciatively.

'They cannit get up to their tricks in here,' he says.

I nod again. And in the end, I succeed in mollifying the couple quite well. Indeed, I entertain them so richly with my anecdotes of building mishaps (I repeat Gavin's story of the bathroom in South Shields) that I am anxious, now, not that they should complain about me to the attendant or to the police, but that they should be too voluble in singing my praises. 'But that nice man, Mr Daley, he said yesterday...' I can hear them tell the Vodaphone receptionist, when the engineer fails to turn up. So I draw our meeting to a close, courteously but a little more formally. 'The office will contact you during the next few days,' I say, without specifying which office or for what purpose.

Having spent longer than intended with the Rutherfords, I am now anxious that I might have missed Fenwick, that he might have gone out, on who knows what errand or family engagement. This would be a great inconvenience. I stood for over an hour today, at the bus stop opposite, waiting for dusk to fall, waiting for their lights to show, the Rutherfords' and Fenwick's. I stood at the bus stop yesterday and the day before that and every day for the past week, sometimes for two hours at a time, waiting so long that those departing at the outset of my vigil were already returning before its end. And waiting in vain, for either the Rutherfords would be in, or Fenwick, but never the two together. Today, my luck has turned and I must make the most of it, because God knows when I shall get such a chance again.

I am in rather too much of a hurry, therefore, as I make my way downstairs and turn into Fenwick's corridor, because I almost collide with a group of women coming out of the lift. I say 'Excuse me', but they aren't interested in me: they are, if I'm not mistaken, viewing the vacant flat, the flat that is for sale, because two of them are holding sheaves of papers, because their eyes betray the curiosity of the stranger, so that I am quite confident when I say, in mitigation of my haste, of my clumsiness, 'Must dash, dinner's in the oven,' and proffer a neighbourly smile as I open the fire door. And as I walk to the end of the corridor and approach the blue wooden door which bears the number 17, Fenwick's number, I even take my own house keys from my jacket pocket, to extend the illusion, because I can see, through the glass in the fire door, that one of the group is observing me still. Her face is familiar, I cannot say why. But she loses interest, by and by, and as she does so I hear for the first time the music coming from Fenwick's flat. It's the Duke. He's playing *Mood Indigo*. I can hear the trombone, muted, and really, really high, because this is the original recording, I'm sure of it, the 1930 recording, with the trombone high and the clarinet low. Joe Nanton. Yes, Joe Nanton on trombone. And I am ready, as ready as I ever shall be, to face him, to ask why. But I'm also beginning to feel, perhaps, that things might turn out for the best after all. That if we can sit down together, if Fenwick and I can sit back and listen to the Duke, to Joe Nanton, let it flow over us for a while, get it all out into the open, that all might be well. Because there's nothing done that cannot be undone.

Tom

1

'Not a nice day to be out, Tom.'

Tom sits in the back of the car with a woman he's sure he recognises but can't for the life of him remember where from. Every once in a while he sneaks a glance at her, wondering what she's doing here, why she's being so familiar. But mainly he looks out of the window, at the level fields blurring to a misty horizon, at the leaves streaming from the trees, and now, on a tight bend, at a long terrace built of yellow sandstone.

'Remember this, Dad?'

Tom's son is driving. There's no-one in the passenger seat but he feels safer like this, his father in the back, where Helen can keep an eye on him. As they slow down, Tom catches sight of the elegant row of arches which fronts the terrace.

'The ice-cream shop,' Tom says, animated by the sudden recognition. 'Are we havin an ice-cream then?'

But by the time he gets the words out, they have already turned the bend and the woman at his side says, 'Bit cold for ice-cream today, Tom, don't you think.'

Tom thinks about this for a while. He looks up at the sky. Because he is a tall man, he needs to bend forward to do this. He looks at the trees, at the bare fields, and nods his head.

'Too cold,' he says. But he has forgotten about the ice-cream.

A minute later, Tom begins tapping his fingers on his knees. 'The geraniums,' he says, because this is what is on his mind now. 'It's too cold, you see.'

The woman looks at him, her lips tightening slightly, as though anticipating what is to follow.

'I need to get the geraniums in.'

Tom sits back and stares at the picture composing itself behind his eyes.

'And the marguerites.'

And then, leaning forward again, and speaking with urgency now, so that his son can feel his father's breath on his neck: 'Or the frost'll get them.'

Tom raps the palm of his hand on the top of the driver's seat.

'We'd best get back now, son, don't you think?'

Tom doesn't see the eyes looking back at him, anxiously, in the rear view mirror, but continues his tapping, wanting the outing to come to an end, needing to tell the driver, this is far enough, this is his stop.

'Dad!'

The woman at his side puts her hand on his right arm and says, in a slow, deliberate voice, as though she is repeating a formula: 'The geraniums are in, Tom. And the marguerites. All the non-hardies are in. Every one of them.'

Tom shakes his head.

'They can't be, man,' he says. 'Not Mrs Robson's. She's too old.'

The woman squeezes his arm gently.

'She's dead, Tom. I'm sorry. Mrs Robson's dead.'

2

'Now there's this old fella lives out Wylam way,' says Tom. 'And it's time for him to dig over his garden, y'see, to plant his seed potatoes.' Tom's sitting in a maroon, upholstered armchair with Queen Ann legs, the middle in a row of five identical chairs arranged in a semicircle to face the large picture window and, through it, the boats, moored in the marina, and the far shore. He's sitting forward, because he's performing. He needs to be able to look around him, to see everyone.

'Now, up until then,' says Tom, 'the old fella had always been able to ring his son, who lived down the road, and say, "Howay over, son, it's time to plant the tatties," and that's what he'd do, his son would come over, every year, to help his dad. But this year, the year I'm talkin about, the young lad cannit make it because he's in jail, y'see, on account of his committin a serious robbery. So what can the old fella do? Well there's nowt he can do but get out his pen and paper and write a letter.'

Tom turns the fingers of his right hand into a pen, the palm of his left into a sheet of paper.

'And in the letter he says, "I'm sorry, son, I've tried me best to dig over the garden, but I don't know if I can do it all meself, it's that heavy. Mebbes I can manage a wee bit at a time."'

'So the son reads the letter,' says Tom, and he writes back straightaway and says, "Dad, whatever ye dee, divvent dig up the garden, cos ye divvent knaa where I've buried the stuff." So he doesn't. No, he doesn't go near the garden, the old fella. He just sits there, twiddlin his thumbs.'

Tom sits back in his chair for a moment and twiddles his thumbs, to show what he means.

'And that night,' he goes on, 'just as it was gettin dark, all the police cars in Northumberland turn up outside his house, sirens screamin, CID, the works. And away they go, diggin here, diggin there, diggin all over the place, spades, shovels, metal detectors, the lot. And what do they find? Eh? What do they find?'

Coming in through the door, as the care assistant is now doing, pushing a tea trolley, it is possible to see only the dome of Tom's head, bobbing from side to side as he speaks, tufts of white hair protruding above his ears. And now, also, the right hand beating a staccato accompaniment on the arm of the chair as he approaches the end of his story.

'What do they find? Eh? I'll tell you what they find,' says Tom. 'They find nowt. Not a scrap.'

He pauses.

'So next day the old fella gets a letter from his son.'

He pauses again, turns the palm of his hand into a sheet of paper, squints at it.

'"Dear Dad," says the son, "Dear Dad," he says, in his letter, "sorry, but that's aall I can dee for the moment. Hope it's aall reet t'stick the tatties in now."'

'Hope it's aall reet to stick the tatties in now.' Tom looks at each resident in turn, first those on the left, then those on the right, and then back again. They are all women. 'Hope it's aall reet to stick the tatties in now.' He repeats the punch-line, beating again on the arm of the chair, thinking the story is worth better than this, it's surely worth more than a few feeble smiles, and wondering, has he left something out?

71

Tom, the newcomer at The Quays, looks much too big for his chair, whereas the others have become too small. The contrast is accentuated by their clothes. Tom is wearing blue denims and a red and blue check shirt, sleeves rolled up as if ready for manual work. The women, in their pale blue cardigans and grey woollen skirts, their blouses buttoned at neck and wrist, are dressed only to sit. They are all one in his eyes. So when he whispers to the assistant, as she pours his tea, 'I meant to tell you, sister, me son's brought us to the wrong place,' it's easy to see his point. Tom looks at the women on either side of him, the as yet nameless women, and tries again. 'I told the lad,' he says. 'I told him, I cannit go back to Shields. There's no work for us in Shields.'

The care assistant smiles and nods. 'Can you reach the biscuits all right, Tom?' she asks.

Time passes.

'So he brought us here instead,' says Tom. 'So's I can be near. You can see his house down there. Coble Court they call it. His flat, I mean. Number seventeen, Coble Court.'

'Nice,' says a woman called Kate, from the end of the row, leaning forward, looking through the window, trying to be helpful. She has seen men come and go in this place and knows they don't cope well, that they can't get used to being cooped up, to being amongst women.

'I said it's nice,' says Kate again, thinking that Tom is cupping his ear, that he is hard of hearing. But in fact there's not much wrong with Tom's hearing, for his age, or with his eyesight, for that matter. And he isn't cupping his ear. He's rubbing it with his index finger, up and down, up and down, gently at first and then more vigorously. His eyes have turned inward now, far away from the potato field, from the bobbing boats. Presently, he pinches the lobe between finger and thumb and gives it a swift tug.

'Cannit get the buggers off,' he says, shifting a little this way and that as though to get a better purchase, a more effective angle of attack. And Kate asks, does he need help, or can she get the assistant, perhaps. And Tom says, pointing to his ear, 'Put your finger there, just there.'

But Kate is too infirm to rise from her chair. Tom sees this and says,

'Sit still, hinny, I'll be there now.' Because he's used to doing jobs for women such as Kate, elderly women who can't fend for themselves. Perhaps he also sees, in her long pale face and white, brushed-back hair, the shadow of something that was once beguiling.

And he gets up, wavering only slightly, placing a hand on the wing of his chair, just in case, and draws himself up to his full height. The women's eyes follow him. He looks around the room in search of a stool, a small chair, anything that will allow him to sit next to Kate. The women's eyes look where he looks. Finding nothing, Tom gives a small sigh of resignation and walks the few paces to where Kate is sitting. He limps slightly. Then, leaning with both hands on the arm of her chair, he lowers himself, first onto his right knee, the stronger of the two, then the left, and bends his head to the level of her lap, where her hands are folded.

'There,' he says, moving his finger up and down behind his right ear. 'The wires. Can you feel them?'

3

'"Look out for the light," he said.'

It's six o'clock. Tom is sitting in front of the window, waiting to show Kate that they can see where his son lives even at night.

'"Look out for the light," he said, "and you'll know I'm at home."'

And he's got to be very careful he gets the right light, because there's that many of them. There's the white lights and there's the orange lights. There's the lights that flicker and there's the lights that don't, they just come on and stay on. There's the lights this side of the river and the lights the other side, and you can't always tell, from up here, looking across, which is which. So he's got to keep he's eyes fixed on that one block, that one floor, that one window, as the dusk gets deeper. And in a short while the light does, indeed, come on and Tom wants to say, 'There it is, see?' because he can stop concentrating now, he can relax, he's done his job. But Kate is asleep, her head on her chest, her

73

face even paler now in the fluorescent light, and there's no-one else in the lounge.

'Not goin down there,' he mutters to himself, meaning his bedroom and knowing that's where everyone else has gone, for a nap before supper, or just to be alone, because being with other people is tiring. 'Plenty of time for sleep when you're dead, hinny,' he says, looking at Kate, whose eyes are still shut. Her lips mouth something inaudible.

'Seven bells soon,' Tom says.

But mainly he doesn't like going to his bedroom because it's downstairs. It's not right, he thinks, going downstairs to bed. Like going into the fo'c's'le. And it's hot in the fo'c's'le. Under the hatch. Hot and cramped. Even now, he thinks, in the dead of winter, when you cross the Line. No winter there. On the Line. Sleep on deck rather than go down there, he thinks, with the flies and the bugs and the mosquitoes. It might be better, he thinks, if he could open his bedroom window, but he's on the ground floor and he's seen lads going by through the day lobbing cans into the bushes. At night, who knows? But it's not just that, not just the window, the heat. There's more room up there too, on the fore-hatch, spread your gear about a bit. Bit of tarpaulin against the sun.

'Three weeks to Buenos Aires, mebbes four,' says Tom, noticing that Kate has stirred a little. 'Fray Bentos,' he explains. 'For the meat.'

Kate has woken up now. She looks at him.

'For the corned beef,' he says.

'That's nice,' she says, weakly, thinking he means supper.

The bell rings.

'Seven bells,' says Tom.

'Six,' says Kate. 'Six we eat here, Tom.'

'Aye, aye,' Tom says. 'You might as well. You might as well.'

Time passes. Another day.

'I told you, man,' says Tom. 'I told you. There's no point sendin us back to Shields.'

'They won't listen,' says Molly, who's in a wheelchair. A care assistant has just brought her to the window.

'Come again,' says Tom, unaware that anyone was listening. Unaware, even, that he has spoken.

'Kids.'

Tom sits up and looks around the wing of his chair. Molly has been placed a little behind him, so that he must crane his neck to see her properly. He is surprised at her wavy hair, her lipstick, her round face; he is surprised, in particular, at the absence of hawk in her face. And he thinks, They've got you too.

'You got boys, then?' asks Tom.

'No. Two girls. That was your lad just going out, was it?'

Tom is taken aback by the speed of the reply. He knows he's expected to say something in return but, for the life of him, he can't think what, so he just says, 'He's brought us to the wrong place, y'see.' Hoping that will do.

'The wrong place?' Molly says.

And there he is, on the back foot again. So he's got to give it another go.

'He says she's brought them in herself, but I don't think so.'

'Brought what in, Tom?'

'You don't know?' says Tom, surprised. But thinks, then, no, you wouldn't, would you, because you're new here, too.

'He says she's brought her geraniums in, but she's too old, y'see, she's gettin on for ninety, Mrs Robson. The geraniums. Yes. And there's others. There's others need bringin in an all.'

Molly waits, to see whether Tom means to name any more flowers.

'So you're a bit of a gardener, then,' she says, flatly, telling not asking. And Tom would like to show her that he's really a lot more than that, he's more than a bit of a gardener, yes, he could show her a thing or two about gardening, but she's altogether too fast for him. So he begins to work his index finger up and down the back of his ear, up and down, up and down. Yes, he would like to tell her a thing or two, but today he can only say, with a bit of a chuckle in his voice, because he doesn't want to make too big a fuss, 'It's the blasted wires, y'see. That's what did it.'

But Molly's not interested in wires. She says: 'There's gardens in the Dene. Jean takes me to sit there when it's fine.'

And she tells Tom to go and look out of the window, because she can't get up.

'All the way up the bank,' she says. 'Tulips. Wall flowers. And... and...'

She stops and thinks. Tom gets up, places a hand on the wing of his chair, stretches to his full height to get rid of the stiffness, and walks over to the window. He looks out. At a ferry crossing the river, down to his left. At the far bank and its jumble of warehouses and new flats. And then, over to his right, the reclaimed grain store, jutting out into the river. Coble Court. He thinks, the light will go on soon. At the end, right by the river. Not the top floor, but the next one down. He looks at his watch. Half-past three. No, a while yet. By the time it gets dark. By the time he gets back from work. Tom leans on the handrail and wonders why he's standing here, what he's supposed to be looking at. It's too soon, he thinks.

'And pergoliums,' says Molly, decisively.

'Pelargoniums,' says Tom.

'Not now, of course,' says Molly.

'Come again,' says Tom, looking back at her, taking his left hand off the rail.

'Not in November. You wouldn't get them in November, would you?'

This is a question. So Tom answers it. He tells Molly about pelargoniums. He tells her about the several varieties. About the Red Cascade, which will certainly have faded by now, but also about the Bredon, which flowers throughout the year in milder latitudes. And the Dolly Vardens, of course, which are prized more for their foliage, but which are rather delicate and need to be wintered indoors. And Tom starts to fret again, not about the Dolly Vardens, he doesn't recollect having any Dolly Vardens out this year. Nor about Mrs Robson's geraniums, because Mrs Robson is dead. But about the others. About Doris Simpson over by Kirkley Mill, whose mignonettes should have been put in cloches by now, and her phacelia too. All that blue so late in the year. And the Nesbitts at Heugh House. He needs to plant next year's daffs and crocuses and tulips and grape hyacinths, he needs to fill all those gaps in the borders, or else what will there be to look forward to, what a disappointment it'll be, come springtime, with nothing to see, and no colour anywhere.

4

Tom is not the only man at The Quays. There's Sid, for example. But Sid spends a lot of his time in the back lounge, where the television is on all the time, where nobody speaks very much, and Tom doesn't go there. Or else he'll be in his room, having a fag, which he's not supposed to do, blowing the smoke out of the window. Sid's room is next to Tom's, and this is another reason why Tom dislikes going to bed, because Sid coughs: thick, growling coughs from deep inside his chest. He does this in hourly spasms, more or less, throughout the night. Tom might not hear the first short bark, or even the second, but the third always lifts the mind's flap, just a touch, so that when the phlegm rises, collects, and then, a few seconds later, Sid gobs into the sink, Tom is back in the stokehold, trying to keep up steam, heaving up the ashes, crossing the Line at 120°, eighteen days gone already and eighteen more to go, a bad trip, the water on rations and nowhere to wash but down in the engine room, the bucket slopping down into a hot well of grease, rising again with a suck. Like washing in hot oil. So that, even though he's not there at all, he's tucked up in crisp cotton, Tom fingers the salt water boils on his hands, he scratches the prickly heat rash around his neck. And when he's spat, Sid says, 'That's you gone to the devil, you bastard,' and lies back on his bed and sighs and says, 'Fuck it'. And that's when Tom wakes up, in a lather.

Tom's sitting in the River Lounge again, facing the window, when Sid enters. Kate is there, too, but she's talking to Jess, whom Tom hasn't seen before. Kate turns to Tom every now and then, to include him in the conversation, but he can get no purchase on it. He doesn't know who Dot and Phyllis are, he doesn't understand why Kate laughs when Jess says, 'He thought Il Divo was the Three Tenors!' and when they start talking about Kate's grandchildren, who are coming this afternoon, Tom would like to say, yes, I've got grandbairns too, and a great granddaughter, over Monkseaton way, a bonny wee thing with tight little plaits, and he conjures up a mental picture of her, as best he can, trying to home in on the eyes, the coat she wore, the look of her hair, and Kate, still trying to encourage him, says, 'Ee, the bairns grow up fast these days, don't they, Tom?' But it's the name he needs, before he can do any of this, because you've got to have a name first, the name comes before everything, of course it does. And it won't come. His own great granddaughter and the name just won't come. Just at the moment when he might have chipped in, he can't get hold of it. It's there somewhere, a slippery fish of a name, but there's no hook, not one.

So he just watches and smiles.

And in a minute or two he's drifted off anyway, because he didn't sleep well last night.

'No, Smiths Docks. Next one down river.'

And when Tom hears Sid's voice, from the far side of the room, he thinks, why have they put the television on so early? Because he hasn't really heard Sid speak before: it's only on the television he hears men's voices these days.

'We'd clock on for the night shift and do a bit work...'

And even when Tom wakes properly and sees Sid's thin, stooped figure standing in front of the television, which is not on, even when he sees the nicotined fingers curled around the handle of his walking stick, and the slow, watery eyes looking directly at him, he doesn't realise that this is Sid, because Sid is a cough, an expectoration, a curse in the night.

'We'd hop over the wall and do a bit filletin at the Fish Quay...'

So it's only the cough that gives him away, a short burst of dry coughs that comes on as Sid raises his right arm and pats the top of his head with the palm of his hand.

'We'd tap wor heads. Like this. Let everybody know.'

He speaks in gulps, surfacing for air at the end of every few words.

'Let everybody know. Gaffers were comin. Cos of their duts.' And he taps his head again. 'Their duts.'

Tom has missed most of the story but he smiles and nods, to keep up appearances. Sid is encouraged.

'You a Shields lad, then, er…'

And Tom knows the answer to this one, although he's a little taken aback by the directness of the question.

'Long time ago,' he says. 'No point goin back there now.' And he looks out of the window.

5

'George had an allotment up on Cleveland Road.'

Jess is a tight little ball of a woman with no neck and the sound of budgerigars in her chest. She's leafing through a colour magazine.

'Me husband,' says Jess. 'That was his name. George.'

She's been told by Molly that Tom is a gardener and she's pleased about this, because it's something they've got in common, in a manner of speaking. Because it gives her a way in.

'He could walk there easy from Scorer Street…'

And because it means she can tell him about her husband, she can show Tom, who she thinks is really quite tall and presentable, and so fresh from the outside world, she can show him that she knows the ways of men.

'More than I could do now,' says Jess, patting her chest, wheezing, leaving a gap for some response.

Tom nods. Which is enough.

'Got prizes for his leeks and marrows,' she says. Then, with a smile, she puts the tips of her fingers on Tom's hand.

'But they say you're more of a flower man, Tom.'

Time passes. The daily medications are brought around. Molly is taken to have her hair done. Kate notices that there is an ambulance in the forecourt. 'I didn't know anyone was ill,' she says. 'Not really ill,' she corrects herself.

'He'd terrible trouble with pests,' says Jess.

'Come again,' says Tom.

'On his veg,' says Jess. 'Caterpillars all over his cabbages. Eatin the middle out of them without you knowin it.' She makes ten caterpillars of her stubby fingers.

'Cabbage moths,' says Tom.

'Moths?' says Jess, sceptically.

Tom turns to face her.

'Caterpillars only eat the outer leaves.' Tom speaks slowly, deliberately. He knows about vegetables. Of course he does. Who said he only knew about flowers? So he speaks like a book, to show he knows. 'But the moth grubs go to the heart of the cabbage.'

Jess can't question what Tom says, because he says it with such authority, in a voice she hasn't heard before, a bit short, that's what she'd say. And that's what she will say, when she sees Kate. He's a bit short tempered, that one. But she can't disagree. Who is she to disagree? All the same, she moves her hand back to her lap, feeling uncomfortable, feeling it can't be right, surely, that her late husband is being contradicted and is in no position to answer back. And disappointed that she can't make a better job of fighting his corner.

'He sprayed them, mind. That got rid of them.'

Tom shakes his head. But this time she doesn't ask. She just waits.

'Ladybirds,' he says.

Jess hesitates.

'I thought you said cabbage moths.'

'Ladybirds. That's what'll get shot of them for you.'

'A bit late...' she begins, irritated now, because it wasn't advice she was after, that wasn't the point. Especially this advice, which just sounds daft.

But Tom says, 'No, no, you wait for the warm weather, when they'll have plenty to feed on, they'll do the trick then, you mark my words, if you can get them, of course, you've got to get them first, aye, that might be a bit difficult...'

And Jess is still trying to hold on to the thread, to follow it through to the next bit of the conversation, because there's lots more she'd planned to talk about, she hasn't really got to the bottom of anything yet, and she doesn't want to give up, no, even though it's harder work than she'd expected. But Tom's started to fidget, like she's seen him do before, flicking his ear, his eyes somewhere else, a long way off.

Men, she thinks.

6

'She's a bonny wee thing, isn't she, Tom?' says Matron.

Tom is sitting in the corner of the lounge furthest from the door. The television crackles and hisses in the background. At Tom's side, on his personal table, there is a half-full pint glass of beer. In front of him, on a long pine coffee table, are his cards and presents. Only minutes after his visitors have left, these are already disturbing his sense of order. He gathers the cards together, seven of them, and stacks them in a neat pile to his left. He puts the pen back in its box and places this on top of the three books which he has already stacked in front of him in order of size, the crossword puzzle book on top of the John Grisham, and these, in turn, on top of *The Diary of a Cottage Gardener*. The wrapping paper he folds neatly and sets apart to his right. The clock, however, is a different matter.

'Your granddaughter, Tom?'

'Great granddaughter,' says Tom, as he puts the folded brown paper and the blue ribbon into the box marked

COCKPIT CLOCK & BAROMETER SET
Mounted on a mahogany effect board

'Daft buggers,' he says, under his breath, but then chuckles because he's feeling quite mellow now, after the beer, to which he's become unaccustomed. 'What d'they expect us to do with this?' He looks up at Matron, shaking his head, chuckling again.

'So you were at sea, were you, Tom?' she asks.

And Tom says yes, a long while back though. 'Crossed the Line twelve times,' he says. And he wants to go on, but there are too many threads to gather together, he grasps one and the others fall away. 'Thirty-six days one time,' he says. And thinks, was it that time? Was it that afternoon, a Friday afternoon, when he pulled alongside, no money, corny hands, blisters, coal dust in the cracks of his neck, in his eye sockets, under his nails, in the whorls of his fingers, so he couldn't shift it. Was it that time?

And Tom says, 'Yes, every day, six in the mornin till ten at night, shovellin the coal, out of one deck, into another, down into the stoke hold. Not much money, but we'd a whack of cigarettes, all out of bond, y'see. Peso for a hundred tabs.'

And he remembers then. He remembers Badger saying, two pesos'll get you a canny wee milonguera, and grinning at him, knowing he's as green as they come. All in their Sunday best too, which was only dungarees, but clean, and clean sweat rags round their necks. And Badger asks, where we're goin tonight? And Spike says The Arches, and Scouse Bill says The Rags, and Stump says The Flyin Angel, and Badger says, where'd you fancy then, bonny lad, looking at Tom, who hadn't a clue, but it's The Boca they end up in, down on the front, big tin shack of a place, all yellow and blue. Full of Germans and Itis an all. But that was '37, so what did they care?

'Aye, back in '37. The first time,' says Tom.

And that's when Badger teaches him how to say hello. *Rechinar la cama*, he says, *rechinar la cama*, and makes him repeat it, *rechinar la cama*, and Tom knows he's pulling his leg, of course he is, he's just about splitting himself trying not to laugh. Badger they call him because of this streak of white in his hair. So Tom doesn't say it, not this time, not the first time, and it's her that speaks anyway, the *milonguera*, and he doesn't understand a word, not then, not yet, only a lad then, but he knows what she means alright.

And Matron says, '1937? ' and Tom stops because he realises that some of his words have broken away from their moorings and come bubbling up to the surface, and he's not sure which ones, and his glass is empty and there's a crack in the door marked Officers Only and a bald head is peeking out, 'Back aboard, back aboard,' it squeals. 'Leave expires at midnight.' And Tom says, 'Matron, there's somethin behind me ear.' And he lifts his right hand to the side of his head. 'Y'see it? Y'see it?'

7

Snow is gusting across the Tyne. It's already settled on the grass in front of The Quays, on the roofs below, on the warehouses and flats on the far bank. And Molly says, looking at Tom, 'I remember it freezing over. The river. The year Jean was born.' But Tom isn't looking at the snow or listening to Molly. He's waiting for the light to come on because this is the day his son's due back. He turns the pages of the pocket diary in which his son has marked the days he'll visit and the days he'll be away. A tick means that he'll call, a cross means he won't be at home at all, so there's no point even looking for the light. The other days are blank. Most days are blank. No visit, that means, but probably a light. A sequence of ten crosses ended yesterday. Holiday, La Gomera it says at the top. He had a postcard yesterday, or perhaps the day before, with a picture of a white house on it, a white house in a green valley full of bougainvillea, and a message reminding him that he'll call on Tuesday. Helen's better, it said. Tom has no idea who Helen is. But the diary confirms the date. Ten crosses, and then today, Tuesday, a tick. Today he's back. Today the light goes back on. And he will call.

Because Tom is engrossed in his diary, he does not notice Sid, who is now sitting at the end of the semicircle of chairs, watching the thickening plumage of snow cover the window.

'Aye, I remember,' says Sid. 'The dock froze over.' And he clears his throat. 'The Albert Edward. And snow, an all, on top of it. Just like today.' Sid knows that only the dock froze over, not the whole river, but he inserts his correction delicately, so as not to cause offence.

Molly says that Jack, her husband, worked in the Albert Edward during the war, before it was bombed. And Jess, not to be outdone, says that her mam and dad were ARP wardens. There is a silence, then, during which each of them ponders the other memories, the harder ones. It is true that all of these have been rehearsed many times before, so many times that they do not need repeating, they can be taken as read. So you would guess that the silence, which descends every once in a while, might be enough. Might even, in its own way, be thought eloquent. Despite this, silence rarely is enough. Because, it seems, there is always some residual itch in one or other of these recollections that, on occasions such as this, demands to be scratched. Perhaps they fear the memories will dissolve, like the snowflakes, unless frozen into words. Or, as now, there is someone new who needs to be initiated, shepherded into the fold.

And with this in mind, Jess might, for example, turn to Tom to say how they grew most of their own veg in those days. And this, in turn, might prompt Kate to say, yes, and rabbits, too, they kept rabbits for food, and how her dad would make excuses for why they'd disappeared, one by one. Yes, and how he'd go to down to Tynemouth as well, him and Archie, her older brother, to gather bits of coal from the beach, and how the sea coal would spit on the fire and shoot embers onto the mat and her mam would set her to cut out the burnt bits and stitch new bits in. Yes. And then, looking out at the darkening sky and just hearing, through the double glaze, the faint moan of the wind in the eaves, Kate might say, 'Barrage balloons. D'you remember the singing noise? The noise the cables made?' Because these things have all been said before.

But today, this does not happen. Because each of them – Jean, Kate and Molly, and the others too, the nameless others who have been inclined to keep their distance from the outset – are wary of Tom. He has been a little abrupt today. His tics and fidgets have been more frequent, more insistent. And no-one wants to create a scene. So, instead, Jess says to Sid, 'You're too young to remember, I suppose, a young lad like yourself.'

And Sid, to begin with, just smiles. But it's a mischievous smile. Because Sid has his own stories as well, of course he has. And Jess knows this, which is why she's teasing him. And he's got to draw them up from his lungs piece by little piece, because the words are so heavy, the rope so worn. Just nuggets of stories, really, like bits of black clinker. How he and his friends would go around the bomb sites. Shields, Wallsend, over the river sometimes. How they'd collect bits of AA shells from the rubble. Splinters mainly, he says. But sometimes big chunks, too. And Sid pretends to hold a chunk of shrapnel in his hands, to show how big and heavy they were. And he'd keep them in his dad's shed, Sid says, these bits of bomb. Because his dad was away, in Egypt or somewhere like that. And he got wrong off his mam when she found out. Of course he did. Her sister'd been bombed out herself, hadn't she? Hair turned white overnight. And the three women nod in sympathy, because this is a story they can follow. It's a man's story, which is nice, it's a change, but it's got women in it, and Sid tells it in a nice gentle voice, but broken, so that he needs them, the three women, to keep it going, to stop it from falling back through the cracks in his lungs.

'So I went into the ACT then,' says Sid. 'Grew up fast then.' He coughs, and collects his breath.

And Tom, who's still waiting for the light to go on in his son's flat, says: 'I was a ladybird miner, you know.' He looks back at Sid and Kate and Jess and the others and says: 'Before the bombs. Long before any of that business.'

Jess tuts quietly to herself, thinking how rude this man is, how uncomfortable he makes her feel. And now, she thinks, nobody knows whether they should be listening to him or to Sid. But everybody's eyes are on Tom, Sid's too, because they're not sure they've caught it right, because it doesn't make sense, and how can they say anything, how can they even ask a question when it makes no sense?

Tom is unaware of any of this. In fact, he's caught no more than a few words of Sid's stories. Instead, his attention has been wholly occupied during the past few moments by the striking display of gerbera which a care assistant has placed on the small pine table in the recess of the bay window. Or, rather, not so much by the flowers themselves as by the contrast between their bright yellows and oranges and the snow beyond. He shivers inwardly at the extraordinariness of it. But only briefly. Because then he thinks, it's not right. It's out of season. Such colour in February, he thinks. Such ostentation.

But there is something else, too: something about the way, from

Tom's vantage point, the tall blue vase, the flowers and the deep green foliage are set against the framed whiteness. And this is the reason why, with a sudden gasp of recognition, he says, 'I was a ladybird miner'. And this, also, is why, a moment later and to the surprise of his fellow residents, who are expecting some explanation, he rises from his chair and leaves the room, smiling all the while, saying to Molly, in passing, 'I'll show you now.' And to Jess, 'You'll see now.'

8

Tom must go down on both knees to pull open the bottom drawer. He does this slowly, in stages, but quite instinctively, this being his usual gardening posture, first leaning on the wooden chair to steady himself, then lowering himself onto the right knee and finally, when he's sure of his balance, drawing down the left leg, the stiffer of the two, the one he must try to avoid putting too much weight on because he knows it won't hold. On opening the drawer, he is bemused to find in it an array of woolly pullovers, neatly folded, because although they are familiar enough, they are out of place here. He looks at them, he places a hand between them, under them, in the folds. Pullovers. Nothing but pullovers. He closes this drawer and opens the middle drawer. Here he finds, on the left, socks, and on the right, gloves, six, seven, eight pairs of them, two in fine calf leather, soft to the touch, scarcely worn, then a thick woollen pair and then some lighter cotton ones. And the rigger gloves? Tom notices that the riggers aren't there. The rubber ones have gone, too. But then, he thinks, they'd be outside in the shed anyway, both the riggers and the rubbers, being grubby, not being meant for indoors, so he's not bothered and in any case they're not what he's looking for.

Tom doesn't open the top drawer as he knows it contains only underwear. Instead, he gets up again, precisely reversing each of his earlier movements, more slowly, of course, as he is now straining against gravity, and settles himself down on the wooden chair, to gather his strength. He looks around the room, at its shades of light pine and beige.

At the wardrobe. At a clock with two faces which, he is sure, has been put there since he was last in the room. At the door of the en suite, which Tom prefers to leave ajar, so he will not confuse it with the other door, the real door. He looks at the fire notice on the back of this door. And then his eyes return to the table on which he is now leaning. He sees nothing here but a diary, a postcard from La Gomera and a potted hyacinth. Nothing. Nevertheless, he fingers its dark polished wood, its worn edges, aimlessly at first but knowing that his fingers often know better than his eyes. And in a few moments they locate the small metal handle which is concealed by the table's overhanging lip. Of course, Tom thinks. Daft bugger. He pulls open the drawer and takes out the brown envelope. He holds one end between thumb and forefinger and shakes out the contents. And there they are, the oranges and the snow, tumbling onto the table. He feels another shudder, somewhere deep inside him.

FOOTHILL ORANGE GROVE IN WINTER. CALIFORNIA   C-1233

Tom picks up the card, runs the tips of his fingers across its shiny surface, the gaudy colours. The oranges, Tom thinks, are so close, he can almost pluck one from its branch just by leaning forward, opening his fingers a little. And Irma must be there too, somewhere off to the right, out of sight, in the packing house. Irma, in her white gloves, wrapping the thin tissue around each fruit, folding it tight below the stem so that the Sunkist stands out. And her hands moving that fast, filling her 16 cent boxes, that fast, you can scarcely see them, tweeking the ones on the outside so the Sunkist shows through the slats, pressing them down just a touch, just a touch, mustn't bruise them, so there's a bulge in the middle, that's how you've got to do it, she says, that's how the customers like it. So fast.

Tom turns the card over.

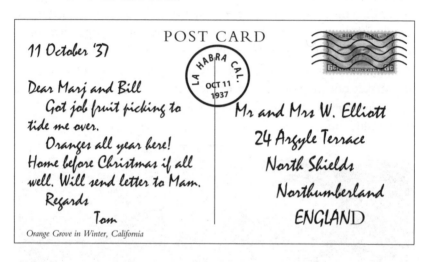

The letter, Tom thinks. Where's the letter? Because there's so much more to say, so much more to tell his mam, much more than he could put on this old scrap of a card. And he realises it's not the card he's after, now, he doesn't know why he was bothering with that. So he looks through the other bits and pieces that have fallen out of the envelope, he sets them out in a row on the table, neat and squared off, all the other cards, a passport, long expired, his Seaman's Identity Card, his pink CRSI card, and he puts a hand on each item in turn, to make sure. But it's not there. He holds up the brown envelope again, turns it upside down, pushes his fingers inside, right to the corners. Nothing. He looks on the floor, in case it has fallen. He goes down again, on one knee, then the other, hurrying this time, looking under the table, feeling under the bed.

And Emilio. Of course, Emilio.

'So we're up in the hills, high up,' says Tom to Molly and another woman, with dark glasses, whom Tom hasn't seen before. They are the only ones left in the window lounge. 'We're up high, me and Emilio. The first winter. Start of November. Before the snows come. To mark the trees. That's where they'd be, y'see. Under the trees. Down amongst the pine needles. Gettin ready for winter. Stick your hand in and it'd be crawlin with them. So that's why we'd mark the tree. To know where to come back to. D'you mind?'

Tom picks up his biro and draws a ‡ in the margin of Molly's Chronicle.

'Emilio's mark, y'see. His own mark. To show it's his bed.'

Tom looks at Molly, but her thin lips remain closed, her eyes looking at the mark, giving nothing away. So he turns to the other woman and says, 'Excuse me, I was tellin your friend about...' But there are no eyes there, behind the glasses, none that he can see, no eyes at all, and anyway, Tom has lost the thread. He looks hard at the newspaper on which he's just drawn the mark, wondering why, wondering what's in it that interests him. And the bell goes for supper, and Molly and her friend are already making their way to the door.

'Seven bells, Tom,' says the care assistant. 'You're gonna be late for your watch.'

9

'Like I was sayin,' says Tom, thinking that Kate's nod and smile are meant for him. 'We were up above the Kern, I think it was the Kern, that's the river there, y'see, aye, and there's me, up front with the burro and all the gear, workin me way up and down, followin the track through the trees, and these fellas come up to us, three fellas and a dog, all with fishin rods, aye, the fellas, I mean, not the dog, ha! And one of them asks us, "Goin minin down there?" Because they were still minin for gold then, y'see. Back in the thirties this was. Everybody wantin to make a buck, like they say. Hard times. Aye. Old fella he was, lot of stubble. Grey stubble. Out with his lads. And I says, "Well, in a manner of speakin." And I tell him what we're doin and he says, "Ah, you're buggers, are you?" Ha! But he doesn't laugh. No. That's what they call them there, y'see. Bugs. Ladybugs. Ladybugs they call them, not ladybirds. And if you go and collect them, well, you're a bugger. Ha! So I says to him, I says, "We're ladybird miners, us. That's what we are. We're ladybird miners." And he laughs then. Aye, he laughs. So that's why I call meself a ladybird miner, y'see. That was in the summer. You wouldn't get that many people out in the winter, not fishin. Not buggin either. Summer, though, it was crawlin. Fishin in the Kern, minin, buggin, all sorts. Everybody out for what they could get, make a dollar. Aye. Emilio says, "Tom," he says, "you know where ladybugs are, you don't tell your wife, you don't tell your burro, you don't tell nobody, or –"'

Tom turns towards Kate and draws his finger across his throat.

'Aye. A hundred beds in summer, that's how many he worked, Emilio. Secret, he said. But you knew where the beds were right enough, knew where everybody's beds were, there were branches all over the place, fir tree branches. He says, "tell them how we do it and – "'

Tom turns to Jess this time and again draws his finger across his throat.

'That was Emilio's job, y'see.' says Tom. 'Cuttin down the branches. Me, I'd go off to get the water. Back and forth I'd be, all day long, carryin water from the creek. Back and forth. And he'd pour the water over the ground then. He had a kind of waterin rose to do it, y'know, like you get on a waterin can, except he had it on the end of a rubber tube. Aye, and he'd pour it over the ground. Ha! Over the ground. I says to him, I says, there's nowt but leaves there, man, Emilio, what you pourin water on the leaves for?'

Tom looks at Jess, then at Kate. To show them how he looked at Emilio. Wide-eyed. Incredulous.

'"What you pourin water on the leaves for, man?' I says to him. "You wait," he says. "You wait."'

Tom leans over the arm of his chair and taps the side of his nose with his index finger.

'"You wait," he says. And right enough, a minute later, up they come, hundreds of them, thousands of them. "They think it rains,

Tom," Emilio says. Aye, that many of them, the leaves all turn orange. Orange spots, y'see, they've got orange spots there, the ladybirds. So y'cannit see the leaves any more. And that's when he says, "Get the branches, Tom." So we get the branches and spread them all over where we've been pourin the water, all over where the ladybirds have come up.'

Tom spreads the branches in the air in front of him, looking at Kate, then at Jess, making sure they are paying attention.

'"Catarina likes keep her feet dry," Emilio says. Catarina he calls a ladybird. Mexican, y'see. And they do. They like the dry. Because I see them all climbin up into the branches, onto the needles, to get out the wet, y'see, and all we've got to do then is shake them off, shake them into the bags. Aye. Summer, y'see. It was that easy in summer. Sieve them then. Like what d'you call it, like how you sieve gold, panning, aye, panning. That easy, y'see, in summer. Long as nobody gets to the beds before you.'

And Tom looks to the left, at Kate, to the right, at Jess, trying to gauge whether they've followed this bit.

'Of course, I've told you all this before, haven't I?'

10

Somebody's opened the window. There's a draft. The sound of bells.

'Bells,' says Jess, pleasantly surprised.

'Church bells,' says Kate. 'They sound like church bells.'

Tom clears his throat. 'South Shields,' he says.

'South Shields?' says Jess, and looks at Tom. 'Surely not. Not over the river.'

'South Shields,' he says. Because where else?

Tom sees Molly in the far corner, by the table, talking to a nurse. He wonders why the nurse is here, in the lounge, sitting down, drinking tea. They're too far away for him to make out what's being said, except for the odd word, and even then Tom's not sure whether he's hearing them or the voices on the television. He tries to piece something together from the way Molly's shaking her head, tight-lipped and frowning, from the way the nurse is rummaging in her bag, pulling a piece of paper out of an envelope, placing it on the table. But he can't make any sense of it. So he has no option but to get up from his chair and walk over to where they are sitting, taking care to go around the back of the room so as not to interrupt the other residents' viewing. He draws up a seat at the end of the table furthest from Molly and the nurse, which he thinks is a respectful distance, and waits for a lull in their conversation.

'Excuse me,' says Tom, after a while, catching the nurse's eye, sensing that she knows he is waiting, 'I hope it's not too late to see you?'

And when the nurse says, 'I'm very sorry, love, I'm just here visiting my mother,' he's puzzled, and then a little put out, thinking it's not right that the nurse's mother should have all the attention. So he perseveres.

'It's me ear, you see. Just the one ear. It'll not take a minute.'

Molly, who has her back to Tom, turns her head a little and says, 'Jean works in the hospital, Tom. She starts her shift at eight.'

But this won't do, either. How can he get to the hospital at this time of night? And why should he, anyway? If the nurse can come out for this woman, why can't she come out for him?

'You remember my daughter, Jean, don't you, Tom?' And Jean says, 'I'll have a word with Matron before I go. See if we can't get someone to take a look at you. Alright, Tom?'

And what can Tom say but, 'Right you are, then. Thank you, nurse,' and make his way back to his armchair? But he's going to tell Kate about it. Yes. Even as he sits down, the words are already forming in his mouth, 'They wanted me to go into hospital tonight, have you ever heard of anythin so daft?' But then he thinks, no, wait a minute. He's seen the ambulance before, outside by the front entrance, of an evening, mebbes that's it, mebbes that's to take you to the nurse. And thinks again, 'But how'd you get back?' Because he's not seen it come back again, nor heard it, which he would have done, surely, with its lights and its siren.

When Tom sits down again, next to Kate and the woman with the dark glasses, he's still trying to gather the threads together. But Molly, and the nurse too, have disappeared from view and, in any case, what he can see, mainly, through the lounge window, are the lights: some the other side of the river, some this side, perhaps even some on the river itself. So he sits back and tries to make sense of them, to see some pattern in them, like you would do with constellations in the night sky. 'Aye,' he says: 'There were no camp fires after dark there, mind. No, not even there. With the war, you see.' And, as always, he looks for the one important light, in Coble Court, one, two, three floors up, there, at the back, on the water's edge. The lodestar. 'Aye,' he says. 'And the snow.' Because, having failed to find his light, he's now considering the snow, only patches of it left now, on the edges of the roofs.

'Not that you'd want to be caught outside,' says Tom. 'Not in February. You couldn't light a fire, y'see. No lights, not even there. No. Back to the trail head we'd go, every mornin. Get up at sunrise. Two hours out. Two hours back. You couldn't hang about. Only four hours left to collect your ladybirds, y'see, so you've got to put your foot on it. And that includes the sievin. Hundredweight of ladybirds we'd gather on a good day, if they were well clustered and not too deep in the snow. Me droppin them into the sieve, Emilio shakin them through, gettin rid of the twigs and leaves and suchlike. Couldn't 've done more, even with two burros. Not enough daylight, y'see.'

Tom turns his head towards Kate who, surprised that the story should have stopped there, that there's a gap needs filling, says, 'Well, maybe we'll get out soon. Once the snow's gone. With the days getting a bit longer.'

Tom continues to look at her. He wants to say, no, that's not the point, you're not listening. But she's still talking. She's saying his name, 'This is Tom'. She's saying it to the woman next to her, the one without eyes. 'Tom's been to sea, Beverley. Isn't that right, Tom?' And the other woman says something, mumbles something, Tom can't understand what, and he notices that her mouth isn't quite where it ought to be, the left side of it anyway. So he thinks, well, no wonder, must make allowances, be patient, explain himself more clearly. He leans forward and speaks loudly at the dark glasses.

'I couldn't get back, y'see. Couldn't get a ship. The bombin. The convoys.'

93

But no, he thinks, that's not where it begins. And what do they know about ships? About convoys? So he tries again. 'They stole me papers, y'see. And me money.'

But was it La Boca? Or was it Johnny the Greek's? Or was it the Seamen's Mission, even? And thinks, yes, that's right, the Seamen's Mission, because he'd met Billy the Rope there. And Badger. And Charley. Aye, Charley Unger, he was there an all, Charley from Hamburg, who'd sailed on the Adel Trapper.

So Tom says, 'They stole me things, y'see. Outside the Seamen's Mission.'

Yes, that's it. He's got it right now. And the organ's still playing 'Lead, kindly light' when they leave, Tom and Charley and Billy and Badger, and Tom says, 'I could do with a drink,' and Charley says, 'We go to Johnny the Greek's.' And that's right. That's when they went to Johnny the Greek's.

'And then,' says Tom, looking at Beverley, seeking out the eyes, trying to bring her into the story, 'And then, what d'you know, I'm lyin crumpled against the wall. Nobody in sight.'

And Tom thinks, has he got the wall bit right? Perhaps it wasn't that one but some other wall, up by the Arches, perhaps. But lying down, anyway, and his ankle's twisted and he can taste blood in his mouth and there's grit on his tongue. And Emilio's there, looking down at him, saying something, but in Spanish, so he can't make it out. And his hand on his arm. Where did you come from? he thinks. And where have the others gone? And Emilio says, "You OK now."

Yes, that's it.

And Tom says to Beverley, 'That's when he turns up, y'see. Emilio. And he says, "I hit him good. Now you OK. Now you come with me." But not me money. No. Not me papers. They were gone.'

11

Tom wakes, looks at his clock, a round white plastic clock with an illuminated dial. It's three thirty-five. He's had four hours sleep. Four hours on, four off. Down in the engine room, up in the fo'c's'le. That's how it is. No, that's not how it is, thinks Tom. Because he doesn't normally sleep four hours. Because Sid's there with him in the next bunk, coughing up his lungs. That's how it is. You put up with it. Long passage. Where else can you go? Except that Tom can't hear Sid now, hasn't heard him all night. He looks at his clock. Three forty. So he decides. At four o'clock he'll get up. He'll check. He'll put his ear to the wall. That'll do the trick, probably. But if not, then he can go out into the corridor and listen at Sid's door. And then, if there's still nothing, he can always ring the red alarm bell above his bed. So that's what he decides. He looks at his clock. Three forty-two. Four o'clock he'll get up. His watch then.

Tom's bladder's tight. The tightness is so deep inside him, he doesn't at first realise what it means. He thinks, it's like a piece of wire lodged inside him, twisted, fastened, tightened. But when he puts his hand down there, below his stomach, to ease it, loosen it, it's like a drum, and so tender he can't touch it. He reaches out his left hand and pulls the light cord. He eases himself up on one elbow so that he can see where the tightness is, because he's sure it will show, the skin will have turned purple, like a bad bruise, like an over-ripe plum ready to burst. Mustn't let the wire break through, Tom thinks. That'd be the end of it.

As Tom raises his body, the pressure moves downwards, to the urethra, and he knows he needs to get to the toilet. He lifts off the quilt but even this slight raising of the arm pulls on the stomach muscles and makes him wince, the brow, the lips, the whole face tightening. He must use his stomach muscles, too, to move his legs, first the right, then the left, out of the bed and on to the floor. The floor – its support, the softness of its carpet – gives him some relief. We're getting there, he thinks. No, he can't quite stand upright, the wires inside him will snap if he stands up too straight, but that's alright, he can ease himself gradually, half-bent, towards the bathroom, one hand on the wall-rail, the other holding the tightness. That's it. Easy does it. And although Tom keeps the bathroom door open at all other times, he closes it now. He always closes it when inside, out of habit, just in case.

And he forgets about Sid. About the silence next door.

12

'Aren't we gettin up today, Tom?'

Tom's eyes are open and he's sure he can hear a voice, but he hasn't yet noticed the care assistant standing at the side of his bed.

'You got visitors today, Tom?'

Tom looks at his clock. It's turned nine. He thinks, this is a mistake. The clock is wrong. She's come too early. She's new, she doesn't know the ropes yet.

'Is it today?' Tom asks.

'I don't know, pet,' she answers. 'Why don't you look in your diary? That'll tell you. You keep everythin in your diary, don't you, Tom?'

And Tom thinks, how does she know this, how does she know his business?

'I'm very sorry, dear,' he says. 'I know you're only doin your job. I told him, y'see. I told him there wasn't any point. There's no point takin us back to Shields, I said.'

'Where d'you keep your glasses, Tom?' asks the care assistant, handing Tom his diary.

'But that's why, y'see. That's why he brought us here... Instead of... On the shelf somewhere... Are they there?'

Tom fingers through the pages until he reaches the end of February.

'There,' he says, and points to the crosses. 'That's when he was away, y'see... The crosses... And there.' He points to the tick. 'That's when he's comin to visit.'

'Tomorrow,' says the care assistant. 'Tomorrow afternoon. So are we gettin up now?'

And although Tom feels there is something she's not telling him, he can't at the moment put his finger on it, so he says, 'Right you are, then. Be with you now. In two jiffies.' And thinks, you're not just goin to stand there, are you?

13

Tom is sharing a table with three women he's seen before, one with dark glasses, one with a round face and lipstick, and one, he thinks, with little claws. He's got an idea the one with the round face, sat diagonally across from him, might be called Jess. His tongue plays with the name, trying it out for size. He thinks of names similar to Jess. June? But he knows no Junes. Jean? He remembers there being a Jean somewhere, but that's not it either, can't be, because he's sure there's an 's' in the name, because it's in her chest, too, as she speaks. Ssss. So he thinks, give it a go. He tries to pick up on what she's telling the woman in the dark glasses, about the way to make a shepherd's pie, to make it properly, not like the one they're eating at the moment, all mush, Jess says, and the veg too, all mush, and how she used to put cheese and leeks together on top, the leeks on the potato, and then the cheese on top of that, and how she'd bake it till it had a nice golden crust, really crisp, not mush like this.

So Tom asks her. 'Jess,' he says, 'so you were a cook, then, were you?'

And Jess is so surprised to hear him use her name, that she's happy to say, 'Well, no, Tom, not as such, but my George enjoyed his shepherd's pie.' And smiles, and then adds that her George grew his own leeks, because she remembers telling Tom about George's allotment the other day. 'And his own potatoes.' And she remembers, too, that she'd let George down, that other time, but she feels better now, she's made amends. George would be pleased with her, he'd be pleased that she was telling people how good he was, fighting his corner.

The woman with dark glasses says that her husband liked roasties best. Some people just have them at Christmas, she says, but they'd have roasties every week, in their house, with the onions in as well, and then says something else which Tom can't make out, because her mouth isn't moving right, and the one with the little claws just keeps on cutting little pieces, her knife and fork much too big for her, thinks Tom, too big and heavy, poor thing, and eating nothing, nothing that Tom can see, not a morsel. He thinks, put it in your mouth, woman, just put it in your mouth. Because although Tom has tended the gardens of many old women, he has never shared their table.

'Are you fond of cooking, Tom?' asks Jess, which takes Tom by surprise. 'I mean, were you... Did your...'

Now Tom would like nothing more than to reciprocate, to present his equivalent of Jess's shepherd's pie, of the roasties. And he could, it's true, tell them something about how his wife used to cook for him, but that was so long ago, almost beyond memory. And he knows, in any case, that it wouldn't be the same kind of story. The story of eating a meal is not the same as the story of making a meal. And he didn't grow his own vegetables, not then. So that won't do. He must go back further.

So Tom says, 'Poordo. That's what they call it there. Camp food, y'see. Nothin special. No. You make do with what you get, out there.'

Jess nods. Because although she doesn't fully understand, Tom is making an effort to answer her question.

''You've got to make do, Tom,' she says. 'That's right.'

'Aye. And what y'get is what the mule train brings,' Tom says, encouraged by Jess's response. 'Once a week, if you're lucky, if there's no bridge fallen, you know, if there's no blizzard. That was my job. Emilio'd be seein to the burro, takin off her load and her saddle, checkin her shoes, givin her hay, all them jobs. His burro, y'see, his job. And me, I'd set about gettin the stove ready, preparin the food. Poordo they called it.' Tom heaps shepherd's pie onto the back of his fork.

'Poordo?' says Jess.

Tom places the food in his mouth, chews and swallows. 'Well, it's whatever y'had to hand,' he says. 'Potatoes, onions, bacon, this and that, aye, I cannit give you a recipe, not really, and you just boiled it all up together. Poordo. That's all it was. Camp food. For the end of the day.' Tom pauses, looks down at his plate, wondering where to go next. 'Tasted good, mind. End of a hard day. Warm fire.' He pauses again. 'Worked up an appetite by then.' Yes, he thinks, a long day. 'And long nights an all, mind,' he says, getting a bit of a second wind, finding there is a way to go, after all. 'No telly in them days, y'see. Not even the wireless up there. Mebbes somebody up for the fishin, in the Kern, you'd get two or three every now and again. Bit crack then. Odd

mule train carryin this and that. Not much in the winter, though. The wranglers off fightin, y'see, most of them. Off in the war. The wranglers. That's what they call them, the men who look after the horses.'
Tom pauses. Takes another mouthful. Chews slowly. Swallows. 'Couldn't get back meself, y'see.'
He looks at Jess, who nods. The woman with the dark glasses smiles, and although the little bent woman with the morsels shows no reaction, Tom thinks, well, that's alright then.

14

Five to six. Sea-gulls screech outside the window. But it's the light has woken Tom. Just a grey ooze of light. Enough, though, because the curtains are thin, much thinner than he's been used to. He thinks of Irma. About her Menudo. About her Pozole. Not the names, of course, he doesn't remember the names, but something of their deep red, and the green bowl she'd put them in. About how the chillies burned his mouth. Way, way back in La Habra.

15

'"My friend." That's what he used to say,' says Tom. 'Everybody thinks they say *amigo*, but "my friend" is what Emilio said. Mexican, y'see. All Mexican there in them days. He says, "You find good wife, you keep her." His wife was back down the valley, y'see. Irma. Aye. Emilio's wife. And he says, "You find good burro, you keep her too." And Emilio says, "Way back," he says. Ha! "Way back, me and me burro were bein chased by Indians." Aye, Indians,' says Tom, repeating Emilio's words, knowing that his audience need to hear this bit or they won't understand the rest. 'Aye, Indians. Ha! Way back, y'see. "We were stood there, on this high bluff," says Emilio, "the Indians behind us, the bluff in front of us, a thousand foot to the bottom." Aye. "So what do I do?" says Emilio. "What do I do? Well, I have good burro," he says. I cannit do the accent. "I have good burro," he says. "Very good burro. She is best of all burros. You tell her, Come! She come. You tell her, Cross creek! She cross creek. You tell her, Find way back to camp! She find way back to camp, Tom, no trouble, no matter snow, no matter rocks, no matter bears. She very good burro. So we jump," says Emilio. Aye, they jump,' says Tom. 'They jump over the edge of the bluff. Y'know, like a cliff. That's what they call them there, a bluff. They jump over the cliff edge. "So we jump," says Emilio. "We don't want scalp the head, no," he says. Ha! So down, down, down they go. "Like big stone," he says. "Like big stone. Down, down, down. And half way down," he says, "Half way down the bluff, I bend over and shout into burro's ear, I shout, Whoa, burro, whoa! And the burro stops. *Si*, she stops. And burro and me float to ground." They float to the ground,' says Tom. 'The burro stops in mid-air, y'see. They float to the ground. "*Si*, it is true story." That's what he says. That's what Emilio says. True story.'

16

A stout woman of fifty or so, with red hair and big hoops of earrings and a long green dress, walks slowly around the room, singing into a microphone, stopping every few seconds to encourage each resident to join in.

'*Some enchanted evening... you may meet a stranger.*' She puts a hand on Phyllis's arm – Phyllis, a small bent pin of a woman who cannot speak and is propped up on three sides by cushions – because even Phyllis is joining in, in her own way, moving her lips.

'*You may hear her laughing... across a crowded room.*' Tom is having difficulty getting to the pitch, with so many women singing, singing so high, and in any case he isn't sure of the words. But he does his best. The woman winks at him as she passes, smiles. A big, toothy smile, with red lipstick. '*Once you have found her... never let her go.*'

Tom smiles back. And he wonders why she needs a microphone, in a room like this. But he's also relieved, because he can hide his voice behind hers. The pianist, in the far corner, plays a refrain between verses. And Tom thinks, that's her son over there, playing the little electric piano. He can see the resemblance, the red hair, the round face. A young lad, just a school kid really. Yes, he, too, is smiling, enjoying himself. And Tom feels, well, this is alright.

Tom rarely comes into the big lounge, especially on a Wednesday night, the social night. He's not one for quizzes and cards and bingo and suchlike. He prefers to sit in the small lounge, where it's quieter, where he can do a crossword, have a natter if he wants one, or not if he doesn't. And because he's uncomfortable in crowds, feels hemmed in. He's come tonight because he's getting on better with Jess, whose name he remembers, and because he has visitors tomorrow. On both counts he's disposed to feel more sociable.

It's only when the woman with red hair finishes her song that he looks around him and sees he is the only man there. He thinks, that's a pity, it would be better if there were more of us here, to balance things out. But what snags Tom's mind is not this, is not the desire for male company, but rather the realisation, which only slowly dawns on him, that this should not be the case, that someone else should, in fact, be there. He looks around the room again, which he can do easily, as all the chairs have been set back against the walls. The singer, having finished her song, is talking to the pianist over in the far corner. He's fingering the pages of his book. As he does so, he laughs, then clears his throat.

And it is now that Tom remembers, with a jolt, who should be there. That he has not heard Sid's cough for some time. He looks around, in case he is huddled out of the way somewhere, but there is nowhere to huddle here, everyone is out in the open, propped up, backs to the wall. And the door is shut. No late-comers here, thinks Tom. But hasn't anybody else noticed? Hasn't anybody raised the alarm? And he has half a mind to go and complain to Matron now, he is already framing the words he is going to say, which will give voice to his concern but also to some measure of indignation because, he thinks, why should *he* be expected to shoulder responsibility for somebody he barely knows? Is it because he sleeps in the next room? Is that it? Could that be possible? Could it really be his job, to report such matters to the relevant authorities? And he thinks, aye, mebbes that's it, there's mebbes something he's missed there, something in the small print.

But it's too late now, the lady has started singing again, and there's no easy way out. The door is over there, by the piano, in the far corner, beyond the piano player, and he cannot go behind the chairs, no, because there's no room. So he must bide his time. The woman is coming his way again, smiling, winking.

'*But I always knew I would live life through...*'

When she gets past, thinks Tom, when she gets past. And he smiles back, fulsomely, thinking, on you go, on you go.

'*With a song in my heart for you...*'

He smiles again. That's the way, he thinks, on you go.

The woman next to Tom has dark glasses, but that doesn't matter, he thinks, that doesn't mean she doesn't know things, hear things. So Tom touches her elbow with the tips of his fingers.

'I say,' Tom whispers. There's no response. He leans over a little, draws nearer. 'I say,' he whispers, a little more loudly this time. She turns her head towards him, just enough for Tom to see, yes, of course, that this is the woman whose mouth isn't right, and he thinks, no, pet, you can't tell us anything about Sid, can you? So he smiles and says, in his proper voice now, because the song has come to an end, 'Back in a minute.' He thinks, I can excuse meself now, nobody'll mind now, surely, I'll just say 'Excuse me' and I'll go.

So this is what Tom does. He crosses the room and makes his way directly towards the door. He smiles at the pianist and, doing so, notices that he isn't the young lad he'd imagined him to be, far from it, he could easily be the singer's husband or brother. The brother, of course, he thinks. The family resemblance. Yes. He's got the red hair. The round face. The same mouth, big, fleshy. A bit like a fish.

And Tom is so preoccupied with the sudden and dramatic ageing of the pianist that he leaves the room without remembering to say 'Excuse me'. And then, when he finds himself on the other side of the door, looking down the length of the corridor which leads to the river lounge and the dining room, he must pause awhile to consider what he should do next, indeed why he is standing there at all, leaning against the wall-rail. He looks back now at the door through which he's just come because he can hear a voice, the voice of a woman speaking, then singing. And then he remembers, yes, I'm going to hear the singing tonight. That woman will be there. Jess. That's her name. And out of politeness, he waits there, in the corridor, until there is a pause. He waits there, humming along to the song, which is familiar and sweetly nostalgic. And then, smiling broadly, he makes his entry.

17

The snow is deep. 'But only one day left,' says Emilio, 'and got to make the most of it.' Tom needs to get a shovel, just to dig a way out of the cabin, the snow's drifted so high against the door. 'Coffee and go, my friend,' he says. There's half an inch of ice on the water in the barrel. Not good. And the burro lost a shoe yesterday. Had to cold shoe her when they got back. Not good at all.

Perhaps that was it, thinks Tom. The shoe loosened, the hoof slipped on a slab of granite, iced, polished, out of sight under the new snow. Or a branch. That's what he'd said at the beginning, first day up here. 'New snow, my friend, watch the trees. Snow make branches heavy, they break. They break you too.' Mebbes that was it.

The burro goes first. 'She good burro,' says Emilio. 'The best. You treat her like you treat your woman and she good to you. She cut back on rock, you put alum on it. She have bad mouth, the calomel. She strain leg, the linament, you rub it in like this. Whatever she want, you give it to her,' says Emilio. 'You doctor to burro. You brother to burro. You husband to burro. Then she good wife to you. But listen, Tom, listen. Watch out she don't kick you!'

So easy in summer, thinks Tom. Blue skies. Warm nights. Open camp. Start out at dawn, get to the beds early. 'She know the way, my friend, you let her go, you just follow.' But there again, mebbes a bit too eager in summer, just a wee bit too eager, always looking for the sweeter grass. 'So be on the safe side,' Emilio says, 'tie her, tether her, you don't want to spend half your morning looking for her, do you, my friend? No, hobble her, she's safe then. You want her, she's there

103

for you. Like good wife. Like good wife at home, nice little home in Mazanillo, by the sea, by the river. She don't wander, your wife, no, she no dirty *taconera*, my friend, she good burro.'

'You not getting up today, Tom?'

Tom remembers.

'You've got visitors today, haven't you, Tom?'

Tom remembers but thinks, bide your time, mebbes it's not too late yet.

'Is it today?' he asks.

'D'you want to have a look at your diary again, Tom?'

But Tom says, 'No, no, no time for that.' And thinks, mebbes it's not too late. Mebbes Matron doesn't know yet. Because he's pretty sure the care assistant doesn't know, or she'd have said something, wouldn't she? She'd not be going on about visitors, not if Sid, not with him…

'And the wee girl?'

'Is that today?' he asks.

'That's today, Tom. Visitors today.'

Tom goes to the bathroom, gets dressed, tidies his pyjamas under his pillow and makes his bed. He carries out these tasks with greater urgency than usual, because he has other, more important duties to see to. But he does so with less care, too, so that in his haste to press on, he forgets to shave, he doesn't notice that the collar of his shirt is turned up under his left ear, that his hair is sticking out in tufts. He walks over to the wall furthest from his bed and stands there, his ear cocked towards the next room. Nothing. He presses his ear to the wall. Nothing. Just the emptiness, the absence of Sid's cough, the rush of blood in his own head. He turns around and tries the other ear. And hears the same. So he opens the door, walks the three paces to Sid's room, stands and listens again. He knocks. Nothing. He knocks again, more firmly. Nothing. He puts his lips near to the door jamb and says, 'Sid! You in there, Sid?' And puts his ear where his lips were. And thinks, You've given us the slip again, you sly bastard.

Tom walks to the lift and presses where it says 'Press'. He presses again. And again. He knows it's a slow lift, that some residents are nervous getting in and out, that little cracks and gaps, little changes in the texture of the floor, can stop them in their tracks, that the doors may be held open for a full minute or two whilst these are negotiated, that he must be patient. He knows this. Nevertheless, when the doors do open and Kate appears, together with a woman in dark glasses, leaning on her arm, he is too intent on his own mission even to exchange greetings, so intent, in fact, that he tries to enter the lift before the woman with dark glasses has properly made her exit and Kate must say, sharply, 'No, Tom, no,' before he realises that this woman is attached to Kate and that they cannot be separated. Kate puts a hand on Tom's left arm, to restrain him, while the other woman, fearing she is going to lose her balance, grabs at his right, so that for a moment all three are caught up in an anxious parody of ring-a-ring-o-roses.

'Very sorry, very sorry,' says Tom, as if suddenly awakened from a dream. 'Got to... Things... Things to do...'

When Tom reaches the first floor, he walks straight past the dining room because he has heard the clatter of bucket and mop and because he can see, through the open door, that the tables are already being cleared, that breakfast is long over. He looks at his watch and thinks, Of course. Daft bugger. So he makes directly for the Garden Lounge which is, he knows, Sid's place. When he's not in his bedroom, or in the dining room, that's where he is. That's where he'll be. So Tom walks on, down the corridor, confident that this matter will soon be resolved. And as he approaches the Garden Lounge, Tom is encouraged by the sound of a cough. So when he opens the door, he just stands there for a moment, trying to work out from which direction it has come. Thinking, that's it, that's all there's left to do. He'd like to hear one more cough, to get a proper bearing on it. Just one more would be enough. But the room has changed. It's lost the order it had last night. Some residents sit with their backs to him, so that they can see the television, others are in a small cluster near the window. And because of these new arrangements, Tom can no longer scan all their faces, so that he's not sure who's there and who's not. And the cough has gone, as quickly as it came, to be displaced by other sounds, by the television, chuckling thinly to itself, by a car alarm, somewhere in the distance, by voices, by one voice in particular, phlegmy, wheezy, which Tom now realises belongs to a woman standing near the window, a woman he thinks is called Jess.

And as he walks towards her, because she's the only one whose name he knows, whom he can ask about Sid, she clears her throat and says, 'Come to see the flowers, have you, Tom?' And she looks through the window, at the dene, at the stream cascading through the rockeries and hedged lawns, at the pond, at the children on their swings and climbing frames, and especially at the daffodils and crocuses, the narcissus and scilla and aconite, except that some of these are too small to identify at a distance and appear only as bright splashes of colour.

'Everything's come so early this year, Tom, hasn't it?' she says, thinking that Tom, the gardener, will appreciate these things.

But Tom doesn't hear. Tom is following a care assistant who is administering the morning medication, is placing the pills and phials in each resident's tray, checking them against the prescription details on her clip-board. And although she says, 'I'll be with you in a couple of minutes, Tom,' he continues to follow her, from table to table, armchair to armchair, waiting his turn. The assistant's progress is slow, punctuated as it is by residents' queries and concerns – about a change in prescription, about going out today if it's not too cold, about the window, always opened in the morning to change the air, says Matron, but letting in such a draft, says one, and that blessed alarm thing, says another – by retrieving a tablet dropped on the floor, by adjusting blankets and cushions. So that Tom, trying to be helpful, goes to close the window – 'just a touch', as the assistant says – , he passes a glass of water here, he offers a smile and a greeting there, so that the girl says, 'You after my job, Tom?' and he laughs. And at the end of the round, when she asks, 'You stayin here for yours, Tom?' he thinks, good, my turn has come, and sits down to receive his Aricept, his Glucosamine, his Detrusitol, and three other medications, all of which he knows well by now, not by name but by colour, shape and consistency. And he says, 'I've still got the dry mouth, y'know,' and the girl asks does he want to see the nurse again, and Tom says, 'Aye, alright,' and then, as an afterthought, 'Not the one in the hospital, mind. If it's all the same with you.' He rubs his chin and thinks, I'll need a shave first.

18

I told him, her load's too heavy, man, too big. But he wouldn't listen. She'll bust it, man, I said. Because I knew there was an overhang there, low over the path. You had to bend double to get under it. She scragged on it on the way up, even without a load. And it's freezin now. What was crisp snow ten this mornin, took a boot, give a bit grip, was ice by four. Gettin dark, Emilio said. We wait any longer, it'll all be ice. I want out of this shit-hole, he said. She done it before, she do it again.

And I tell him, it's not like before, man, she's ridin too high. And I'm about to say, take it off, man, take the load off, we can put it back on when she gets round the spur, but he's away off, out of sight. Last load. Last day. Last bloody day. I hear him shoutin at her, way above. 'Whoa! Whoa!'

That's all.

And then she's in the air. Not a sound, just the burro flyin through the air, hooves up, panniers hangin down from the saddle. Only a second she's up there, I know, but for that second it's like she really is flyin. Like a circus act. Just wait a bit, you're thinkin, and the pannniers'll turn into wings and she'll be off skywards again. Or the rider'll shout, 'Whoa, girl, whoa!' into her ear and down she'll float, light as air, onto a ledge. Aye, you even start lookin for the ledge where she'll land. Or failin that, failin all else, there'll be a net, there's got to be a net, they cannit do this without a net, man. But there's no rider. There's no net. And she's not flyin, she's fallin, down, down, down, and not a sound, doesn't know a thing, doesn't know what all this air means, why it's blue under her hooves, half a mile down and doesn't know a thing. Just a small *thwap* then, like a pine cone droppin in snow, *thwap*, when she hits the bottom. Then quiet again. Nothin.

'Emilio! Where are you, Emilio?'

You bastard.

19

'That's the boat for Amsterdam,' says the boy at the window as he watches the blue and white liner come in to view. He turns to face Molly, in her wheelchair, and a younger woman sat next to her and says again, 'That's the Amsterdam boat, Mam.' A girl, who has been reading a magazine at the table, walks over to the window and for a minute all four watch silently as the vessel parts the black water. Like a great cliff. He can see the funnel approach, higher than all the flats on the riverbank. But paper thin. Like it's just a huge cardboard cut-out of a boat, cutting through the water, without sound, so big, so smooth, like somebody's pushing it from behind.

'The Bergen boat, dear,' says Jess, who's sitting at the other end of the semi-circle of chairs facing the window. 'It's the Bergen boat goes from Shields.' She turns to Molly. 'Bergen,' she says. 'In Sweden.' Molly nods, smiles. The younger woman says, 'The Oslo–Bergen Quay they used to call it, didn't they?' The boy is unhappy with this. He walks back to where his mother is sitting, fingers the beading on the wings of the chair, shifts from foot to foot. He wants to tell her that the little fat woman with the wheezy voice doesn't know what she's talking about, that she's a stupid know-all that knows nothing. But he can't say that. He can, however, state the facts. Nobody, he thinks, has a right to complain at that. So he says, 'The Bergen boat goes on Tuesdays and Saturdays, Mam.' And leaves it at that. And the boy's mother says, 'Yes, that's right, the Bergen boat.' She turns to Jess and says, 'Always gone from Shields, hasn't it, the Bergen boat?' And they all look at the boat again, as it passes by. So high out of the water, so improbably high, and wondering, what's holding it up? Why doesn't it fall over?

Tom is back in the River Lounge because he's expecting visitors and he wants to see the light go on and then, as his son is about to leave home, go off again, and he'll know he has ten minutes. That's the usual time. No doubt there are doors to be locked, windows even. Yes, even though it's high up, you can't be too careful. There's probably a burglar alarm. A lift to wait for. A road to be crossed. It all adds up. But ten minutes as a rule. Tom looks at his watch. Twenty to six.

'Might be Norway, mind,' says Jess. 'I get mixed up between them, sometimes. Between the different countries, y'know.'

Molly nods. Her daughter looks at her watch and tells the children to get ready because it's late and their dad'll be expecting them. 'Give him my love, won't you, Sally,' Molly says to her daughter, quite cheerily, not wishing to give anything away in front of the children. But Jess has the bit between her teeth and she's reluctant to let them go just yet.

'I've never seen the point, mind,' she says. 'Cold places like that. Never seen the appeal. Cold enough here, I should think, without spendin your holidays... y'know... without lookin for colder. Once...'

'I remember when it froze over,' says Molly. 'The river, I mean, frozen over, here to South Shields...'

'We went to Majorca once,' says Jess. 'Me and George... now that was warm. That's the sort of place you'd go for a holiday. Don't you think?'

And even though Jess's question is directed at Molly, Tom has noticed that the light is now on in his son's window and, being buoyed up by this, feels an urge to respond; besides, he has something to say on the matter. He has sailed on much bigger ships than this, and been to warmer and more distant places, too, so he seizes the opportunity.

'I was a Mexican once,' he says. 'I mean...'

Jess and Molly look at Tom, but there is no surprise in their faces, because neither is puzzled any longer that he says such things, because this is what they've come to expect. He's a gardener one day, a seaman the next, and then a ladybird miner, whatever that might be. So it's no surprise, not really, to find that today he's a Mexican. But Jess is put out that her question has been ignored. That Tom has muscled in again.

'I mean... in a manner of speakin,' he says.

'How'd you mean, Tom?' asks Molly. 'How'd you mean, in a manner of speaking?' But meaning, don't be silly, Tom, you don't know what you're talking about, do be quiet. And Jess says, under her breath, 'It'll be his wires again. I wouldn't bother.'

The children, however, are curious that they have someone in their company who was once a Mexican. The boy, being a little older, is less wide-eyed than his sister because he knows already that this is a place of delusions, but even he turns his head towards Tom, wanting more. And

Tom, seeing that he has a more eager audience than usual, responds.

'I could've been Chinese or Japanese, mind,' he says. 'Or Filipino, even. If Emilio hadn't been Mexican, I mean. If he'd been somethin else, and I'd gone back to his family, like. Cos they're all separate there, y'see. Live separate. Work separate. Mexicans here, Chinese there, Yanks somewhere else. That's how it is there. That's how it was. What's your name, lad?'

And because the young boy doesn't speak, seems not to realise that this old man is speaking to him or can be spoken to, the young woman says, 'This is Darren. And this is his sister, Julie.'

Julie, embarrassed to be put on show like this, carries on reading her magazine.

'You'd have to change your name if you were Mexican, mind,' says Tom. 'You couldn't be Julie. No. You'd have to be somethin else.' And he thinks. 'How's about Julietta? Aye. That's what you'd be in Mexican. Julietta. And your dolly, we'd have to give her a name too, wouldn't we? What's your dolly's name, pet? Has your dolly got a name?'

Tom looks to the girl's mother, who says, 'Tell the nice man dolly's name, Julie.' And the girl says something into her chest, indistinctly, not lifting her eyes, so the mother has to say, 'It's Baby Lisa, isn't it, Julie?' And Tom says, 'Well that's a nice name. Lisa. Sounds Mexican enough already to me. I think you've got a real little Mexican baby there. What do you think, Julietta?'

Tom looks around the wing of his chair at Julie, who is standing now, having her coat put on by her mother.

'Not sure what the lad would be, mind. I don't think they've got a Darren there. How'd you fancy somethin different, Darren? Eh? How'd you fancy bein a Pablo? Eh? Or a Pancho, mebbes? That's a good Mexican name. Aye. Pancho. Pancho and Julietta. Aye. And Lisa. Don't forget little Lisa.' And thinks again. 'I was Tomás,' says Tom. 'Not Thomas. No. Tomás. Tomás. That's what Emilio called us. Tomás. How about that? Eh?'

Tom winks at Darren. And then, realising that he's not really explained who Emilio is, that there's so much more to tell, and because the children are standing by the door now, with their mother, he says: 'Hang on a minute. I'll be back in a minute. Just a minute.'

Twenty minutes later, Tom leaves his room, clutching a brown envelope, not even bothering to close the door behind him. He walks along the corridor towards the lift, holding on to the hand-rail, passing Sid's door, the other doors, and thinks, yes, he can tell them so many things. And if at the moment he doesn't remember the words, none of them, that doesn't matter, because he sees the things themselves, sees them with such clarity that he's sure he'll find the words he needs, when the time comes. Because he's there with Emilio and Irma, with the others, hundreds of them, walking through the Campo, and the candle's wax, he can feel it, the candle's drip hot, then hard, tight, on his hand. He's there as they arrive at the hall, he can hear them singing

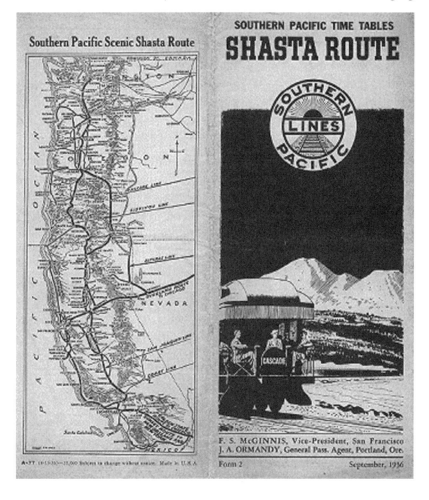

inside, he can see them now, the girls in their bright white and tinsel, and so hot, even now, in December, with all the candles.

But most of all, because they're just kids, he'll tell them about how he'd lower the... about how he'd lower the... And he sees it, in his mind's eye, something like a pot, hanging on its rope, except it had a name, and the name won't come. And that was his job, because he was strong, with him having been a stoker. Tomás, you strong, you lift the... you lift the... Yes, he'll tell Pancho and Julietta, 'Put your blindfolds on now,' he'll tell them, 'It's comin down now, it's comin down, the...' And he really needs the name now, because the story won't be the same without the name. Howay, Pancho! Come on, Julietta! See if y'can break it! See if y'can get the treats out! Because that's what's inside, y'see, your Christmas treats. Julietta first, that's right. That's it, with your stick, try to hit it with your stick, pet, go on.'

But where, thinks Tom, is he going to get a stick in this place?

When he returns to the River Lounge, the children have gone, their mother too, even Molly. Tom's sure he'd asked them to stay, just for a minute. He's ready to say, I've found them, I've found me papers, me photos. He thought they'd been stolen, he thought Sid had stolen them, but now he's found them. The words are already there, on his tongue. Look, he's ready to say, Look, y'can see the oranges in this one, and that's the mountains behind, you've got sun and snow together, y'see? And here, the train, this is the train I'd catch to get back. I even kept the timetable, look. Y'see how I tried to get back?

But now there's no-one to say these things to.

20

A care assistant finds Tom sitting by himself in the River Lounge and says, 'Tom, you not coming for tea tonight?' But Tom is still waiting for the light to go off in his son's flat, so he says: 'I've got visitors today, pet. I've got to stay here for me visitors.' And the girl says: 'You've got to eat something, Tom. I'll bring something through for you.' And Tom says, 'Thanks. That'd be nice. Thank you. Yes.'

Tom looks at his watch. It's a quarter to seven. If his son left now he'd be just ten minutes. Five to seven, he thinks. Seven at the outside. And so many things to say. Too many. So just one at a time, he thinks. Hold on to it, keep it tight in your fist, don't let it go. But his fist is already full. Full of the burro, upside down, drowning in too much air, and his own voice, shouting 'Emilio! Emilio!'

And surely that's all he's got to do, thinks Tom, is follow the tracks. So he stops shouting. And at first it's easy. There's a saddle to cross before you get to the rock, just a few trees, the prints deep and clear, the snow with a hard crust on it now, freezin harder by the minute. And the burro's prints are dead straight, she knows where she's goin, even in the snow. Emilio's a bit this way and that, sometimes in the burro's prints, sometimes just to one side, better grip that way, mebbes, make your own steps. Whatever, the steps are clear, all the way to the rock.

But when you get to the rock, thinks Tom, it's all different. There's drifts in the gullies, but there's no prints there. There wouldn't be, of course, no, not in the gullies, you'd go waist deep in some of them, you'd stay well clear. Aye. So you'd stay on the rock. And that's right, that's the way I go, because there isn't any other way, and I can see them now, the prints, because I'm steppin into them, cos that's the only way, just three or four of them, the burro's prints, on a ledge. Three or four. And beyond that, bare rock, long shiny granite, all black and white, and hardly any snow at all. And I'm slitherin all over the place here, man, it's icin up rotten, like black ice. Slip in a bad place and you're off the mountain. So you wouldn't come this way, would you, Emilio? No, not even you. But what other way can you go?

'Thank you, er...'

The care assistant leaves a tray on the table by Tom's chair. He turns the corner of a sandwich. Cheese and pickle. Good. She knows he likes cheese and pickle. And takes a bite. And looks at his watch. Ten to seven. And the light still on. Perhaps he's on his way. But he's left the light on. So perhaps not yet. But soon.

Tom studies the wedge of rock. End-on, that's what it is, a single wedge, slightly tilted. On the left it banks, eases, down to the forest, to snow, to nowhere, and more and more of the same, forest and snow, as far as you can see. He pans across to the right. But there's only a

113

jagged edge there, and a void, and under the void, way down below in the evening shadow, the black snake of a river, and you can't lean out to see more or you'll go over the edge. Is this it? thinks Tom. Is this where the burro went over? He looks round and can't see any prints. He examines each ledge, each spur of rock, each patch of snow. Nothing. So that's it, he thinks, that's the burro gone. It slips, it cannit stop itself, just gettin faster and faster, under its load, shoots off the granite, woosh! No sign of a fall, mind. But then, what would that sign be? How can you find skid marks in the air?

End-on, thinks Tom, a single wedge. But you know it's not. You know that it's really like two turrets of a castle. And that's the way the path goes, it zig-zags between the turrets, it's the way you came this mornin. No other way. So where are you, Emilio? You bastard, where are you? But when you get to the second turret, when you stoop under the overhang, holdin onto the rock wall, watchin every step because the path narrows here, is all iced up, you think, mebbes, just mebbes, he's tried to find another way off, avoid the drifts, avoid the ice. Mebbes he's seen the burro go, sailin off into nothin, and took fright. Who knows?

So Tom turns back, retraces his steps, back to the first turret, and thinks, if you're down in that shack when I get there I'll ruddy swing for you. And thinks, then, what if he's gone down after the burro? What if he's gone down to rescue the load. To get the ladybirds? Because that's the sort of thing he'd do, isn't it, the mad bastard? So you look over the edge again, but you know you can't go any further. You look back. Is that his footprint in the snow, or is it yours?

'Here's your tea, Tom.'

The care assistant has returned.

'Your visitors late?'

Tom looks at his watch. Just turned five to. Plenty of time yet.

'On their way,' says Tom.

'That's good,' says the care assistant. 'Need anything else before I go?'

And Tom says: 'No, thank you. Nice sandwiches. Very nice. Just how I like them. With the pickle. Very tasty. Aye. And I've kept me bit cake to have with me tea.'

And then, just as the girl is leaving the room, as Tom is reaching for his cup, he remembers. He says, 'Excuse me, er... Aye, there is. Sorry. I meant to say. Meant to ask.' And he thinks, spit it out man, you've come this far, spit it out. 'Have you seen Sid?'

And he's sorry that he barks these words, that they come out like an accusation, he hadn't meant them to. But the care assistant doesn't seem put out, and Tom's glad of that.

'Didn't you know, Tom?' she says. 'Didn't anybody tell you?'

And Tom is relieved to hear in these words more sympathy than surprise. 'I thought you'd have known,' she says.

Tom looks at her, wondering what he's supposed to have known.

'Sid left us last week, Tom,' she says.

'Ah,' says Tom, thinking he understands, then realises he doesn't. 'What? You mean, gone away?'

'He died, Tom. Sid died.'

'Ah,' says Tom. 'I see.'

'He was very ill.'

Tom thinks, aye, that explains it. And although he doesn't admit it to himself, he's a little relieved again, not that Sid is dead, but that things have fallen into place.

'In hospital was he... I mean, when he...'

'Yes, in hospital.'

'I see.'

Tom looks at his watch. It's three minutes past seven. He takes a sip of tea, a bite of fruit loaf, and settles back in his chair. Any minute now, he thinks, any minute, have to ask the lass to fetch another cup of tea, two cups if he brings that woman, the woman whose name escapes him at the moment, but who's been to see him before, he's sure of it. 'Two more cups, please, for me visitors,' he'll say, quite pleased that he can get others to do his bidding. And there again, he might be a bit fast, Tom thinks, he might have set his watch ahead a bit, to be on the safe side.

So is he dead, then? Is Emilio dead? But who can you ask? And it's you they'll be asking in a bit. *Hey, Tzompan, where's Emilio? He not with you?* And what will you say then? All night, in the shack, you think, what will you say then? You lie awake, hearin noises, thinkin, it's him, he's found his way back, but it's a branch breakin, or mebbes a coyote, scavangin, and you're hopin it is, then, you're hopin it's not Emilio, because what would he say to you, what would you say to him? And all mornin, as you're checkin the sacks, weighin them, settin them out, you're thinkin, what do I do with these? What's a sack of ladybirds worth now?

The mule train comes up the track, as you knew it would, sooner or later. Watch the branches, one of them shouts. Just like you, Emilio. That's what you'd said, watch the branches, heavy, ready to break. New snow. And still thinkin, what do I say? What do I tell them? And he dismounts, the first one, the one who's been doin the shoutin, says 'Howdie,' says, 'Hope you got the coffee going in there.' And you shake your head. 'Things are bad,' you say. 'Very bad.' And bide your time a wee bit, till the others tie up the mules, till the three of them are inside, out of the wind.

And you say it.

'Emilio didn't make it.'

You look down, you shake your head.

'Out by the South Fork,' you say. 'Bridge got washed away... Lost his footin... River too fast, y'see, too deep... Couldn't get the rope to him...'

And everybody knows that the South Fork is five miles away, that it's too far to go in this weather, that the river runs west from there, away from the rail head, that they've got a schedule to keep to. And the first one says he's sorry to hear that. Very sorry. That's tough, say the others. Real tough. Good thing you made it yourself. Has he got kids? You shake your head. They shake their heads, too, and the first one shrugs, says 'It happens'.

And that's your grievin over. You pack up and set off. It's done, it's all said. And that's when you realise it's not them you've been worryin about. They fuck their burros just like you did, Emilio, what do they care if another chunty cops it in some fuckin iced-up river in the back of nowhere? Plenty more where he came from. It's not them you've been worryin about, never was.

Tom squeezes the last morsels of cake between his thumb and first two fingers and places them in his mouth. He washes them down with the now lukewarm tea. He takes his glasses from his shirt pocket, adjusts them on his nose, this way and that, until they are comfortable. Then he opens the timetable, lays it on his lap, and tries to work out the route back to La Habra. Because he must tell Irma, tell her that Emilio wan't be coming back. Tom moves his finger down the list of stations. He does this quickly at first because he expects it will be easy, the route will be clearly mapped out, he'll just have to check the times. But more slowly, then, because he realises that not all the lines are shown here, that he can't even find La Habra. And thinking, well, he changed trains, he must have done, so he'll have to go and ask elsewhere, in Bakersville. Or Sacramento. Except that Sacramento's too far north. So Bakersville it is.

I'm sorry, Irma, he'll say. Emilio didn't make it. And something in the way he'll say it, he'll be right up close, to show her that he's there to see she's OK. He'll tell her not to worry about money, he'll make sure she doesn't lose out on the last contract. (The mule train picked it up, Irma. Yes, yes, I admit it, I helped them. We weighed ladybirds, even though Emilio was still out there, somewhere. But I'd no choice, y'see.) Yes, up close, so if she needs to hold on to him, he can be there, arms ready to hold her, comfort her. He'll have to use his Mexican to say this, because Irma's English isn't that good. Where is he? she'll say. And mebbes she'll cry. Aye. Mebbes she'll shout at him, even. He hadn't thought about that. Because she needs a body to keen over, to light candles for, to bury. She'll need to tell his mother back in Manzanillo, so she can grieve too. How can I tell his mother? she'll say, through her tears. How can I tell her that her son's dead but we can't bury him? Aye, she'll say it, but will she really mean it? Will Irma really cry? Cry inside? Well, thinks Tom, mebbes she will. Because she doesn't know he fucked burros, does she? Probably doesn't know any of them fucked burros. So he'll go through the motions, he'll help her do what she's got to do. But thinking, you know he was a bastard, don't you?

But when Tom gets to La Habra he doesn't see Irma, it's her brother he sees, as he gets off the red car, walks out of the station, he's there, kicking his heels outside the Cobacha bar, and he knows already. He says, 'Why you bother to come back, Tomás?' And Tom says, 'To tell you. To tell Irma.' But the brother just shrugs. Looks away. Says, '*Va con el Sancho.*' Nods in the direction of the main street. 'Over in Placentia.' Rubs thumb and forefinger together. 'Dollars. Many oranges, *limones*. He look after her.'

Tom looks at his watch. Ten past seven. He smiles at Jess and two other women who've just come in to the room. Ten past seven. And Tom thinks, perhaps he's stopped off at a shop on the way. He's not done that before, not as far as he can remember, and he doesn't know if there is a shop near here, he can't see one, but it's possible. Two other women come into the lounge and sit down beside him, one with dark glasses and, beyond her, a woman in a wheelchair with a round face and lipstick. The one with the lipstick bends forward so that she can see Tom better and says, 'Where did you get to this evenin, then, Tom?' And, looking at her, composing his reply, Tom glimpses someone else, now, on the far side of the room, by the television, someone he hasn't seen before, a little man in a sloppy beige cardigan, with heavy black spectacles and a hang-dog face. 'Just been waitin for me visitors,' says Tom, but wondering, what are you doing here? What have they brought you here for? 'They're due now. Any minute.'

And he wants him here now, his son, because he's got things to tell him. But he must get them in the right order first. Just one at a time, then, hold it tight in your fist, don't let go. Wants to say to his son, I'd have told you earlier, if I'd had the chance, if I could've got back. No, that's not it, that's not right. I got back. But it was difficult. That's it. It was difficult, no money, no papers. Not that I didn't try. Look, here, the card, he'd say. 'Home before Christmas.' Aye. That's what he wants to say, I'd've come back if I could've done. Of course I would. 'Will send letter to Mam.' It was all in the letter, son. T'your grandma. Y'see? Y'understand? But you never knew her, did you? Daft bugger. She was dead long before you... Before you were...

But that's the point, y'see, thinks Tom, that's the point. And it's so clear this time that Tom feels a rush of excitement, just thinking about it, a sense of anticipation so strong that he starts beating his fist on the arm of the chair, steady, rhythmic beats. Because this time he's held on to it, it's still there, tight in his fist. Y'see, son... Y'see, son, if I'd come back, I'd have been there meself, with me mam, with your grandma, and the rest, all of them, under the rubble, I'd've been there meself, and you, you'd not... And that's when he'll show him the map. There, he'll say. And he'll point to it, number 63. There it is, he'll say, that's where it was. But Emilio comes along, y'see, gets us up on me feet, says to us, he says, Come with me, you OK now. Cannit do the accent, son. Never could do the accent. But y'see what I mean, don't you, son? Y'understand?

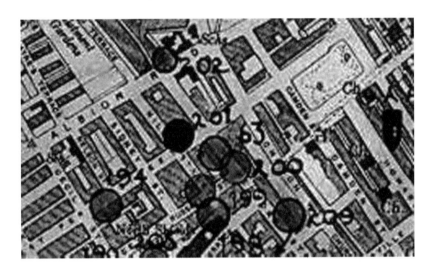

Nicky, Val, Barry

Nicky

It began when I heard the *dunk dunk* sound out in the back yard.

I'm lyin in bed, listenin to me music, on me pod like, cos me mam's
in the front with Daniel and it's late, turned one, I think. And at the
beginnin it's like the *dunk, dunk* gets mixed in with the music, cos
mebbes I'm half asleep, just driftin off, so it's like inside me head, not
out there at all. Then it comes again. *Dunk, dunk.* And it's not in me
head, I know that now, it's out the back, in the lane or the yard or
somewhere. And I know it's metal. You can't mistake metal on concrete.
Not a tin can, though, summick the cat might knock over, you know,
so that you'd get mebbes a little rattle afterwards. No, this is more of
a thud, like somethin's bein put down, not knocked over. And heavy.
Cos your ear can weigh things. Funny that.

Must be the back end of August, cos I've just had me birthday. I
know this cos the first thing I do when I get up is go and put me dressin
gown on, the big white thick one that me mam got for us. 'To see you
through the winter,' she said. It's hangin on the back of the door and
I've not really worn it yet, not much, cos it's still summer. 'Got meself
one as well,' she said. Which is another reason why I've not worn it
much. And I don't want to be ungrateful, but I'm thinkin, why've you
got to do everythin the same as me, Mam? Why didn't you ask me
first? Cos I might actually have wanted somethin different. Hol's got
a long kimono thing which her dad got her, from away somewhere,
cos he works away lots, abroad. Her dad knew what to get her. Even
her dad.

Anyway, I go and look through the side of the curtain. I don't put
the light on because I don't want anybody to see us. And he's there, this
big bloke in orange overalls, I can see him by the light in the back lane.
No, not big, just lanky, long legs and a long bony face and a woolly hat
on his head, and I'm thinkin, why's he got a woolly hat on this time
of year? But mebbes he's got no hair. Mebbes that's why. And he's
walkin through the back gate, carryin a chair under each arm, just like
this is what he does, you know, this is his job. Big metal chairs, an all,
not the poxy little ones you fold up.

And that's when he sees us, cos of the curtain movin, probably, or the white sleeve of me dressin gown standin out against the dark, I'm not sure. So he stops. He puts his chairs down and looks up at us. And he says, 'Bit past your bed-time, isn't it, pet?' Not bothered, like. Not shoutin it out. And I can hear him cos the window's open, with it bein warm. 'Back to bed now, little girl,' he says. 'There's nothin to see down here.' Which pisses me off. But I do go back to bed, cos what else can I do? And anyway, I don't want to wake me mam up. And I just carry on listenin to the chairs. Dunk, dunk. Like countin sheep. Till he's finished.

Like I say, that's when it all kicks off. When me mam gets up in the mornin and sees all these chairs in the back yard. Twenty of them. All green. All with fancy patterns in them. And she stands there countin them. 'Why you countin them, Mam?' I ask her. But she just says, 'We're out of here, Nicola.' And she's got the For Sale sign put up the next day.

Val

Look, Nicola. You see the way the sun shines on it, makin it all warm and soft, like it really wants you to live there? That's the way they shoot it, I know, it can't be sunny all the time. But every now and again would do. Just think. To come back to that every day. All that space. All that light. And that beautiful stone. Like honey

Come and have a walk around, Nicola, just for a minute, I'll get your tea ready after. Look, there's even a stream runnin through the garden. Can you believe it, your own stream? And the moors behind. And back then, you see, it takes you right round, it follows the path through the trees, past the garage, then back to the front door, and in you go.

Look, Nicola. We're in the kitchen, now. There it is, the Aga, just like you'd expect. And the big oak table. And the dresser. And isn't it just like you're there, really there? As if you're walkin from room to room, feelin what it's like to live there, for it to be your own place. You can see everythin. And it'd be nice to hear it as well, I know. To have a few sound effects, a footstep, a tap runnin, a door openin and suchlike, perhaps a sheep bleatin in the background, and you would be there, as good as. But that'll be next, I bet it will.

Just think of it, Nicola. All that space. All to yourself. Have a look, Nicola. Imagine yourself there.

Nicky

I've got to tell her twice.

'Mam, Jessica called us a fat slag today.'

Cos she's not listenin. Cos she's lookin at these pictures of houses on the computer. Sayin 'Mm' and 'Ooh' like as if she's stuffin pieces of chocolate into her gob.

'Mam, she called us a fat slag.'

And what does she say? She says I'm fourteen now and I've got to live with it. And what does that mean? Did I miss summick? Eh? Did summick happen on me fourteenth birthday and nobody told us? A law was passed that any old bitch like Jessica could call us what she liked and it'd be alright, cos I was fourteen? I'm fourteen. I've got to live with it. That's what me mam says. And goes back to her pictures.

'Live with what?' I say. 'Bein called a fat slag? Or bein a fat slag?'

And she looks us up and down, like she just can't decide if I'm a fat slag or not, like she's only just set eyes on us, like I'm a total stranger.

'Look OK to me,' she goes, in that can't be bothered voice she puts on when she wants to be really irritatin.

'OK? What d'you mean, OK?' I say. 'OK as in, Well, she's fat, but I suppose she'll do? Eh? Is that what you mean, Mam?'

And she shrugs, just like a kid, just like Hollie does when she's got a cob on. And then she really goes for it, like she's been savin the worst till last.

'Look at me,' she says. 'Just look at me.'

Like she's sayin, you might as well give up now, pet, you've got no hope, it's in your genes, just lie down and blob out. And how can I answer that, when she's sat there, me own mam, lookin like Mrs Blobby, and she's not bothered? Actually thinkin it's alright. Thinkin, if it's alright for me, it should be alright for you an all. Look at her? How the hell could I miss her?

And she goes back to her pictures again. 'How'd you fancy that, Nicola? Up Bellingham way.' Like we've never even had the conversation, like I'm a little puppy dog or summick and she can just hoy us a ball and I'll go runnin after it and everythin'll be alright.

How do I fancy it? All I can see is hills and trees and some manky old barn in the middle of nowhere. As though she can distract us with a fuckin barn. So I tell her not to be daft, I ask her, how are we gonna live up there, with her workin in Shields? And what am I gonna to do in the middle of a poxy field? And Daniel, what's he gonna do? Play in the stream? I don't think! Like it's me that's her mam.

And she's sat there, with her head on one side and her hands folded on her lap, like she does when she's pretendin to listen. And I'm thinkin, why've you got to do that, that pretendin to listen thing, and your hair, my god, your hair, cos I've just noticed it now, she's had this crop thing done to her hair, and I want to ask her, why've you done that crop thing to your hair, Mam, you never did that before? I want to tell her, Get a life, Mam. Your own life, not mine. For fuck's sake, Mam, even the hair.

'Why'd she call you a fat slob, anyway?'

'Fat slag, Mam, fat slag.'

Cos she's not listenin, you see.

'It's all words, pet. Slag, slob, slob, slag. Just yackety yack.'

Not listenin. Just takin the piss.

Val

There's no harm lookin, is there? I mean, it gives you an idea what's out there, what you can aim for. Cos you've got to want somethin, haven't you? You've got to know what you want, or you'll never get it. Don't waste the next twenty years workin that one out, Nicola. That's what I want to tell her. No, that's what I want her to feel. Tellin her's a waste of time. So just a couple more, just the saved ones, to have a last look, at the pictures and the maps, to click the button, to request the viewin, to know that things are startin to change.

Barry

Bumped me first Ruko today. High security. At least that's what it says. So that's why I was keepin it till last, bit of a challenge, like. I've done the rest of the batch, a couple of regular Yales, a Banham and a Chubb. Piece of piss, even the Chubb, could do them in me sleep. The five-pin Ruko's different, though. Stubborn bastard. And I'm bangin away at the key this way and that, from the right then from the left, fast and slow, hard and soft, like they show you in the video, and I just can't get it. And I'm startin to think, I've not got the right bump key, cos you need different keys for different types of lock, you see, and there are that many types. Just a wee bit difference in depth and it'll not work, it'll not catch the pins. Or it mightn't be the key at all, it might be the lock. It's old, I can see that, all polished, like, where people've been fingerin it. So it's worn inside, bound to be. And what can I do about that? Or there again, mebbes me hammer's not right, wrong weight, bit narrow at the head, whatever. Cos it feels weird after you've made do with a screwdriver for six months. But it's cost us fifteen quid so I'm stickin with it. I change the spring. I try a dampner instead. I try two dampners together. I'm thinkin, what the fuck else can I do? This is what it's like, bumpin locks, you've just got to keep on tryin.

But it's not the tools. It never is, is it? Bad workman blames his tools. And I'm thinkin now it must be the turnin pressure. When you bang the key with your hammer you've got to press one side of it with your finger. Just a touch, like. And just at the right time. Or your thumb, of course. Some people on the Forum use their thumb, say it's easier to hold the lock still. But I use me finger. So I start pressin the key clockwise, just a touch, and tap, tap, tap, with the hammer, short sharp taps. Nothin. Press again, a wee bit higher on the key, tap, tap, tap, and not so hard this time. Nothin. Press again, tap, tap, tap, down this time, but I know I'm pressin too hard now, I can feel the tension in me wrist, and it's hard to use your hammer with your right hand and keep that pressure really light and gentle with your left. Imagine pushin a dead beetle over a pane of glass, it says in the manual. That's how light. So I stop. I take a deep breath, like they tell you, let the muscles relax. And I start again. Nothin.

So if it's not the pressure, it might be the hammer. No, not the hammer itself, but the way I'm holdin it, the way I'm swingin it. Or the angle. There's that many things to think about, that many things to remember. So I start tappin the key on the top, not the back, cos they tell you that, to try everythin, every combination, and not really even a tap, just a clip on the edge. Pingin it. Not bangin it. Not pushin. Pushin's worst of all. Ping. That's all. Ping. And fuck me, that's it. I hear them, I hear the clicks. Three, mebbes four of the top pins, settlin back. I'm not there yet, but I'm on the way. And that's the best bit, just before you get there, and you know next time you're gonna make it. So I ease off the key a wee bit, just a touch. Keep it light. Don't be too keen. Cos the proper turnin pressure wouldn't leave a mark on bluetack, that's what they say. And that's all it takes, in the end. Feather touches, they say. Cos it's only tiny, tiny pins you're movin. Not every time, mind. But this time, for sure. And I do it again, straightaway, in case it was just luck. It opens. Nee bother. And it feels that slack, that free, like it's been there for us all this time, just waitin, not really offerin any resistance. After all that time. And again. I do it again. Cos I've got the hang of it now. The knack. The feel of it just sticks in your fingers, your wrists. Cos every lock's got its own feel.

Jaz asked us if it was a garage lock, the Ruko. And I said I've got no idea, and I've not, cos it was all a job lot, like, on eBay. And he says, What's the point of that, man? Meanin what's the point of bumpin locks, any old locks. Meanin, you daft fuck. On the Forum it says if you become a master of locks you become a master of freedom. But Jaz wouldn't understand that. No more than me dad would. That's why I keep them at the bottom of me wardrobe, out of sight, all me locks and keys. That's why I tell Jaz, I'm practisin for the real thing. 'You just wait,' I tell him. That's why I tell me dad nowt.

128

Val

Start off with five things you can see, he said.

I can see the window frame, the front gate, the wall, the For Sale sign, a car. Five things.

Then four things you can hear.

I can hear. What can I hear? I can hear the wire pullin on the sign. I can hear. I can hear a car goin past outside. I can hear. I can hear the water in the central heatin, an air pocket, a gurglin sound, whatever. I can hear. I can hear another car goin past. Four things. But does that count? Does the second car count? Would he let me count that?

Then three things you can feel. Count three things that you can feel. Which is easy. Me bracelet, me watch, me hand. Three. Three things.

And two things you can smell. I can smell. I can smell. I can't smell. And this is the one, this is the one that slows you down, that really does the biz. What is there to smell? So little, you've got to hunt for it. The back of me hand. Moisturiser on the back of me hand. What else? What else? What do curtains smell of? Let's see. They smell of damp and fags. Cos they hang there, just soakin it all up. Damp and fags and tiredness.

And finally, he said, one thing you like about yourself.

One thing I like about meself is. Is. Is. One thing I like about meself is, that I have a little boy who likes seein us come home. Does that count?

There, now. Does that feel better, Mrs Robson? Do you feel calmer? Can you breathe more easily?

But why do they leave out taste? That would be the best one. Taste.

Nicky

'Wave bye-bye to Mammy.'

And I lift him up to the window so that he can see his mam goin out the front gate. So she can blow two kisses, give him a wave. The wind's strong, really strong, so she's got to hold her jacket hood with her hand . She's got to lean into it as she walks, blinkin against it.

'So what d'you want to do today, little Daniel, eh?'

Cos there's only a few days left and it's back to your Auntie Gillian then, and back to school for me. And I'm thinkin, well, that was Christmas, but where was me holiday?

'Wanna go beach.'

'Tomorra,' I tell him. 'If it gets out. If you're good.'

Cos the wind'll blow you off your feet. Although that leanin thing she did, holdin her hood on, all that stuff, she does that for effect. To show she's got the worst of it. Guilt trip. Mammy goin out to work, for us, not for herself. Out into the big wide world, Daniel, just for you and me.

Me mam's got a job down the leisure park on the quay, which is just like a big flash swimmin pool really, with chutes and things. And like lives there, just about. Cos this is their busiest time, she says, when the schools are out. And with her bein Assistant Manager now. She's got a plastic badge she wears with Val Robson Assistant Manager on it, and her picture, all smilin like, cos she's chuffed she's got the job. 'Things are lookin up,' she says. Meanin she's got to do lots more work, evenins and weekends and that, but it'll be worth it. Cos we can move somewhere better.

That's what worth it means to me mam. Gettin another house. Cos the chairs are still in the back garden, tellin her that's what she's got to do, cos who knows what it'll be next. That's what she says. And I'm thinkin, well, aye, what next? What's the next step up from garden chairs? Firebombs through the letterbox mebbes? Sniper fire from the roof of the post office? What planet are you on, Mam? They're too fuckin monged out their heads to fart round here, most of them. 'It can only get better now, pet,' she says. 'Look on the bright side.' And I'm thinkin, when, Mam, when? And *my* school's out as well, you know. So where's *my* holiday?

'Don't put your mucky paws on the wall, Daniel!'

Cos she's told us to keep the place straight. No clutter, she says. Not that she was ever fussed before. But that's what they tell you on them house-movin programmes. Get rid of your clutter. And that means Daniel's toys. Why, Mam? Why've we got to put his toys away? Cos it distracts them, she says. So I've got to get them all out and I've got to put them all back every time he wants to play. Distracts who, Mam? Who is there to distract? And it means no pots or pans or plates in the kitchen, no coats on their hooks, no shoes in the passage, no dressin gown on me bedroom door, and no pictures on the walls, none of mine, anyway. So it's like a fuckin hospital. And I tell her, who wants to live in a hospital?

But he's got to put his mucky paws somewhere. So I wipe his prints off the kitchen wall and get him ready to go out.

'I'll have to strap you in tight, Daniel. Stop you blowin away.'

Nobody wants to live in a hospital, that's who. And nobody wants to buy this place. So learn to live with it, Mam, will you, and give us a break.

'Wanna go play with Chloe, Daniel?'

And we go to Hollie's, cos it's nearer than Emma's or Kelly's or Jen's, where we might have gone, if it hadn't been that windy out, that miserable, and if I didn't have Daniel with us. Hollie lives on the other side of the park, by the Metro station. She's got a sister called Chloe who's six and likes playin mammy and baby with Daniel. Well, doesn't mind anyway, for a bit.

'Look, Louis, Daniel's come to play.'

Except that Hollie calls her sister Louis, not Chloe, because she's had enough of people sayin, 'Ee, are you Alan Shearer's bairn?' And she can't believe that her dad didn't know that Alan Shearer's kids were called Hollie and Chloe. Her mam, mebbes, but not her dad.

'How's your mam, Hol?'

Cos I've got to ask. Although I don't really want to know, not if it's bad news. And Hollie doesn't like talkin about it either, I know that, so I'm glad when she says, 'Still on the chemo,' and leaves it at that. Cos that means somebody's doin somethin, somethin that might work, if we just bide our time.

Anyway, Chloe calls herself Chloe, because she likes it when people think Alan Shearer's her dad.

'So we go into the front room,' I tell her, tryin to take her mind off things, and that's all I've got to tell her really, cos we don't do owt else these days, me and me mam, except go and look at other people's houses. 'We go into the front room, and the family's all there, sittin there, eatin their food in front of the telly, like a bunch of monkeys. We've got to walk round them. Don't mind us, they say, don't mind us. And it smells of farts and baked beans and fag ash, like all mixed together, and the old fella's gawpin at me belly, pretendin not to, like, not movin his head, just his eyes, really sly like, you know, cos I'm wearin me crop top. And he's all fat and slobbery.'

And Hollie wrinkles her nose.

'That's gross, Nicky. Really gross.'

Which is the sort of thing that Hollie says. In fact that's all she says, really, like nothin ever happens to her, or nothin she can ever be arsed to tell you about. But at least she's not in me face all the time. Not like some of the others. Not like Jessica. Jessica called us a slag just because I asked her boyfriend if he was goin to the Motorettes gig. Like as if she owned him. Like I had to ask her permission just to speak to him. Weedy lookin creep anyway. What do I care if he goes or not? Hol wouldn't do that. Wouldn't go off on one. But then, Hol couldn't, could she, cos she's not got a boyfriend. So what I'm sayin is, bein with Hol's alright, here anyway, in her house, cos she's not in me face.

And me mam. Hol's not like me mam, either. And I tell her this, that it's a relief to get out, cos livin with me mam's like livin with a nerdy teenager. Mothers, who'd 'ave 'em? I say. And she really laughs at that, even though I shouldn't have said it, mebbes, not with things bein as they are. With her own mam, I mean. Laughs at it, like it was somethin really funny.

'Your Barry in, Hol?'

'Gone to Newcastle. Won't be back till tonight.'

I can see Barry in Hol, just a bit. They've both got these droopy eyes, sort of slopin downwards. Makes them look like they're sad even when they're smilin. And that an all. They've both got this way of smilin, a really wide smile just like a smiley, just lips, no teeth. So cute.

A big sad smiley. And that other thing, that far away thing. They can switch off, go back into their heads, a long way away. That's what it looks like. A long way off. But what do I know? He's seventeen. What the fuck do I know what goes on inside his head?

'Gone to the sales?'

And I know it's a daft question, because lads don't do shoppin, but it's out and I cannot pull it back in and I'm lookin up at Hol, expectin her to say, What do you want to know that for? Cos why would I? Why would I want to know what her big brother's doin of a Thursday afternoon? And I'm gettin this little prickle of heat around me ears, waitin for her to say it. But she doesn't. Of course she doesn't. That'd be somebody else. Cos Hol just takes anythin I say, no questions asked, like that's all it's about.

'No,' she says. And then, 'Well, sort of. He's got a packin job in Masons.'

No questions asked, cos he's just her big brother. So what am I talkin to Hol about her big bother for? Fuck knows.

'You heard back from Chebsie?' I ask her.

'Dunno,' she says.

'You looked?'

She shakes her head.

'You wanna look?'

She shrugs.

'So you want to sit here like a puddin all day do you, Hol?'

And she shrugs again. But by now I'm openin up the computer meself, keyin in the address. Then she does this whiney thing she does when she can't be arsed to do owt else.

'But what if he's just a kid?'

'What kid thinks Rihanna comes from Ireland, Hol?' I ask her. 'Duh!'

She shrugs again.

'What kid says, "I want to hang out with nice friendly girls cos I haven't got a sister?"'

Cos like I say, this spaced-out far away thing's just Hol not bein arsed. And come to think of it, Brian does that an all. The shrug. I can see him doin it. Like as if to say, I don't mind if you do and I don't mind if you don't. Except that's not what Hol's sayin. Hol's sayin she's in a grump.

Anyway, when I get in to the chat-room there's only Trilz and dBoi and Krissay havin a stab at Smokey, who promised to 'come on line half an hour ago. So I key in, 'Has Chebsie been on?' Although as I'm doin it I'm scrollin down and I can see he hasn't. And Trilz just says, 'I'm room hoppin cos this tit's doin me head in.' So dBoi says, 'c/t go fuck yourself,' which just leaves Krissay, and Krissay just wants to know how she can upload her holiday photographs and says, 'Who's Chebsie?' And I think, fuck this.

Then somebody called Hardcorefix comes on and says, 'Hi, I'm Jed and I'm so sexy,' and I start to key in 'WANKER!!!!' But then I think, no, why give him the satisfaction? So I ignore him. I just say, 'Where y go on holiday K?' And leave it at that. And Krissay says, 'Ibeetha' and she can show us the pics, but how does she send them? So I ask Hol if it's OK to give her her email address.

'Suppose …' she whines. 'Suppose.'

Whiney cow.

'Tell you what, Hol.' And I'm thinkin, alright, I'll give you just one last shot. One last chance to get off that sad fat arse of yours. 'How's about we go up the sales tomorrow?'

And she thinks about it.

'I've got Louis,' she says.

'I've got Daniel,' I say. 'So what?'

'I've got no money,' she says.

'I'm goin anyway, Hol. Come if y'want.'

Sad cow.

So I let her stew for a bit. I go into the kitchen to see why Daniel's whimperin and I find Chloe tryin to prize a bottle of washin-up liquid from his fingers. There are gooey slug trails across the floor tiles. So I get a couple of pan lids from the cupboard, a wooden spoon from a drawer, and I show Daniel how to drum with them. Here you are, little man, I say, and I'm thinkin, God, boys are a real doddle, that's all they need, to bang away at a couple of pan lids, that's all they need to keep them happy. And I set about spongin the floor. But Chloe says, 'Can I do that?' So I think, what the hell? And let them get on with it.

When I go back to the front room, Hollie's curled up in her armchair, pickin her feet, suckin a pen, starin at one of them daft word puzzles you do when there's really nothin else to do but die. And I'm thinkin, that's where you want to be, Hol, down there in your gloomy pit, pickin your feet, suckin your pen, suits me fine, but don't expect me to join you.

Krissay's pictures have come through. Just a lot of beach scenes, pool scenes, dad-actin-daft scenes. Nice, though. Sunny, warm. And this picture of a party, outside some big pink house. On the terrace, that's what they call it, with the pool just off to one side, I think, out of sight, but I can see those long white plastic chair things and some scrumpled up towels. I can feel the heat on their bodies, just standin there, squintin in the sun, glowin, soakin it in. Like there's nothin happenin anywhere else. Just them, there. Nice.

Hardcorefix is back in the chat-room. 'Fancy go on holiday w me?' he's askin Krissay. Cos he's got a pool too, he says, and he'll buy her tequilas, and he'll bring a ship load of cowies with him. And that's when I realise that Krissay has sent this wanker the photos too. Fuckin slag. Trilz comes back on line, full of it, wantin to get her oar in as well, sayin that her mam and dad have done a house swap with somebody in Orlando, boat, swimmin pool, the works, even a maid comin in every day, and I think, Oh aye, pull the other one, who you tryin to kid?

And I've dropped out of the loop. As fast as that. Cos that's what happens if you just sit there, watchin, if you don't keep bangin away, you become invisible. And I know that Hardcorefix is a wanker and a freak, but if he can ask that slag Krissay to go on holiday with him, why can't he ask me? Only so I can tell him where to stuff his fuckin holiday, mind. But still, why can't he? It's like he knows, that's why. Cos I didn't get back fast enough. Cos I didn't send any pictures. Cos I've not got any pictures. It's like he knows, even without seein us, that I'm a fat slag, a bigger fat slag even than that Krissay bitch.

So I'm bangin away again, cos I've got to, cos I've let it slip and it's like me fingers are sayin it for us, I don't have to think. 'We've fixed a place in Brooklyn for summer.' Not cos I've got any idea where Brooklyn is, but I know nobody else will either, and anyway it's me dad's voice in me head now, fuck knows why, sayin that's where it started, that's where he'll go when he scrapes the cash together, the Big Boogie, Nicky, he'd say, in the Big Mecca, see what's crackin. The waster.

And I don't care where it is, I don't even care if me dad's made it up, that's where I want to be now, a long way away, a long way from Hardcorefix and Krissay and Daniel bangin his pan lids and Hollie sittin there like a puddin and me mam and all this shit.

Val

'What do you mean, Mam, get used to bein called a fat slag?'

And I can't believe she's rakin this up again, at half past eight in the mornin. Daniel's plasterin his mucky paws all over the fridge door. I've got to be in work in twenty minutes. Why now, Nicola? Why this?

But then, if it wasn't this it'd be somethin else.

'Nothin, pet, I didn't mean anythin. I don't want you gettin upset, that's all.'

But thinkin, why are they callin you a slag? How much is there I don't know, Nicola? How much is there you're not lettin on? So I ask her, 'Why'd they call you a slag, pet?' In a really gentle voice, really tryin to understand, tryin not to ruffle her feathers. 'Why'd they call you a slag, pet?' That's what I say. Just that. But that's not the question she hears. And mebbes I should have thought it through a bit more, but I'm puttin me coat on, I'm lookin for me keys, which aren't in me purse, where they ought to be, and if Daniel's had them God knows where they are now. So I don't think. I don't have time to think. And when she shouts 'You what?', I don't understand. And she shouts again. 'What did you say?' And then I do understand. She thinks I'm implyin somethin, yes, I see now how she might think that. Like I'm sayin, they call you a slag, so they must have their reasons. Like, there's no smoke without fire, is there? Do they know somethin I don't? Somethin like that.

So I start to say. 'I don't mean...'

But no, that's not it at all. That's not what she thinks.

'So you do think I'm fat!'

Cos that's what she hears. She hears me sayin, Yes, you're fat, forget about it, now talk about the slag bit.

Next time I'll know to say it different. I won't even say, 'Why'd they call you that, pet?' Tryin to be neutral, not implyin this or that. Cos even that's wrong. It's askin for explanations. And her mam shouldn't be doin that, askin for explanations. So when she next tells us, so'n'so said this, so'n'so said that, I'll just say, No! And sound astonished, like who would ever believe such a thing? The bitch, I'll say. The old cow. Cos that's what she wants. And it's not the words. The words are just words. It's her mam she wants, there with her. Tellin the world it's a bitch. So she doesn't have to take it all on by herself.

But she's still shoutin when I leave the house. And I stand there, cos she's normally brought Daniel to the front window by now, by the time I'm closin the gate, to blow him two kisses, to wave bye-bye, but she doesn't do it this time. And I stand there a bit longer, waitin, lookin at the paint peelin on the window frame, the crack in the renderin under the sill and the For Sale sign tuggin at its wires. And I'm wonderin, what the hell is me daughter doin wearin eye-liner on a Friday mornin?

Barry

Jaz has got this upstairs flat, where his Auntie Jess lives, except she doesn't any more, she's in a home, but his dad's fucked off and his mam's busy shaggin her boss, and there's nobody else to worry. So that's where we go, me and Liam and Alex and mebbes a couple of lads from work, and Jaz, of course, cos Jaz is the only one with the key and he's not gonna give it to anybody else, is he? 'I divvent need a key, man,' I tell him, 'I can bump it.' 'I'll bump ye if y'dee,' he says. And he would an all. So when Jaz is about, that's when we go. And when me dad's around. To keep out of his way. Me dad works security on the ferry to Bergen, so he's away three nights in ten. Bergen and that other place. Stav summick. Three nights in ten for five years. And the bastard hasn't sunk yet.

And anyway, Jaz is there most of the time cos he's got nowhere else to go. I mean, he can go home, of course he can. But you wouldn't want to, would you, you wouldn't want to stop home if your mam was shaggin her boss all the time, would you? And that's not all. He's been banned from the Metro. All he did was hoy up on the platform cos he'd had a dodgy curry. And then fall over this lass gettin onto the train. That was it, probably. Not the pukin, the fallin over. Fuck me, you can't fall over these days without gettin fuckin nicked. So that's Jaz's contribution, like, the flat, for gettin together, havin a laugh.

And Jaz says it's good for bringin lasses back an all, bein how it's full of his Auntie Jess's things, it's like all cushions and knick-knacks and pictures and that. And there's these cups Jaz's Uncle George won, on top of the telly. Years ago. For his leeks. Lasses like that, Jaz says. Can't see it meself, mind, why lasses should like lookin at Uncle George's cups. Not threatenin, you see, he says. Not cool, but not threatenin. And lasses like that, he says. Some lasses. It's cosy. And they like it when Jaz tells them he's lookin after his auntie's flat for her, while she's in hospital, or on holiday, or seein her sister, or whatever he thinks up, thinks the lass wants to hear. That's what he says. Some lasses just think he's a loser, mind. Which he is, in a manner of speakin. But how can you get a job when they'll not let you go on the Metro? Aye, and the buses an all, cos it's the Metro owns the buses, so he can't catch a bus neither. He keeps the place clean. You've got to give him that. Clean enough.

So that's what Jaz has chipped in. The flat. Cos he's skint. Except for what he knocks off.

'Yer mam aal reet?'

Jaz always asks that. Thinks he's got to, probably. But I don't come here for that. So I just shrug me shoulders. Cos who the fuck knows anyway?

Nicky

I'm meetin Hol on the 1.13 Metro from Shields. This gets into Percy
Main at 1.18. Percy Main is Hol's station. I've texted her, just in case
she's gone back into a grump or can't peel her arse off the sofa or has
just plain forgotten. 1.13. So that gives us an hour and a half, a bit less,
which is OK, if I get a move on.

'Off to see your daddy now, Daniel.'

'Daddy,' he says. That's all. Not givin anythin away.

'Just our secret, Daniel, alright?'

Cos I haven't told me mam. Of course I haven't. And to be honest,
he wouldn't have been my first choice either. But who else is gonna
look after Daniel on a Friday afternoon?

And that's why I'm runnin a bit late, what with puttin everythin
together, the nappies, the spare clothes, the food and drink, and writin
out the things to do, the things not to do, cos I can't leave anythin
to chance, not with me dad. Cos he forgets. Cos I wouldn't trust him
anyway. Who would?

It's not easy, pushin the buggy with one hand and the bike with
the other. I don't think you *can* steer a buggy with one hand. It keeps
veerin this way and that, like the wheels've got a mind of their own.
But the bike's worse, cos the pedals keep bangin against me calf, against
me ankle, especially at the kerbs, cos I just can't lift them both at the
same time, and the buggy goes out one way and the front wheel of
the bike goes the other, and you'd never believe there was that many
kerbs, just goin to Chirton Rise. And I'm all of a lather by the time I
reach me dad's, and me wrists are ready to snap.

You can tell which flat's me dad's cos the windows are painted lilac.
And cos the flats next door are boarded up. Bein refurbished, me dad
says, every time. Like he knows anythin. But not completely empty
either, can't be, cos you can see where people have got in, have got the
boards loose, and if they can get in once they can get in again, stands
to reason. He's waitin for us at the top of the stair-well.

'Hiya, Nicky. Come on up.'

But I've not got the time. And I don't want to think of any of this
now, his crap flat, who's next door, what the hell he's gonna do with

Daniel. So I just tell him I've got a train to catch. I've got to be away. 'Mebbes later on,' I say, tryin to sound like I do really want to. Cos I can deal with that later.

I've collapsed the buggy, so that's one thing less for him to do. But Daniel's clingin to me neck now, bawlin, squirmin. And I'm tryin to pass him over, tellin him, 'Daddy's gonna take you out today, Daniel, aren't you, Daddy? Tell him where y'gonna take him, Daddy.' And me dad does his best. He says, 'Come on Daniel, we'll away down to Mickey D's, see if we can get you an extra Big Mac, what'ya say, soldier, eh?' But he's bawlin worse than ever.

And then it strikes us that mebbes Daniel's not sure who Daddy is. Or doesn't even recognise him. Me dad's cut off his brown curls, which was the closest he could ever get to an Afro, and I think, God, I wouldn't've known you meself if I'd seen you anywhere but here. So I give up. I pull Daniel's hands off me neck. I put him down by his buggy. I just say, 'Back by six, Dad. See you later, Daniel.' Cos he's got to learn. Cos I'm not his mam. Or his dad. But feelin a bit guilty, all the same, cos he's cryin real tears now. 'Like the hair,' I tell me dad. And I'm on me bike.

Barry

It's not that I *couldn't* bump it, mind. I can do them old Yales standin on me head. You barely need a bump key, they're that slack. Any old key'll do. So it's not the lock. It's just that you never know when Jaz is gonna be there. Or if you get in all right, seein there's no light on an' that, when he's gonna come in, find you there. There's no tellin. So I've got to be careful, bide me time. But Corinne would be up for it, I know she would.

And it's not that we couldn't do it with Jaz there. I mean, Liam had that Becky lass there last night, and Jaz was out of it, cos he'd been smokin blow all day, and Craig and Kieron were just watchin the footie on the box, couple of cans of bella, so Liam and his lass just slope off like, to the spare bedroom, just slope off, like it was their own place, cos that's how it is, if you're in with Jaz. Only the spare bedroom, mind, cos Jaz'll not let anybody use his Auntie Jess's bedroom, even though it's got the best bed in it, even though she's never gonna sleep in it again.

Glad they did, mind, cos she'd been bitin his face off for half an hour and I couldn't concentrate on the footie, with them writhin around there, and me gettin all horny meself, and thinkin what I'd like to be doin with Corinne. And Kieron askin them, 'Woudn't you like to retire to somewhere more comfortable?' In that voice he does. And Craig just says, 'Aye, hadaway an' fuck, will yiz, man, and leave w' in peace.' So everybody laughs, except Jaz, who's still out of it, and I'd say she's laughin more than him, aye, Becky's laughin more than Liam, cos Liam's a bit bashful, when it comes to the crunch, cos of his bein Catholic. 'Hadaway an' fuck the Pope for fuck's sake,' says Kieron, 'he's not had a shag in two thousand years, man.'

And mebbes, if I brought Corinne here, with everybody round, we could laugh like that and it'd be OK. Bit blow first. No rush. Settle in. Natter about this and that. Corinne would get on alright if Becky was there. Aye, I'd have to fix that. For Becky to be there. Bit blow first. Except I don't know if she does blow. And if she doesn't, then she's gonna think, God, what a waster that Jaz is, which he is, like, I'm not sayin. But how do you get from that? How do you get from sittin there, Jaz monged out on the sofa, and Kieron and Liam and Craig downin their bellas, watchin the footie on the telly, listenin to that Martin Tyler wanker, or mebbes Becky's there an she's got that fuckin Skin the Pig on or some other depressin shit. How do you get from that, from sittin down to standin up to goin to the bedroom? What happens? Who says what? Who looks at who? And if Liam's the Pope, who am I? And do you laugh, Corinne, when Kieron says, 'Hadaway an' fuck, man, will yiz?' Cos we're not there yet, me an Corinne. We're just not there yet. So I've got to bide me time.

And that's why I'm thinkin, if we can get in there by ourselves, just the two of us, me and Corinne, in Jaz's flat, that'd be easier. No Jaz, no Liam, no Craig, no Kieron. And no Corinne's mam and dad, neither, lookin at us like I'm summick on the bottom of their shoes, stickin their nebs in. Just the two of us. That'd be nice.

141

Nicky

I look at me watch and I think, I'm alright, ten minutes is enough. And then I think no, ten minutes is enough to get to the Metro, but then I've got to lock me bike up, buy me ticket and get to the platform. So mebbes it's not enough. So I ride as fast as I can, standin on the peddles, goin down the back streets to avoid the traffic. It's not that I'm bothered about bein late. It's bein late if Hol's on time. That would just be humiliatin. And I know it's me own fault, cos I'd forgotten how slow I was pushin the pram and the bike, how Daniel would play up, how things never work out like you want them to. So it's me own fault. But it's me dad's fault an all, cos this is his bike, the bike he left behind, and ridin as fast as I can on me dad's bike isn't that fast. The chain keeps jumpin and the top gear slips as soon as I really get goin, so it doesn't matter how hard I pedal, I can't go any faster. And that would be alright, but it makes this clankin sound all the time, somewhere between the pedals, like it's all gonna fall apart in a minute, and the faster you pedal the worse the clankin, and everybody's lookin at us, laughin at us, laughin at this fat bitch on her nerdy bike. Her dad's bike.

Even so, I might still be alright, I've got a couple of minutes to spare, me watch might be fast, the train might be late, and I'm thinkin, yes, I'm gonna make it, I'm comin to the turn into Nile Street and thinkin, I'm gonna make it. But just to make sure, cos Nile Street's sometimes busy with taxis, blockin the road, and mebbes I'll not be able to turn straightaway, I could be stuck there just waitin me turn, so just to make sure, I go up onto the pavement, just by the bingo, just by the last stretch, knowin I'm gonna make it.

And I've come this way, down Russell Street, cos it's quiet and there's nobody on the pavement, almost nobody, just this one bloke, and that's alright, cos there's plenty of room and I'll give him a wide berth, and I've not got a bell but fuck knows I'm makin enough racket, so he's bound to hear us behind him, clankin, and he'll keep out me way, he'll step to one side, of course he will. And I'm gettin closer, knowin he's gonna shift, or mebbes look over his shoulder first, just to see what's makin all the racket, and then shift. They always do. But he doesn't. I know he will, cos why wouldn't he? But he doesn't.

Cos he can't. Cos he's too fat. Like a big fat Tellytubby. All squidgy. And he's got this daft way of walkin, sort of waddlin, and his briefcase swingin in his hand, bangin against his leg, cos that's how he's walkin, like fat people walk, how they waddle, tiltin to the left, then tiltin to the right, just like a Fimble. And that's why he doesn't shift out the way.

But no, he's not a Tellytubby, no, I can see now, cos he's turnin round. At last, he's turnin round. Just his head, he's turnin his head, that's right, cos he's heard us now, he's heard the clankin, I knew he would. And he's not a Tellytubby, he's more like one of them characters on South Park, you know, cos he's wearin this funny hat, like a Russian hat with flaps down over his ears. Kyle. That's the one. That's who he's like. Kyle in South Park. A fatso with a funny hat.

Or he would be like Kyle, except he's got this beard, like a big fluff ball round his face, so that when he opens his mouth, which he's doin now, it's not like a mouth, it's just a hole in his beard. And I'm thinkin, he's turned round, he's seen us now, so he'll step out the way, he'll shift over to the right, cos that's the way he's lookin, over his right shoulder. So I swerve to the left. And he sees us, he sees us swervin, I can see him lookin at us, like followin which way I'm goin. And I know he's got to move, and really quick. He'll move to the right, cos I've moved to the left. I know he will. But he doesn't. And I can't believe it, cos he's movin the wrong way, he's stepped right in front of us. He's even holdin his briefcase out by his side, to make sure I can't get past. And I can't believe it.

So there's no time to think. I've got to slam on me brakes. But the brakes don't work properly, do they, cos this is me dad's bike, so what can I do but jam me foot down, drag it along the pavement, try to stop meself. And jammin me foot down sends me body forwards, so that I'm leanin over the handlebars now, still holdin on to them, cos there's nothin else to hold on to, and they're turnin now cos I'm leanin too much one way, too much to the left and me right foot's up, out of it, somewhere by the saddle I think, and down I go, clankin into the gutter, me and the bike, cos I'm still holdin on to the bastard handlebars.

So I'm lyin there, tied up in me bike and feelin the pain come through, in me ankle, in me shoulder. And thinkin, he'll turn round again now, he's bound to turn round again, and he'll see us lyin here, he'll come and give us a hand. But when he does look round all he does is grin at us. Not than I can see his lips, but that hole in his beard gets bigger. And he nods. He grins and he nods at us, two or three nods. And I can't credit it. Like as if to say, you weren't expectin that, were you? And he's off, around the corner. So that when I shout at him, I know he can't hear, but I've still got to shout, cos look at the state of us, look at me jeans, look at me jacket, look at the fuckin state of us. So I shout. I shout, 'You fat pig. You just wait. You just fuckin wait.' As loud as I can.

Val

Click

Episode 3: Leicester
Kirstie and Phil house hunt for three generations of one family - one big house for one big, extended family, mother-in-law included. To make matters worse, they can't agree on where they want to live.

Today I'm havin me lunch break with Kirstie and Phil. And I don't normally let meself do this, have a peek at what's comin next week, but it's what I need now, today. And I'm lookin for me own episode here, the one that'll show us how to do it, wonderin how it would work out, if it would work out. But this isn't it.

Click

Episode 4: Southampton revisited
Kirstie and Phil helped Andrew McKay and Ian Fish find a terraced house two years ago. Back then they had crippling student debts and couldn't afford a deposit. How have things changed for them?
And seein how people cope, how they get by, how it all comes right in the end, doesn't matter what shit's thrown at them, it's all right in the end. Two years, this lot, and no money, but it still works out. Yes,

that's how things have changed for them, I can tell you that for nothin, cos they always do work out, wouldn't be entertainment otherwise. And that's alright, it shows what's possible. Except for one thing. They've got each other, haven't they? Andrew's always got his Ian. Kirstie's always got her Phil. That's the difference.

Click

Episode 5: Ipswich
Faint-hearted first-time buyers Jennifer and Peter have lost three houses in the last 12 months, and want different things: Paul wants a renovation project but Helen wants a ready-made home.

So they're always fallin out. Right, it should be easier for me, that's what I'm thinkin. I haven't got that Peter bastard, hankerin after his renovation project. I've got rid of mine already, Kirstie, I've told him to sling his hook. Except he wasn't called Peter, he was called Terry. Peace and quiet, that's all I want. And I'm not some faint-hearted wimp, either. This is me talkin, Kirstie! Can you hear me?

Click

Episode 6: Somerset
Joe and Rebecca Nosworthy, their children, three camels and other sundry wildlife need more space - eight acres of it, in fact - on a £700,000 budget...

Come off it, Kirstie, you're pullin me leg now.

Click

Episode 6: Yorkshire
Lara and Roger Huggett have won £1,800,000 on the Lottery, but with a budget set at £650,000, how will they react when they see that they won't necessarily be able to afford a mansion?
Well, poor Lara and Roger. Now listen to this, Kirstie. This is my episode now. Val Robson, single mother, and her two children, Nicola and Daniel, no husband, definitely no husband, so nobody wantin a

renovation or an extension or a camel, and just the two generations, last lot dead and cremated, out of the way, so a tidy little jackpot, not the Lottery but more than you'd expect, at my age, enough to buy some peace and quiet, you'd think. That's all, some peace and quiet. So, come on, Kirstie, do your stuff. What are you waitin for?

Nicky

So I texts Hol to say I'll meet her under the Monument at two, cos I've had an accident, which means it's not my fault that I'm late. And she texts us back, U OK Nk? And I answer, Tell u in town. I feel a bit better then.

But when I get to the Monument it's not just Hollie there, with Chloe, it's Jessica as well, and Kelly. And Kelly would be OK, except that she's a friend of Jessica's, except that she's got some kind of big posh Red Indian coat on with a big white fluffy collar that she must have had for Christmas, that makes us feel like a tramp. And except that, just as I'm weighin all this up and before I've had a chance to say anythin, she's clockin us, she's sayin, 'Where the hell you been, Nicky? In the river?'

So I tell her.

'This big old fat bloke knocked us off me bike.'

And as soon as I say it I know it's not enough, cos it sounds pathetic, cos why would I let some big old fat bloke knock us off me bike? I mean, how pathetic am I? So I need somethin bigger, somethin as bad as how I feel now, standin under the Monument, that Jessica bitch lookin down on us, wrinklin her nose. So I just carry on. He knocked us off me bike, I tell her, and he grabbed us and called us names. I thought he was gonna rape us.

And Hol says, 'God, Nick, That's bad. Really bad.'

That's right, Hol. You got it. Really bad. You tell them.

Then Jessica asks, 'What'd he call you, Nicky?'

But Jessica's got no right to ask that question so I just say, 'Fuckin this and fuckin that…' And I'm thinkin, you're enjoyin this, aren't you, but I can't see her properly cos she's standin on the top step, under the Monument, and the sun's behind her, so I'm squintin at her, shieldin me eyes, not seein her right, but I can hear it in her voice. 'What did he call you, Nicky?' Like she wants us to produce a recordin of it, like she doesn't believe a word, and it's all a laugh. Or like, whatever he said, it's bound to be true.

And Hol says, 'That's really bad, Nick. You should report him.'

And Kelly says, 'And what did you say back to him?' But not like Jessica, not like she's laughin at us, but because she wants to know, I can tell that cos she says it fast, like as if she's listenin to a story and she wants to know what's gonna happen next, like when I read Daniel a story and I'm tryin to go through it bit by bit, first little piggy, second little piggy, but he doesn't want the piggies, he wants to get to the bit where the big wolf falls down the chimney and gets boiled. So he keeps turnin the pages, till he gets there. That's how Kelly is, wantin to get to the end. So I tell her, I tell her what she wants to hear. That I got up and kicked him in the shins. That I told him to fuck off, that he was a fat old perv and that I'd clocked him and would creep up on him one of these nights and cut his bollocks off, so he'd better fuckin watch out if he knew what was good for him. And left him there, rubbin his leg where I'd kicked him, wishin he'd never set eyes on us.

'Like that Kyle in South Park,' I say. 'He had this daft hat on, with flaps, just like Kyle.'

And now it's me laughin. And as we walk into the Eldon Centre, I'm feelin better, a lot better, I'm even feelin that mebbes me clothes aren't that bad after all, that the dirty patches on me sleeve and me jeans are dryin out now, lookin less muddy. And anyway, they're part of me story. And mebbes I won't clean them off, not just yet.

Barry

So Corrine says, 'Got any more nice white goods for us to see today, Barry?'

Cos me and Corinne've got this thing goin. We've had this thing goin ever since she came to work here, back in October. Well, just about, anyway. I was here first, I'd been here three months before Corinne came, so that meant I could show her round, introduce her to the crew, make her feel at home. And it was sort of my job, in a way, helpin her to settle in, showin her the ropes, cos the rest of them were here today gone tomorrow types, most of them, part-timers and casuals and suchlike. But I'm full-time permanent staff, me, so I know me way round.

Goods-in. That's my job. Mainly fridges and freezers and dishwashers and cookers and washin machines on this side, where I am today, but I do the furniture an all, the chairs and tables and beds and wardrobes in the next bay, dependin on how many deliveries are comin in, who's on. Just unpackin at the minute, makin sure they're in the right bays, settin aside the orders, to go out again. But I'm sittin me Forklift Certificate next month, so I'll be doin more then.

Anyway, that's where Corinne comes in, when I'm takin a delivery, cos it's her job to do the quality control, to check the goods against the specs. Not just her, mind. There's three other lasses doin the same sort of thing, cos it's all women on the QC. Lads on the deliveries, you can understand that, with it bein heavy work, and cold, and dusty, but only lasses on the QC. Don't know why. She checks goods out an all, returns, damaged items, that sort of thing. But I don't have owt to do with them. That's another bay.

And we've got this thing goin on between us, between me and Corinne. Like, I'll say, 'Fancy seein what's inside me big box, Corinne?' And she'll say, 'Only if you help us collate me figures.' That sort of thing. Kind of banter. Kind of teasin. And daft, really. Cheesy. But it's good. And I could tell she liked us, cos she'd hang about, even though it's cold down here, and noisy as hell, and the other lads really pushin it. Like, I mean, if there's anybody half fit on the QC team, they let her know it. Fuckin sexist crap. You know what I mean? And Corinne's fit. Like, you'd probably say she was way out of my league, but what the hell? Anyway, she'd pretend she was checkin the stock, reconcilin this and that, but how long does it take to read a model number? So I'd help her then, I'd shout out the numbers and she'd key them in, and I'd get stick for that from the other lads. 'Your number come up again, Bazza?' That kind of thing. But you could tell they were jealous.

And I asked her last week, I asked her if she fancied goin to Legends sometime, or mebbes the Ikon. Great, she said, just like that. Great. But can we go down the New Monkey instead, cos it's really mint there, you can stay till seven in the mornin, and she likes it there cos it's all loved up, that's what she said, all loved up, and they come from all over, just for the atmos. And she's lookin at us, and she can tell I've never been there. So I tell her, Aye, all right, game for anythin. But it's in Sunderland and I've got to be in at eight for the early delivery, and I can't throw a sicky cos Liam's throwin a sicky tomorrow and I'm coverin for him. That's how it works. So I've got to say, 'Next week all right?' And she says, 'If it's Friday night, I'll be there.'

And today, this afternoon, she comes in and asks us if I've got any more white goods for her to look at, and I'm thinkin of a funny way of answerin her when Hollie turns up, out of the blue, and Chloe an all, and that fat lass who Jaz dumped the garden chairs on, and I'm thinkin, fuck me, it's happened, it's Mam, it's fuckin happened.

Val

I'm up on the third floor, seein what I can do with the emergency exit, by the top of the flume, cos it keeps blowin open in the wind, just a touch, but enough to get the mams sayin, It can't be good for the bairns, goin down into the warm water then comin back up to this. Look, this one's sayin, Look at how he's shiverin. And there he is, her little Johnnie, his boney shoulders all hunched, his bottom lip quiverin. Although I'm thinkin, thank God for the fresh air, because it's usually all steam and chlorine up here, enough to knock you out. And that's when Brian shouts up, 'Somebody on the phone for you, Val.'

And it's him. Terry. The waster. Sayin Daniel's fine, nothin to worry about. Like as if just hearin him sayin that isn't plenty reason to be worried. Sayin he's been ringin Nicky's mobile, otherwise he'd not have bothered, but he couldn't get an answer so he didn't know what to do. And stammerin, cos he's in a rush to get the words out. And he says it all again, like the first time he was only practisin and he messed it up. Just ringin to say Daniel's fine, Val, not to worry, they've been down to Micky D's and then he had a sleep and then... But what's happened to Nicky, he asks, and will he bring him home now? Cos he's not sure what to do, he'd expected Nicky to be back by six. And what should he do? Should he keep him there? Cos he can keep him till nine if I want him to, he says.

And I can't tell him, can I? How the hell can I tell him that I hadn't the foggiest idea Daniel was with him in the first place, that I'm gonna knock the livin daylights out of Nicola when I see her, that I'll never let her look after Daniel again? How can I say any of that? And I can't say, Alright, Terry, keep him till nine. I can't say that either, can I? Thank you so much, Terry, if you don't mind, that'd be very nice. How can I say that?

So I just say, 'I'll be there now.'

And I feel so tired.

Nicky

It's five o'clock when Kelly and Jessica say they're gonna hang out in Kathmandu for a bit, mebbes meet up with some mates down the Salsa. So I think, whatever. Go meet your hippy friends, and thanks for the invite, I don't think. But I'm a bit relieved an all, cos it's easier for us to say, 'Hol, when does your Barry finish work?' And when Hol says, 'Six, I think,' and doesn't seem fussed, it's easy enough to add, 'Howay then, let's go and surprise him.' And cos we're only down the road from where Barry works, and cos Chloe's complainin that she's tired and her feet hurt, Hol says, 'Aye, alright. Fancy goin to see Barry, Louis?'

Hol doesn't know exactly where Barry works in the shop, so she starts driftin around among the accessories, lookin through the bargain gloves and scarves and belts, on auto-pilot. And I'm thinkin, you're always gonna be like this, Hol, aren't you, half a bloody mile behind everybody else, goin nowhere? And I've got half a mind to tell her that, to tell her what I really think, cos I'm feelin a bit edgy now, I'm buildin up to it. But that's when Chloe starts whingein again, so it's easy enough just to say, 'Aw, poor little Chloe. Let's go and ask the nice lady where your brother is, shall we?'

And that's what's good about takin a little girl shoppin with you, because you can say to the nice lady, Can little Chloe go and see her big brother, please, just for a minute? And she'll take notice of you. Where is he? she'll say. Oh, I think he's in packin or unpackin or somethin like that, you'll answer. Then she'll say, Of course you can, pet. And she'll turn to Chloe, she'll bend down a little, she'll ask her, 'What's your name, then?' And Chloe'll smile and go all coy and just whisper, 'Chloe'. And then, 'So, Chloe, What's your big brother's name?' And she'll say 'Barry', louder this time, cos she likes sayin it, she likes people knowin she's Barry's sister. And the nice lady just won't be able to resist her.

And that's how it is. So the lady, who's wearin a badge with Joyce on it, says 'I've got to go with you,' meanin Health and Safety, but probably cos she's bored and it's somethin to do and she's taken a shine to Chloe. So we go through the door marked 'Staff Only' and I take hold of Chloe's hand, cos we're walkin into a big space, full of crates and boxes and suchlike, and a wind blowin through it, a cold wind, cos it's open at the far end. I can see that now. And Joyce is goin, 'Now don't you run off, Chloe, will you, or we'll never find you.' And it's when I take a hold of Chloe's hand that I realise me own hand's gone all clammy and I know that in a few seconds me mouth'll go dry and me tongue'll be like a dead slug. And I realise I don't want to be in this place any more, it's all been a mistake. And I just want to get out of here.

But it's too late, cos the nice lady is showin Chloe things, she's tellin her that she can walk up to the yellow line, but not any further, cos that's where the trucks come to, the trucks that carry the boxes of things that Mammy and Daddy come to buy, and does she know that Santa Claus comes here too, just before Christmas, to collect his presents for all the children? And Chloe wants to know if she really means all the children, in all the world, and whether Santa Claus is still there. And that's when I see him, in his orange overalls, just standin there, and he's probably been there all the time, but there's lots of them there, in their orange overalls, and it's hard to make them out cos the place is too big and there's too many things in it, boxes and crates, all mixed up.

151

And Barry looks over and I get this hot prickly feelin above me ears, cos I know we shouldn't be here, and cos I don't know what to say, and I'm hopin Hol will say somethin, Hol who never says anythin. But she doesn't need to, cos Chloe's full of it, sayin to Barry, look at the wristbands she's got from Accessorize, and has he seen Santa Claus, and that's all good, thank you Chloe, you're a star, you're my favourite little girl. But there's no stoppin her, so she says this and she says that, and she says, Did you know that a big fat man kicked Nicky off her bike and raped her? Yes, and Nicky kicked him back, didn't you, Nicky?

So that just as I'm feelin I've hacked it, I'm fadin into the background, this isn't my case, I'm right back there, under the spotlight, and I've got to say somethin. So I say, 'Well, no, not that bad, not really.' But I can see what Chloe's thinkin now. She's thinkin, this is her story now, cos she's lookin at us, like as if I've let her down, and she looks right into me eyes. 'You said he was a fat old perv, Nicky.' And then she looks at Barry, tryin to make him believe her. 'And he had a Russian hat on,' she says. 'Like Kyle's hat. You tell him, Nicky.'

And Barry looks at us, but not at me face, and I can tell from the way his eyes are movin, that he's noticed the mud on me jeans and me top. He says, 'This a joke?' And I'm tellin meself, I've blown it. I'm such a fuckin dopey cow. So I say, so I've got to say, 'He told us he'd have us next time.' Then I wait a bit, 'Honest, Barry,' I say, 'I was that scared.' And I shake me head. Cos that's all I can do. I shake me head and shut up. And Barry asks, 'You know this guy, Nicky?' And I can feel meself startin to shake, cos I can't tell where this is leadin, cos I've pushed it too far, cos everythin's mixed up, got no shape. And I can't say anythin, even though he's asked us a question, cos the shakin would break through and I don't know what words would come out, and everythin would get fuzzy again. So I just shake me head. I keep me lips tight, I look at him and shake me head.

But that's alright. Cos I'm only shakin on the outside. Inside, where it's real, it's all become hard, the edges are bright and sharp. It's like Barry's just picked us up, like you'd pick up a shell on the beech, and he's washed the sand off and the grit and the rest of that shit, just rinsed it off in a pool and it's all clear and shinin now and you can barely remember what it was like before. It's not what he says. It's his voice, the way he says 'You *know* this guy, Nicky?' Like he's sayin, my story's really important and dangerous. But then comes up light again when he says me name. Nicky. Nicky. Nicky. Cos he doesn't want to make things worse, he doesn't want us to be frightened. He's sayin, not to worry, he'll take over now, everythin's just fine.

And I can't say any of this, because if I opened me mouth now the shell would just get all covered up again with grit and sand, and I don't want that. But it's alright, cos he's lookin back at us now, sayin, 'You see him again, Nicky, you tell me. No shit. I'll sort him out. You hear?' Cos Barry's different, he can say things from the inside, from his shell, and it stays hard and bright, it doesn't get covered with sand and muck.

And for now that's enough, just stayin quiet. Chloe's taken me hand again, cos her big brother, in his big bright orange overalls, has got hold of me story now, is takin care of it, and we're all in it together. And that's good, that feels nice, and I'd settle for that, cos I don't have to do anythin else, I don't have to say anythin, and a bit of me mind is already lyin on a pillow, driftin off, thinkin of how I'd text him. When the time comes, when I see the fat man again. He's here, I'd say, that man with the hat like Kyle, the fat bastard, please come and help. Except I'd have to say more than that. I've seen him again, I'd say. In Morrisons. He's here now, by the checkout. But not that, either. There's too many people about. And I don't want Barry to get caught.

And that's as far as I go, cos I can see now that Barry's not by himself, not been by himself all along probably, just I wasn't lookin, wasn't lookin at anybody, not even Barry to begin with, I was just down here, on the inside, and on the inside you can only peek out a little, cos it's so tight and closed up. So I've not seen this woman, cos she's standin over to one side a bit, and mebbes she was just mindin her business, carryin on with her work, I don't know, cos she's got this machine in her hand, like a big fat calculator. But she's not workin now, she's lookin at Barry, and she's smilin.

And mebbes that's OK an all, for a bit, cos it means she's not been listenin, cos if she'd been listenin she wouldn't be smilin, would she? And mebbes it's alright when she says, 'Come to see your big brother, have you?' and lookin at Hol when she says it, like she can see she's his sister, she can see the resemblance. That's alright, I'm thinkin, cos Barry can explain. Yes, he'd say, they've come to see their big brother. And then he'd introduce us. He'd say, this is me sister, Hollie, and this is me other sister, Chloe. They're me family. But this here, he'd have to say then, this here's Nicky, she's not me sister, no, not family at all, she's a friend, and she's havin a bad time. And the smile would go. It would have to go.

It's not like I want him to explain. Not really. No, I don't really want him to say anythin to her. That's not the point. The point is that's what he should say. And he doesn't. He just turns round and smiles back at her. And she comes over then and she says to Chloe, 'Aren't you the lucky one, havin such a big strong brother?' But she's not really talkin to Chloe, I can tell that, not really, cos that voice isn't meant for Chloe, it's not meant for any little girl, it's meant for Barry, which is why Barry's not talkin now, he's just foldin his arms and smilin in that way he does, just lips, like a smiley, like a big daft smiley.

'Macho man, aren't you, Baz?'

Bitch.

And there's another reason why it's not such a bad thing havin a little girl like Chloe with you when you go shoppin, even when she's whinin because her feet are sore and her legs have gone floppy and she's got to be dragged back into the store. Because I can say to her, 'Look at them hair clips, Chloe.' I can even put one up against me own hair, the one with the bright blue snake on it, and turn me head this way and that, like a model, and say, 'What d'you think, Chloe?' until little Chloe says, 'My turn, my turn'. And after Chloe's looked at herself in the mirror, I can promise that she'll get the same clip for her birthday, but she's got to put it back now, just where she found it, and not to worry if somebody else comes and buys this one, she'll get another one just like it.

So I lift Chloe up and she puts the clip back on its glass shelf. There. Remember where you've put it, Chloe, I tell her, so we can come back and find it again. And nobody notices. Nobody's got a clue. I just drop the scrunchies into me Accessorize bag. Three of them, that's all, and only scrunchies, which isn't much, which isn't really enough. But it'll have to do.

Val

Every day, Mrs Robson, he said. Three things that made you proud. Just three. That's not a lot, is it?

Proud, he says. But I think he means pleased. I was proud the day Nicola went to school. I was proud the day Daniel was born. That's the kind of things people are proud of. But you can't be proud of yourself, can you? Well, not every day, anyway. So, pleased. Three things that made us feel pleased.

One. I didn't go off on one with Nicola. I didn't even say anythin about her dad. I just said, if you want to leave Daniel with anybody, best you tell me first, so I know where he is, so I can get in touch. 'So you can say no,' she said. And I didn't rise to it. I didn't go off on one. I was pleased with that. That's the best I could have done.

Two. I found a woman's keys outside the changin room and put them in reception until she came lookin for them. She was pleased, anyway. So I was pleased. That's how it works.

Three. We had a viewin today. Not that I was there, not that I'm ever there, because it's best to keep out the way when you've got a viewin, give them a free run. And it's just as well Nicola's back at school and Daniel's back with his Auntie Gillian as well, so there's no clutter or commotion, they can see the house without any distractions. So I was happy enough about that, that it was all ready for them. And I thought it was a good sign, havin a viewin this time of year. They must be keen.

And it's best I'm not there anyway, because I don't have to lie. Because there's no need then to tell them about the chairs, that I'm just storin them for a friend, which is what I've told the estate agent to tell them, and I know she's suspicious because who'd store somebody's garden chairs for five months, right through the winter? Who'd have twenty wrought-iron chairs anyway?

'Can't you get your friend to take them away?' she said.

'I'll ask them again,' I said.

So even though I'm pleased we've had a viewin, I can't think of it without thinkin of the chairs as well, and that really stresses us, because it needs sortin out. And I was goin to phone the police when it happened, way back, because people have got no right to come on to other people's property and drop their junk there, have they? But Brian at work said to watch out, because he's got a brother in the force and he reckons he knows about these things. Watch out, he said, you don't want to be done for possession, do you? Possession? Bloody cheek. But I didn't, and now it's too late. And then I thought, not to worry, whoever left the stuff there will just come back and collect it, won't they, and I'll not have to do anythin, because it's not my problem, is it? That's what I thought, back then.

So if I'd been there, for the viewin, I'd have had to lie in front of her, about the chairs, and they'd have known, I know they would, because I get tongue-tied when I lie. And part of us wants to say to them, to the people doin the viewin, this is what it's like here, you don't really want to buy this house, pet, not unless you're desperate, so stay away, don't make the mistake I made. Especially the woman. That's what I'd say to her. You can do better than this. But they'll be desperate, won't they? Otherwise why come here? She'll be pregnant, with a puffy face and a look on her that makes you think she's gonna break into tears any second. He'll be a bit on the short side, with a cocky, know-it-all way about him, and a ring in his left ear. I've seen them before. So what did it for you, pet? Was it the cute curly hair? Did he sing 'It Ain't Hard to Tell', knockin out the rhythms with his fingers, really badly, but you'd never heard it before, so how were you to know? 'It's ghetto grit, babe,' he said. Somethin like that. And you never did like it, did you, cos it didn't have a tune, you just pretended, for a year or two. Until you found out it was all just yackety yack. Cos you even got that from him. That's how he'd say it. All yackety yack.

So that pleased me, I suppose, that we had a viewin, that I stayed away.

Nicky

Chebsie's back on line. So I tell her. 'Chebsie's back, Hol.'

And Hol goes 'Uh-huh,' like she does when she's not listenin, when she's got her head in her catalogue.

'I said Chebsie's back.'

And she looks over at us, but without lookin, if you know what I mean, with these blank eyes, and her head still down there, in this retro stuff she's gettin into.

'You goin goth, Hol?'

'I hate goths.'

So she's listenin at last.

'Chebsie says his dad's got this place…'

'I don't like it, Nicky.'

'Don't like what?'

And I look at her, waitin for an answer, not because I don't know what she doesn't like, but because she doesn't know herself, that's how she is, and I'm ready to stare her out if I've got to, to get her to say it. But it's too easy. She gives in too easy.

'Dunno.'

'Chebsie says his dad's got this place in London. You believe that, Hol?' And she does the shrug thing. 'Says his dad's an airline pilot, so he's got the house to himself lots.'

'What about his mam?'

Which is what Hol would say, of course, you can understand that.

'He doesn't say, Hol. Mebbes they're divorced. Anyway, it's all bollocks.'

So I start tappin at the keyboard.

And she says, 'What you doin, Nicky?' Like she's just woken up. Like somethin matters, at last.

'What d'you think, Hol?'

'We'll get wrong.'

'It's not us that'll get wrong, Hol. Just think, Hol. Think.' And she shuts up again, cos it's too hard to think. So I read out what I've typed. *Hi Chebsie lucky sod. Coming to london wkend tell us wh u live will call by.* 'Will that do?' I ask her.

157

So Hol drags her arse of the sofa and flip-flops her way over to where I'm sittin, by the computer, and she's wearin these fluffy pink mules, like she's just got out of bed, even though it's four o'clock in the afternoon. And she reads the message, like as if she needs more proof, like she doesn't believe us.

'You goin to London, Nicky?'

'Mebbes.'

'By y'self?'

'No, with the Toon Army, what d'you think?' And I shake me head, thinkin, what are you like? And I tell her, cos she wouldn't have worked it out for herself, I tell her, 'I'm not goin to London, you muppet. I just want his address.'

And Hol's mouth is still hangin open, she's still tryin to make sense of what's goin on, when I see her lookin through the window. So I turn round. And there he is, Barry, walkin up the path. And even though I know who it is, cos how wouldn't I, I've got to say somethin. Or Hol will notice. What will she notice? I don't know. This damp feel on me top lip. Me heart, beatin faster. Summick like that, I don't know. But I've got to fill the gap.

'That Barry, Hol?'

And when Hol says yes, and I ask what he's doin back this early, doesn't he work Saturday afternoons, I know I'm jumpin in too fast, too deep. So I shut up, I turn back to the screen. And that's what I'm doin when Barry sticks his head round the door.

'Where's Dad?'

And Hol says 'Gone.'

'Work?'

'Yeah.'

That's all. And I sit there, bitin me lip, starin at the screen, at me fingers, sendin off messages to nobody. But before I know it there's other lads there an all, out in the passage. I can hear them, bangin about, rattlin keys, shoutin at each other, like they do, for no reason, just that's what they do. And Barry says, 'I'm away for a shower,' cos he's still in his work clothes, in his orange overalls. And he's gone. But that's OK, cos I'm busy now, I'm not just pretendin to be busy, I'm feelin comfortable again. And I'm goin through the messages and I can see that Trilz is still tryin to impress that wanker Hardcorefix, and that makes us feel good, cos Trilz is so pathetic, and I'm well out of that.

And that's when the shoutin and the rattlin come closer, cos they're here now, the other lads, they've come in to the room, and there's just the two of them, but they're fillin the room. And the first one, the lanky one, says 'Hello, Hol,' like he really fancies himself, like they do. And they're not like Barry's friends ought to be, neither of them. Not like I expect them to be. Want them to be. And the other one, he looks like a mouse, just a little mouse, with a mousey nose, and he's got this leather jacket on that's too big for him, like he's borrowed it off the lanky one. And then the lanky one comes over, and he's got straw hair and pink eyes and he's standin right by us now, unzippin his fleece. And I can smell the cold air on him. Cold air and fags.

'What yiz deein?'

Like it's any of his business. And I'm thinkin, how are you two drongos friends of Barry's? But they are, and they wouldn't be here otherwise, so that's how it is. And Barry'll be down in a minute, he said so, and Hol's sayin nothin, will never say anythin, and although I don't want to tell him, somebody's got to say summick, so I tell him, 'Me and me mam are doin a house swap.' And I point at the screen. 'See?'

And they're there, right in front of us, cos that's where I am now, that's where Trilz has sent us, to this house swap site. So they're there, the houses, hundreds of them. A Seaside Chalet in Florida, which is pink, cos I can see it, there's a picture of it. And then this big swanky place. A Villa on Vermont's Knight Point, it says, all white wood and lawns. And then this apartment, which is nothin on the outside, just brick, dirty red brick, but inside, through the windows, you can see it all, the skyscrapers, the river, the sun shinin off it all.

And he says, 'You goin to the States?'

But like he doesn't really believe it. So I say, 'Mebbes. We've not decided yet.' Like there's that many choices.

And I just want him out of me face, cos he's leanin right over us now, he's takin hold of the mouse and he's clickin away with his bony fingers and he's touchin me shoulder with his arm, not like knowin he's touchin it, just like I'm not there. And he says, 'Ow, Kieron, look at this.' And the little one's got up now an all and he's standin on the other side of us, so I've got the lanky one on me right and the mouse on me left. 'That's my bed there,' says the lanky one. 'That's where I'll be sleepin. The one with the fuckin gold nobs on it.' And looks down at us, like he's just remembered I'm there. 'Scuse me language, like.'

Tosser.

And then he looks over his shoulder and says, 'Fancy stayin in a penthouse, Baz?' Cos Barry's come back into the room now, he's come back and I haven't realised cos the lanky one's been makin that much noise, but he has, he's come back and he's leanin on the back of me chair, lookin over me head. And I've got nowhere to go now, cos they're on all sides and I can't even hide meself in the computer any more cos he's got it now, with his bony fingers and his pink eyes. And I'm squeezed in the middle of them and I can't get out.

'Nice,' Barry says. 'Very nice.'

And the mouse says, 'What's a penthouse?' And the other two laugh, and the lanky one says, 'It's where we're gannin for wor holidays, man.'

'Very nice,' says Barry again. And I can feel his breath on the top of me head.

Val

'Sorry I'm late,' the estate agent says, all cheery, offerin us her hand. Because of the traffic, she says, and havin the wrong keys, or mebbes just bringin the wrong keys and havin to go back, I'm not sure, because she's talkin that fast, and pressin the bell all the while, sayin, Come on, come on. She'll snap soon, I'm thinkin. She's wound up that tight, she'll snap.

'It's Nicola, isn't it? And little Daniel?'

She knows our names already, of course she does, and where we live, too, she doesn't need to ask, because we're on their books. And because she knows where we live, she knows why we want to move. It's taken as read. And I know her name, too. She's called Barbara, and this is how she is, every time, and there've been that many times. And it's only professional, I know, doin her job, like, but at least it makes us feel she's not given up on us, that I'm not a hopeless case.

'Total security here,' she says, pointin up at the cameras. And we'll have our own intercom, she says, like it's all settled, and we'll wonder how we ever managed without. There's a good community feel, too, you ask anybody who lives here, she says. I've got friends here, yes, and they all say the same thing, good community feel, everybody keeping an eye out for each other, total security, peace of mind. Do I believe her? I'd like to believe her. It's just difficult to feel it, the security, the peace of mind, with Barbara tryin so hard to sell it to me.

And do I like it? I don't know.

The inside's like the outside, all dark brick, and there's girders runnin the length of the passage, like ribs, which isn't what I expected, but I don't really know what I expected because I've not been in a place like this before, a warehouse tryin just to be a house. 'Different,' she says, seein I'm findin it difficult to take it all in. She even pats one of the girders, as if it's a pet dog. 'All the original features,' she says. Like she's talkin about that barn conversion in Bellingham. And I lift Daniel up so he can press the button to call the lift, because the apartment's on the second floor.

And when we come out the lift, it's still the brick and the girders, except we're in the middle of the building now and there's no windows. But that's OK, I think, because it's light enough and the walls have been done in a nice warm colour, got an earthy feel to it, lighter than terracotta, a bit like sand. And it does feel safe, Barbara's right, you've got to give her that, you'd think the world would never get in here. Although I'm also thinkin now, where's everybody gone? Are they all inside, tucked out the way? Are they still at work?

And that's why it's nice, just as we're turnin into the corridor, that we bump into him, one of the residents. Is that what you'd call him? A resident. No, that can't be right, it makes it sound like an old folks' home. One of the neighbours. That's better. A smiley fella with a beard. Anyway, we bump into him and that's nice, not for any special reason, just because he's got a friendly smile and he says, 'Excuse me' because he hasn't seen us comin, turnin out of the lift, and how he's in a bit of a hurry, because he's got his dinner on, somethin like that, somethin neighbourly, and I like that. Although when he says it, at first, when he says, 'Excuse me' I don't really hear the words, what I hear is his voice bouncin back at me off the walls, and I'm thinkin, I'm goin to have to get used to that, that hard sound in the passage.

But by now Barbara's opened up the door with no. 14 on it and she's takin us over to the window, which is a big bright square, goin almost to the floor, so that you feel that you might fall through it if you got too close, and it makes us giddy. And she's askin, Can you see the river, Daniel? Which he can, when she points it out, a bit of it, anyway, over to the right, beyond the car park. And then she shows us how the intercom works, and the extractor fan, that'll keep the air fresh, she says, even at this time of year, with all the windows shut. And the bedrooms, the master bedroom first, with its en suite, which makes life so much easier, she says, especially when you've got kids. Your own bathroom, Mrs Robson, just think of it. Leavin a gap for me to think. And Nicola's bedroom, then, white, empty, ready for her to do it out just how she likes it, and I'm just goin to say, What d'you think, Nicola, when I see she's not here. And she's not in the lounge either. And I don't know where she is. And she should be here, to see her bedroom, to think about her new home.

Nicky

And Jessica, the bitch, tellin everybody she wants to kill herself cos she's gone up to a six. What kind of diet you on, Nicky? she says, pretendin she's not just lookin for the nearest fat cow to make her feel slim again. The not eatin kind. That's what I should have said.

Val

One thing I can see.

Nicola standin in front of her bedroom mirror, on a stool. Can't see
Nicola, just Nicola in the mirror. And she's got to stand on the stool
cos the mirror's screwed to the wall and when she stands on the floor
she can only see her face and shoulders. Can she see me? Not yet. She's
doin the thumb thing with her new Chinos. The thumb test. And you
can tell she's tryin not to cheat, hardly breathin in at all. The thumbs
go round the back, then back to the front. They feel comfy enough,
she's thinkin. You can tell. There's almost a smile on her face.

She's turnin now, half turnin, puttin one foot just behind the other,
leanin forwards a little so the black cotton folds round her bum, and
she's thinkin, me thigh looks alright in this, like you might almost want
a thigh like that. And a little smile again. Cos she doesn't see this as
cheatin, not at all, although I bet if I went up to her now and asked
her, When are y'gonna stand like that in real life, Nicola? she'd have a
job tellin us. She's got her thumbs in the pockets now, thumbs on the
inside, fingers on the outside, feelin the little diamante studs.

And that's it. She sits down. So far so good, she's thinkin. The Chinos
are tighter now, of course, sittin down, and she daresn't bend forwards
for fear of poppin a button or splittin a seam. And she's frownin. That
little cross mouth, like she's bein cheated, like there's somebody else to
blame. She's thinkin, it's the way they've made them. They're cheap.
Made in Taiwan or somewhere. Why couldn't her mam have got
somethin better? Somethin that was made properly? But then, thinkin,
mebbes they're just not worn in yet. Cos she really does want them to
fit. She's wonderin, will they give a bit with wearin? And thinkin, God,
what if they shrink in the wash? Cos they're cheap and nasty. And she's
back to that, then. Her mam's fault. My fault.

Mebbes I should be grateful she's not anorexic. Not bulimic. That's
two things to be grateful for. Pleased about, even. So I can count
them in, next time. Two things I'm pleased about. One, Nicky's not
anorexic. Two, she's not bulimic. She would be, mind, if she could.
Woudn't you, Nicola? Eh? Bet you'd like to have some eatin disorder,

wouldn't you? You could really twist the knife then. But you just can't be arsed, can you?

And that's somethin to be grateful for an all, I suppose. That she can't be arsed.

Nicky

Chebsie's message is still there. Like he's waitin for an answer. Like he's sayin, go on, I dare you. So why not?

My name is Mr Terence Robson and I am Nicola Robson's father. I have already informed the police about you so dont think you can get away with it. I am coming to see you on Saturday.

But I'm thinkin, what happens Saturday when nobody turns up? What happens then? What do I do? So I cut that bit out. The rest of it's good, though. I read it out, and it sounds really good. So I send it. And I'm tryin to picture the look on his face when he opens it. When he reads the bit about the police. I'd like to see that face. And mebbes he'll get back to us and beg us not to do anythin, like it's all been a misunderstandin, summick like that. Beg us to talk to me dad and say, Chebsie's explained it all now, Dad, and it's alright. Later on, mebbes. When he's had time to open his messages. When he's had time to think. Leave him stew for a bit.

But now, I've got to text Hollie. Not Hollie, really. I've got to text Barry. But it's best I send it to Hollie, cos she'll pass it on. Anyway, I've not got Barry's number. And I daresn't be too pushy. Not yet.

Seen perv. Heres hs flat. Coble Court. No 17

And it's a good picture. You can see the number and everythin.

Barry

'Aye, gan on, Corinne,' I tell her, cos everybody else has, they've all got their shoes off, cos it's his auntie's flat. 'Mind ye dee an aal,' says Jaz, 'cos I divvent want your dirty feet aal ower me auntie's best things.' But I can't reach mine. 'I cannit reach me feet, man' I tell him. And I know they're down there somewhere, but I can't see them cos me head's all the way up here, too far away. And me hands. They've gone an all. 'Yes please, Corinne,' I tell her, 'yes please, be a pet, take me shoes off.'

So she kneels down and starts takin me shoes off and Kieron says, 'Ow, look, Corinne's takin Baz's clothes off,' and I can see her, down there, kneelin down, like this hump on the floor in front of us, that's what she looks like, cos of her black hair and her black top, just this black hump, cos Corinne's a bit goth, really, and I never thought I'd go out with a goth, like she's even into Marilyn Manson and that shite. And she's undoin me shoelaces, I can feel her fiddlin with me feet, and Jaz is lookin at her and Kieron's lookin at her and Liam's lookin at her and me hands are full and I've got to go for a piss, like all of a sudden, it's like I've got to go for a piss because Corinne's takin me shoes off. Like, if me shoes come off, I'll start pissin meself.

So I tell her, 'Howld on, man, Corinne, howld on, leave me shoes on.' Cos I'm fuckin dyin for a piss, and I tell her, 'I'll be back now.' But no, I've got these things in me hands, so I say, 'Howld this for us, pet, will ye?' And I give her the bottle. And then I say, 'Howld this an aal, please, pretty please, Corinne, please, pretty please,' I say. And I give her the other bottle. So I can lean on me hands now, to help meself get up, I can do that bit. But I still cannit budge. Cos why? Cos I don't know why, that's why. All I know is that she's not taken me shoes off, cos me shoes are still on, I can feel them, they're still on me feet. But if she's not taken them off, what's she done? Cos I know she's done summick. And I try to get up anyway and I think, God, this is bad, I've really gone, cos it's like me feet aren't mine any more. I can feel them, but they're not listenin to us.

And I try to get up, I push meself up on me hands, thinkin, right foot first, here we go, but it doesn't listen, me own foot doesn't listen, and I fall over, so I've got to start again, I've got to push meself up on me hands, and it's easier now, cos I'm lyin on me belly, and here we go, here we go, left foot this time, but it won't come, and I'm down again, and I need a piss and me feet are sore now, like as if me shoes are too tight, cos that's what she's done, I can see them now, over there, where Jaz is laughin, killin hisself laughin, I can see what she's done, she's tied me laces together, that's what she's done, and I didn't know, I didn't know where me shoes were anyway. If you'd telt us, 'They're on your feet, man,' I'd still be none the wiser, cos I'd no idea where me feet were. But I can see them now, I can see she's tied me laces. And Jaz is killin hisself laughin and Kieron's killin hisself laughin and Debbs, who's Kieron's lass, she's killin herself laughin an all.

'Got him where you want him now, Corinne,' Debbs says. 'What you gonna do with him now?'

And I'm tellin Corinne I'm gonna piss meself, I've got to go to the bog or I'll piss meself, cos I'm laughin that much. But Jaz is pointin at us now. 'Ow, look,' he's sayin, 'it's me Auntie Jess come back t'play war with w'.' Cos he's stuck this thing on me head, which must be his Auntie Jess's hat, cos it just sits there, on top of me head, all floppy. And Kieron's talkin in his daft squeaky voice, 'Now you bairns behave, d'you hear? I'll have no nonsense in my house.' And Jaz is sayin, 'Aw, Auntie Jessie, please let w' play.' And Liam's sayin, 'Please let w' play, Auntie Jessie, we'll be good little boys and girls.'

And then he's in me face, Jaz is in me face, cos he's got somebody's lippy, and he's puttin it on us. And I don't mind if it's Corinne's lippy, or Debbs's even, but I don't want Auntie Jess's lippy on me lips. No, I'd hoy up then. And mebbes it is Debbs's cos it's Debbs sayin, 'Sit still now, Auntie Jess, so Jaz can put your lippy on. No, I don't think it's her colour, do you?' And I've got no idea what colour it is and I couldn't give a fuck cos I just want a piss, so I tell him, I tell Jaz, 'I'm ganna piss ower your Auntie Jess's carpet if ye divvent let us gan t'the bog.' And he says, 'Is that right, Baz? Well we cannit have that, can we?' And Kieron says, 'What'll ye dee, Baz? Eh? What'll ye dee if we let ye gan to the bog?'

And I tell him, I tell Jaz, I can't do anythin like this, with me feet tied together. And Kieron says, 'Let him crawl to the bog on his hands and knees.' And Debbs says, 'Let him hop! Let him hop!' And Craig says, 'Put his hat back on first.' And Jaz says, 'Aye, have more respect for me Auntie Jess's hat, will ye, ye hooligan, ye.' And that's when Corinne says, 'I know what he can do.' And she says it again, 'I know what he can do,' and it's like she's takin for ever and I'm thinkin, Howay, for fuck's sake, man, Corinne, I'm ganna piss meself here. And I tell her, 'Please, Corinne, I'll dee owt.' And she's sittin across me legs now, so I can't budge, so I'm wedged in between her and the wall. 'Anythin,' I say. 'Anythin?' she says. 'Anythin, anythin,' I say. And she says, 'Get his hat.'

And I'm thinkin, whose fuckin hat? But Kieron says it, Kieron says it in his voice, 'Whose hat would that be then, madam?' Cos he's tryin to stretch it out. The bastard. And Corinne tells him, 'The fat perv's hat, the fat perv's funny hat. Cos Baz has promised to sort him out.' That's what Corinne says. 'He's gonna bring back his perv hat to prove it. You do that for me, Baz?' That's what she says. 'You get the perv's hat for me. The Kyle hat.'

And Debbs says, Who the fuck's Kyle when she's at home? Cos she's got no idea who Kyle is. But I'm out of it now. And I tell her, I tell Corinne, aye, alright, anythin, and I'm out of it, cos I've got to go. And Jaz says, 'Got to go? Should've said, man. Should've said.' And Debbs says, 'Better touch up your lippy when you're in there, Auntie Jessie, it's all over your face.' And Jaz says, 'Ee, poor Auntie Jess, she's gone, ye knaa. She's really gone. We'll have t'put her in a home now.'

Nicky

I'm countin it as childcare payment. Like compensation for the fact that I'm not his mother but I've got to look after him like I was. And thirty quid's not a lot, not when you count the days and the nights. Anyway, me mam won't miss it. In fact she'll probably even thank us, later on, when it's all set up. So that's all I've got to do is type in her credit card number and I'm away. In fact, I'm thinkin, she's lucky I don't take advantage, cos me mam always leaves her purse in the house when she's on lates, just in case, and Friday lates are worst of all, she says, even though she always gets a taxi back. And anyway, it's for her as much as for me, as much as for anyone. So just this once is alright. That's what I reckon.

They only allow you to upload two pictures on the basic deal but that's OK cos there's only two I'm happy with really. There's me mam's bedroom, cos the other rooms are too small, like shoe-boxes, except for the kitchen, and who wants to look at a fridge or a cooker? And me mam's bedroom's got a nice picture on the wall, a gondola in Venice, or wherever. And I tried to get a shot of the outside, tryin to cut out the other houses and the TV dishes and the parked cars an that, cos they look naff. But you could still see the For Sale sign and I reckon that'd put people off, like how can we expect anybody else to live here if we don't want to live here ourselves? The garden might have done, but there was still the chairs in the corner and bugger all else, because me mam likes low maintenance, she says, like what's the point growin things if you're goin to be movin any day? And anyway, it looks weird when you put it in a photo, just lots of fence and concrete, like a Guess What This Is competition, when you've got to look at things from a funny angle, work out what they are.

So I went down by the High Lights, got a really good shot there, lookin out over the Fish Quay to the river, makin sure to get the two piers in, and the sea between them, and the big ferry an all, right in the middle, I was lucky with that. Big blue and white boat settin out for somewhere, don't know where. And close enough, the High Lights. They can walk there in fifteen minutes, twenty at the outside.

So I put the two pictures in, the bedroom and the river. And I type out the thirty-word description, cos that's what they allow you, just the thirty words. And I've worked dead hard on that. And you'd think thirty words would be easy, but it's not, cos you don't want to leave things out, and you want to make it sound nice, like nice enough to get them to travel half way round the world. And it's really difficult, gettin the words right. So I've had to nick some words off other people, and that's alright except that lots of them are in the wrong places, in Devon and Cornwall and Ireland and suchlike, so they won't really fit. So I've nicked bits off VisitNewcastle as well. And they'll just have to do. And anyway, if they're not right, who's to know?

And I read it out aloud, to see how it sounds, expectin it to sound crap, knowin it's crap, just a jumble of words.

Traditional comfortable English family home. Elevated position on north bank of famous River Tyne. Beaches, castle, priory, Roman Wall, parks all within easy reach. Buzzing Newcastle nearby.

But it's not crap. At least, I don't think it is. And I can't believe it's not, so I read it out again, to make sure, but properly this time, like I might be doin it on the telly, and it's still not. And I'm really chuffed. And I've still got three words left. So I look through me list again, cos I've printed them all out now, the words, and I've crossed out the ones I've already used, so it can't be that difficult. And I'm thinkin, what's best? *Fantastic shopping, night-life?* Or *Train from airport?* Thinkin, this is really mint, I can get in to this. But the one I go for is *Cultural capital of the North.* Which means I've got to drop two words, so I get rid of *all* and *buzzing.* Cos I reckon, if they're from New York, they'll have had enough buzz, they'll be lookin for somethin different, culture and that.

And I'm almost there. There's only two boxes left to fill. Where would I like to go? So I key in *New York, Brooklyn if possible.* How many will be travelling? That's more difficult. I can hear Hol in the kitchen, with Chloe and Daniel, gettin them fed, and I'm thinkin, that's four already, countin me, and then there's me mam and Barry, so that'd be six. And how am I gonna ask Barry? How the hell am I gonna ask Barry? And Hol's mam. What do I do about Hol's mam? Will they let her fly, the way she is? And I don't know the answer to any of these questions.

So I key in seven, to be on the safe side, cos that's all I need to do now, I can always change me mind after, if I've got to, I can always put three or four in, instead, or whatever. And I'm thinkin, mebbes Barry will come after all, if I ask him the right way, if I tell him it's like a family holiday, a two-family holiday, like no big deal. Or not me. No, not me. If Hol asks him. That's it. I'll get Hol to ask him. If she says, it's for Mam, Barry. A holiday for Mam. That'll do it. Cos

169

how can he say no then? With his mam bein on chemo an that? And I start thinkin, this is gonna work, it really is. But mebbes two pictures isn't enough, after all, so I get me mam's card again. And it's only £10 more, for another picture, so I put the Angel of the North on as well, just one I've found on the net, cos they might recognise that, they might come for that. Even though me dad says it's not an angel at all, it's really a statue of him carryin a surfboard. 'But he's got a bit rusty,' he says. Which was funny, really funny, first time he said it. 'Got a bit rusty.' So that's what I see now, when I look at it: me dad carryin a surfboard. Anyway, that's what goes on. Cos it's different.

Val

Five things you can see.

Well, I can see me purse, cos it's in me hand. So that's one. And when I open it I can see the gap in the front, where the credit card should be. That's two. And I can see Nicola's bed, which hasn't been made, probably because she didn't think I'd be back this early, so it wouldn't matter. So no credit card, no Nicola, no Daniel, no note, no nothin. How many's that? Purse, credit card, I mean no credit card, and bed. That's three.

Three.

And through the window I can see somebody. He's standin in the yard, with his back to us, his hands on his hips, and he's lookin at the garden chairs. I'm lookin at him. He's lookin at the chairs. And this can't be happenin. But that's only four, so I can't stop now, I've got to have five, I've got to see somethin else. Alright, I see his hat. He's got a woolly hat on. It's too dark to see what colour. Five.

Now hear. What do I hear?

I hear a *dunk, dunk* sound. And now I see what he's doin. He's pickin 'em up, he's carryin them away. But this isn't right, cos I'm not supposed to be seein, I'm supposed to be hearin. So close your eyes, then, you stupid bitch.

And what do I hear?

I hear his footsteps, walkin away, walkin into the lane, must be, that'd be my guess. But I'm not allowed to look, so I can't be sure.

Two.

Dunk, dunk again. But that doesn't count. At least, I don't think it counts. Once is OK. But no double countin.

And there's nothin else.

So cough, you bitch, cough.

There.

Three.

Then what?

Clap your hands, you dopey cow.

Four.

Good. So far, so good.

You feeling better now, Mrs Robson? A little calmer?

Much better, thank you.

You're doing very well.

Smell. This is the one. Get through this and it'll all be fine, just hold on, that's all you've got to do.

Well, alright, then.

Nicola's dressin gown. The one I bought her, which she's just left lyin on top of the bed, thinkin that's OK. The collar. It smells of Nicola. Which means what? Soap? Moisturiser? Me own perfume? Where's Nicola in all that? Somewhere, must be.

And then what?

Just breathe in, he said. Slowly. Feel the air as it passes through the nostrils.

No.

Slower.

Try again.

Breathe in. Really slowly this time.

What do I smell?

Is that the smell of air? Of dust?

Barry

I can see the gates are locked when we get to Coble Court but Kieron says 'Nee sweat, man,' and he gets out and walks over to where the gadgie's standin in his office. 'Nee sweat,' he says. 'Just wait here. Try an' look like y'knaa what yer deein.' So I stay put. I pick up me paper. And I listen to Kieron and the gadgie through the window.

'Three Yuccas for Coble Court.'

'Come again?'

'Three potted plants. This Coble Court?'

'Who for, did y'say?'

'Ground floor lobby it says here.'

And I can see him, I can see Kieron pointin at the order sheet. Cos he's good, Kieron, like he's sayin, Howay, man, get yerself shifted will ye, we've got a job to dee here. And it's got Mason's Homestores on the top of it, all orange, like, the same as our overalls. And I can see him. I can see the gadgie puttin on his glasses, lookin at the paper.

'Paid for, see,' says Kieron. 'Three Yuccas. Coble Court. Paid for. You just sign here.'

'I cannit carry owt.'

'Y'what?'

'Me back... I cannit...'

'There's two o w'.'

And I jump, just for a second, cos Kieron's pointin at me now, he's lookin round, and pointin at the van. I can feel me heart gettin faster. I can feel the sweat breakin out on me neck. So I keep on readin the paper, keepin me head down, cos what else can I do?

'You just sign here,' says Kieron.

And the gates open. Just like that. And I can't believe it, but Kieron's back in the van and we're drivin in. And the gadgie's shoutin through his little window now. 'Press the buzzer and I'll let yiz in,' he's shoutin. 'The green buzzer to the left of the door. Y'cannit miss it.' And we're in. I can't believe it, but we're in.

1e book says that bumpin's like Newton's Cradle. Like you drop the 'tal ball at one end and it's the ball at the other end that jumps. The balls in the middle just hang there, doin nowt. Like nowt's happened. And that's what the bump key's like. You bang it with your hammer, and the pins jump up. All you've got to do then is give the key a bit twist and you're away. The lock'll open. Newton's Cradle they call that. Same as bumpin.

It's not as simple as that, mind. Not in real life. Like, for one thing, you'd want to use a spring. Else you'd be there all day. You put the spring on the key, before you put it in the lock, like, so that it'll bounce back every time you bang it. Be there all day otherwise, settin and resettin. Put a spring on, and bang, bang, bang, bang, bang, you can tap away till the pins jump on. Bit twist then and you're away. Key turns. Lock opens.

Except not always. Cos some locks won't bump when you use a spring. Aye, you've got to remember that. That mebbes it just won't open. You've got to keep that in the back of your mind. Just in case.

So anyway we carry the Yucca into the lobby. We've only brought the one cos Kieron says they'd've missed more than one. So just one Yucca, and hope the gadgie's not countin. And we drop it there, in the lobby, and Kieron goes back to the van and drives off. Cos that's how we've planned it. And cos the van's right up by the door, the gadgie'll not se it's only Kieron gettin back into the van. That's what Kieron says. J done and we're away. But I'm thinkin, won't he see I'm not there, I not in the van, when Kieron drives past him? But it's too late now, I here. And it's all brick and me boots are clumpin on the floor.

So I get into the lift, which is right in front of us. And I've got to v a bit, for it to come down, like, and I'm hopin there's nobody in when the door opens. Nobody to ask us what I'm doin here. To s the gadgie, then, Who's that lad in the orange overalls? Is he supp to be here? But there's not. The lift's empty. So I get in and I pre button for the second floor. And there's nobody there, either, o second floor. 'That's why we've gorra dee it in the afternoon,' h said. 'Cos there'll be neebody there. Cos ye can just act norma anyway, Kieron said, that's when he's got deliveries, that's w can get the van. And it's all brick here an all, in the corridor, walls, and I can feel meself startin to walk on tip-toe, like I've g

173

geet big boots on but I'm walkin on tip-toe, like a fuckin fairy. A big fuckin fairy in boots.

Mind you, bumpin a lock in your hand doesn't mean you can bump it in the door. Bump it in your hand and you can get the angle easy, ninety degrees between the hammer and the key, cos that's the angle you've got to keep for the spring to work. Cos if you don't get the angle right the spring'll slip all over the shop. Easy in the hand. Bit of practice and you can do it in your sleep. But in the door. Bangin the key at shoulder height, tryin to keep it straight, tryin to hold the ammer straight. That's different, that's hard. The book says to use me tle finger as a pivot. But there's that many things to think about.

I've bumped me own house, mind. Five seconds on a good day. 'n again, it's just an old Era, and Eras couldn't keep a three-legged ut. Not if it could stand on a ladder, like. And there's nobody inside 't Hollie and Chloe. That makes a big difference an all. You know in't matter if owt goes wrong. If the neighbours look out their vs, like. If they hear the tap-tap-tap-tap. They'll just think, Aw, Barry. Must be summick wrong with the door, they'll say. Pity mam, isn't it? Especially for the little one. For Chloe. How ope? That's what they'll think.

e I say, it's just an old Era. So for the past few weeks I've win me dad's clamp, cos it's in the garden shed and nobody here. I just fix it on a shelf, at shoulder height, and I can y. Yales, Banhams, Chubbs, Rukos, the new Lince dimple the Assa Twin 6000, the lot. I'm down to twenty-three which isn't bad. Canny good, really. I'd not bump me dad's about, mind.

the corner I recognise it from the picture Holl sent with three windows in it, three round windows, and You can't really make it out in the picture, but I can rridor, through the windows. Just a short passage eady to go through yet. I need a minute to think. jh the door, that's it, I've only got a few seconds. us. Hears us. Before I lose me nerve. And I can now. And that's not good. That's not good for keepin a grip. I can feel me heart thumpin, this pressure behind me eyes. And that's what's really difficult, you see. It's not just gettin the angle right. It's not just tappin, gettin it hard enough but no harder. That's bad enough. But this is worse. Thinkin mebbes a neighbour'll hear you, tappin, turnin, tappin. Some gadgie'll say to his missus, Hear that? Not the first tap, mebbes, no, he'll just prick up his ears at the beginnin. But then, after the second tap, he'll say, Is that somebody knockin at the door? And she'll say, Why knock, man, when there's a bell? And who's this, anyway, who's this that's got in without buzzin first? And that's when they'll check. Just as you're gettin ready for your third tap, that's when they'll ring Dennis on the gate, to ask him what's gannin on, because he's not been on the ball, Dennis. Not lately.

And that's what the book says an all. *The main obstacles to in-use bumping are not technical but environmental.* Meanin the neighbours. Meanin your wrist seizes up, your fingers start shakin, and you try to relax, you try to steady yourself, and that's how you come to hit the key too hard, because you lose your touch. You hit it too hard, you hit it at the wrong angle, you press too much, the key jams, it'll not turn, it'll not come out, and you've had it, you're fucked. And the spring makes it quicker, so you use the spring, to get it over with, but the spring makes it noisier an all, cos the spring takes the force of the hammer, so you've got to hit the key that much harder. Else there'll not be enough force, not enough force to go through to the pins. So you want to be fast. But you want to be quiet an all. But you can't be fast and quiet at the same time. So what's it to be? Too noisy? Or too slow? And you're fucked either way.

So I take a look at the lock on the first door. Cos I can still get away from here, fast like, if I've got to, before I open the door. It's a cylinder, I can see that much. Mebbes an Evva, cos I've bumped Evvas before, and this one's got the same oval shape. But is it a five-pin or a six-pin? I've got no idea. And mebbes it's the new type, the Evva MCS, the one with the magnets in it that stop you bumpin them. How would I know? Do they look any different? I put me hands in me pockets, to check for the hammer. It's there, in the leg pocket, with the bag for me overalls afterwards. And the keys, in the right-hand pocket, just three of

them, cos there's no point bringin them all, so just the three, the three
ultimates they call them. Cos if they're not enough, I'm fucked anyway.
And the spring, the Loxpring. It's there, in me breast pocket.

And I says to Jaz, mebbes I'll bump into him in the street, you know,
like me sister's mate did, I'll just nick it off his head, before he knows
what's happenin. Or mebbes I'll see him in the pub, and he'll take it
off, and he'll just put it down beside him and I'll walk past and pick it
up. Might take a bit of time, like.

'Aye, and mebbes ye'll see him doon the New Monkey,' says Jaz,
'and ye can slip him a couple o' cowies and he'll just give ye his hat
cos it's your birthday.'

'Barry's bottlin it,' says Kieron.

'Barry's brickin it,' says Craig.

Or mebbes, I thought, I can just go out and buy one of them hats,
them Kyle hats, if I can find where they sell them. In the market
probably, or the Army and Navy, and nobody'll know. Except that I
couldn't, cos Kieron said he'd get us in, he'd got the van, he'd not take
no for an answer. Piece of piss, he said. And I don't even remember
tellin Kieron, tellin him I knew where the fat perv lived. But there
again, mebbes I didn't, mebbes it was Corinne, cos I tell Corinne
everythin.

I've been practisin in Jaz's auntie's place the past few days, since me
dad come back. I've brought the clamp over and everythin, cos he'll
not miss it. And it'd be lush if I could sleep here, but I can't, cos me
mam's back an all, and me dad says everybody's got to pull their weight,
because he can't do it all himself. And it sounds all right the first time
he says it, like he really means everybody, and talkin to Hollie an all.
But like what am I supposed to do? Cos Hol's looking after Chloe and
what's me dad for if he can't look after me mam? So me dad says it
again, It's about time you pulled your weight, but meanin me, just me
this time, and meanin, You're fuckin useless, you, you've always been
useless. But I know it's me dad that's useless, and that's what I want to
tell him. It's you that's useless, Dad, not me. Do I tell him? Do I fuck.
So I go over to Jaz's place, where I don't have to take this shite.

I know that lasses aren't into locks. At least I don't know any lasses on the bumpin Forum. And when I show her the Brockhage lock, the one you can see through, the one I practise on, so I can tell what I'm doin, when I ask her, 'Can y'see it, can y'see the key turnin, can y'see the pins shiftin?' I start laughin. Or when I show her how to use her finger to set the bump key. 'Can you feel the difference?' I ask her. 'Can you feel it?' And she starts laughin herself then. And we're both laughin. Cos Corinne knows nowt about locks. Like me and death metal. I know nowt about death metal. It's just a joke. So I laugh, we both laugh. Cos it doesn't matter, does it? I do bumpin, she does the metal thing, the goth thing, whatever she does, and that's OK. That's how I see it, anyway.

And mebbes that's it. That's why I like Corinne. Cos she just lets us get on with it. Like as if I'm one of them magicians, pullin a rabbit out of a hat. Tap-tap-tap-tap with me hammer and the lock opens and I tell her, Down to ten seconds now, and she claps, that's right, Corinne claps, and I laugh, and I couldn't give a monkey's then when Kieron says, Aye, very good, Baz, good bump, but what does the lock get out of it, eh? Or Jaz tells Corinne to watch out, cos Baz'll bump owt in sight, won't you Baz? I couldn't give a monkey's, cos nobody else can do it. And they're just jealous.

But so far so good. Cos I'm in the passage now. I'm in the passage and I can't hear owt. No voices. No telly. Nowt. Like there's nobody here. Like nobody lives here. Just like Kieron said. They're all out. And it's there, right in front of us, number 17. I ring the bell and wait a bit. Just in case. And if anybody comes I'll just tell him I've got the wrong flat. But nobody comes. So I ring again and wait a bit more. I stick me ear to the door. But there's nobody there. There can't be. And I've got the bump key in the lock now and me fingers are steady, me wrists are loose. Cos once you've got the key in the lock, all you think about is tappin it just right, not too much, not too little, all you're listenin for is the *click*, *click* that says you've got it taped, you're in charge. And I'm not sure how many taps there's been, but not too many and not too few, I know that much. And the turnin pressure just the same. Just enough to do the job. Like the key's inside me head somewhere. Like it's me mind that's turnin the key. That's where the buzz is.

So when I get into the flat it's like I've already finished the job. And I have, in a way, cos I've done the difficult bit. And it's like I want to hold on to that feelin, cos I know I'm gonna be disappointed. Mebbes it'd be different if I knew this gadgie. Like if he'd knocked us off me own bike. Summick like that. Or if I was gonna nick summick else, summick valuable. And that's why I've not thought, what if the hat's not there? Cos I'm lookin now and I can't see it. I look on the pegs near the door. I look in the cupboards and the drawers and the wardrobe. I go back to the pegs and I start all over again. Pegs. Cupboards. Drawers. Wardrobes. But I do it faster this time, cos there's not much time left. And there's nowt here. There's no Kyle hat. There's no hats at all. Except for a little yellow thing. A kid's hat. Sittin on the glass table in the lounge. And what use is that? What does that prove?

So I look round. Cos what else can I do? I've got to find summick. After all this, I've got to find summick. To prove I've been here. That I've been in the perv's flat. So I go back to the bedroom, to the wardrobes. And one's full of men's stuff and the other one's full of women's stuff. Suits and shirts and dresses and ties and shoes and suchlike. I take a blue one out, cos it looks special, like it's got this shine on it. All silky. And a black one. Cos I reckon these are the suits that count. The ones he wears for posh do's. They're not heavy, mind, not nearly as heavy as I thought they'd be. I thought the fat perv'd have heavy clothes, with him bein a big fat perv, but these are real light. And I start thinkin again, what the fuck am I gonna do with these? What do these prove? Cos they're useless. As useless as a pair of socks. They don't mean owt. So I put them back. And I don't know why, but I try and put them back neat and tidy, all folded again. Mebbes cos I can feel him in them, I can feel the fat perv through his clothes. And that's when me fingers start shakin, when I go to hang his suits back in the wardrobe. And even though I'm tryin to be careful, I start fumblin, me fingers miss the rod, and the suits fall on the floor. And I've not got the time to put them back.

And I go back to the lounge then, and I'm walkin on tip-toe again now, cos it doesn't matter, nobody can see us. And cos that echo's come back, because the floor's all wood, and the wall, the wall with the windows in it, lookin out over the river. It's that red brick again, like the outside's on the inside. And I look around, cos I'm thinkin, mebbes I can take a picture here, just a quick one, I've got me camera phone in me pocket, if I can just find summick, summick that'll show where I am, to prove I've been here, in the right place, his place, the perv's place. Not that I buy the perv thing, mind, I know that's just a joke, that's not what it's all about. But what is there? There's nowt here, just all that red brick. And all the white, the white pillar, the white chairs, the white lampshades, and long low white things, I don't know what you call them. Not tables. Not cupboards.

So I go over to the window, on tip-toe, cos at least I can see the river through the window, and everybody knows the river. And I hold it out in front of us, me camera, workin it this way and that, to get the right angle, so it takes in me and the window and the river, all together. I take one shot and have a look. But me face is just a blur, all dark, like, you can't make out who it is. So I take another one, and another one, until I get the angle. And the face still isn't right, it's really just a smudge, but I'm thinkin mebbes that doesn't matter, not now, cos underneath me face I can see the overalls, like a blob of orange, I can see the Mason's in Mason's Homestores, and mebbes that'll be enough. And I'm thinkin, fuck me, I've still got me overalls on. So I take them off, as fast as I can. And it's like when you try to go too fast, you can't, you're all thumbs, and I'm tearin at the studs and fumblin with me laces. And I'm sweatin again now, me fingers shakin.

But it's done. Me overalls are in the bag. I look at meself in the camera. Just a smudge really. But it'll have to do. Cos there's no time. Cos what else is there? There's nowt here, just the bairn's hat on the glass table. And that looks wrong, lyin there on the table. It shouldn't be there, it should be hangin in the lobby, on one of the pegs. So I pick it up, I go back to the lobby, and I think, which peg will I hang it on? Can you believe it?

And that's where I am, in the lobby, puttin the bairn's hat on the peg, thinkin, that's it, that's all I can do, I'll turn the light out now and I'll be away, when I hear it. The door. Not this door, mind, not the flat door. No, the fire door. I hear the *crick*. And then, aye, then, like straight away, before the fire door's properly shut itself, I hear the flat door. The key turnin. And can you believe it, I still put the hat back on the peg, so that nobody'll think I've been tryin to steal it. And mebbes if I'd not done that, or mebbes if I'd not took the picture of the river, or mebbes if I'd not taken the suits out the wardrobe, then this wouldn't be happenin now. That's what I'm thinkin, although it's too late, of course it's too late. But if I'd not done summick. Or if I'd done it faster. Not the lock, though. No, I couldn't have bumped the lock any faster, that's as fast as it gets. But summick else, then not this, because he's got us by the collar now, and all I want to do is get away, but he's pullin us back inside, back into the flat, he's got us by the collar and he's pullin us back inside. And why, I'm thinkin, why's he doin this, what's the matter with him? And there's no beard and there's no hat, and even now, even here, with his hand round me neck, I'm thinkin it mightn't be too late. I can say, Just give us your hat, mister, that's all I want, your hat. But he's not wearin a hat. And he's pushed us against the pillar now, he's shoutin, I can't hear the words, all I can hear's the shoutin, and the door's still open, I can see it, it's wide open, the key's still in the lock. And he's shoutin that loud, his voice is bouncin back off the walls, and me feet are clumpin on the wooden floor, cos he's pushin us back into the flat again, he's pushed us past the pillar, and I can't stop him. And all this noise he's makin, all this noise I'm makin, after I've been that careful, that quiet. And I think, if I can only stop the noise, just for a bit, just for a minute, if I can just get to the door, if I can just stop him findin the suits. But he's right in me face, yellin, I can feel his spit on me lips. And I don't hit him, not yet. cos all I want to do is get to the door, get out. But he won't get out me way. The daft fuck. And I tell him, 'Let us out, man, I've not done owt.' But he won't. So I tell him again. 'I haven't got owt, man.' And there's somebody else in the passage now, I can hear them. Somebody's voice. So I've got to shut up. I've got to shut him up. And I still don't hit him, I just push him and he falls against the pillar. And that starts him off again, whinin, shoutin. So that's when I've got to hit him, kick him, to shut him up. To get out of here.

Nicky

'How'd you fancy this, Jen?'

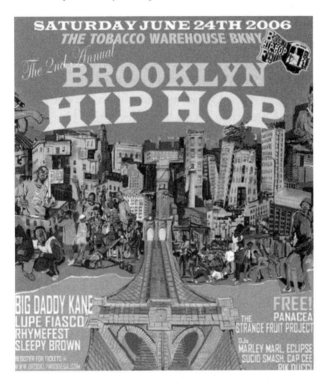

And I'm glad I didn't say anythin to Hol about the Brooklyn thing,
about the house swap, not too much, nothin definite anyway. What
with her mam and everythin. You know, cos she's tied up now.
Cos she can't really leave her, can she, not now? And her mam's
not gonna be comin herself, that's for sure. Which is really sad but
that's how it is and what can you do, cos these things happen. So
I'm glad I've not said anythin to Hol. Nothin definite anyway. I've
not seen her meself, mind, Hol's mam. Cos how could I, the way
things are? But that's what Jen says, cos Jen's mam goes round there
to see her, every now and again. Says it's knocked her back. Really
knocked her back.

'That's Brooklyn, Jen.' I tell her. 'Brooklyn, New York.' And she knows that, she says. She knows things, Jen.

And me mam says, How could he do it? Cos it was in the paper and on the telly and it sounded bad, really bad. That poor man, me mam says, what did he do to anybody? What did he do to get beaten up like that? So I was thinkin it as well, How could you do it, Barry? And I thought, to start with, No, this can't really be you, Barry, it's some other Barry, they've made a mistake, cos you're not like that, this isn't you. But they've not made a mistake. Cos his picture's there, in the paper. And they've said about his clothes, about how they found his overalls in a bag, and there's been pictures of his house, an all, Hol's house, the lot. And everybody wonderin why he hadn't nicked owt.

'Nothing missing,' they said. So how could I go? I mean, with things like they are?

And then me mam says, Why did he do it? What did he think he was doin? But not expectin us to answer, not thinkin I know anythin, just sayin it, cos she can't understand. And that's good, cos if she wanted us to answer her, it'd be really hard then, I'd want to tell her, I'd want to say, Mam, he did it for me. I'd want to tell her, Look, I know it sounds bad, really bad, but he did it for me, Mam. And mebbes, if I told the police that, that it was all for me, that the guy was a perv, that the guy he was lookin for was a perv, mebbes it'd make a difference. And if I could find the real bloke, the one with the hat, and if he could say, Yes, I was there. I don't live there, but I was there, callin on somebody, callin on number seventeen. Mebbes that'd make a difference. But it all gets into a blur then, and I can't think any more.

'So you'll come, Jen, will you?

'Course I will.'

Which is good. And I know we've got to save the money but there's plenty time. And I can tell me mam now. Tell her we're going to Brooklyn. And she'll have somethin to look forward to then.

So I'm glad. I'm glad I didn't promise anythin to Hol. Nothin definite, anyway.

Acknowledgements

Thanks to the Academi for a generous bursary which bought three months of writing time, and to Emma Turnbull, Ruth Dineen and Gwen Davies, who helped me knock the story into shape.

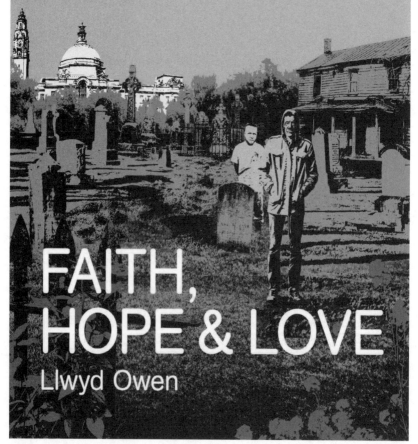

Not unlike the Mike Leigh of Secrets and Lies, pointing out the black holes of family life. An outright talent and natural storyteller. **Martin Davies, Taliesin**

FAITH, HOPE & LOVE
Llwyd Owen

"Well paced, tightly plotted... holds a magnifying glass to the middle classes to highlight their dark underbelly... an unconventional thriller that will linger long in the memory." **Lloyd Jones**

ays the love
of someone

Huw Lawrence

"Compelling, humane, a novel of remarkable delicacy and power."
Michael Symons Roberts

THE

DEER

WEDDING

PENNY SIMPSON

Published October 2010

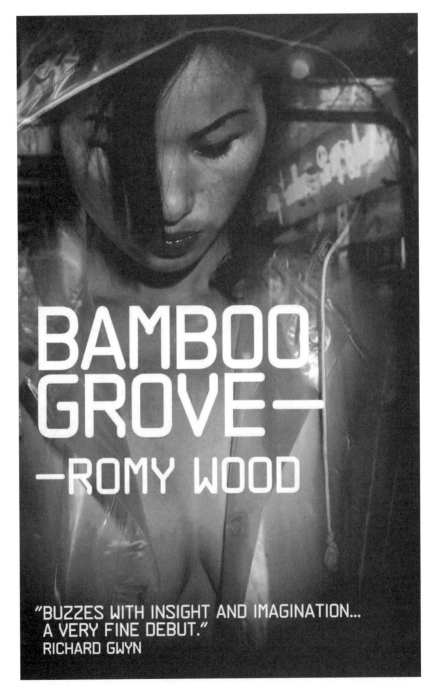

BAMBOO GROVE

—ROMY WOOD

"BUZZES WITH INSIGHT AND IMAGINATION...
A VERY FINE DEBUT."
RICHARD GWYN

Published October 2010

TWENTY THOUSAND SAINTS

Fflur Dafydd

WINNER OF THE PROSE MEDAL –
NATIONAL EISTEDDFOD 2006

Oxfam
Emerging Writer of the Year 09

MxLexia
Woman to Watch 09

SOOTHING MUSIC FOR STRAY CATS

JAYNE JOSO

"Jayne Joso's novel skilfully melds the esoteric and the everyday, the surreal and the banal, to create a strangely gripping narrative full of dark humour. *Soothing Music for Stray Cats* marks the debut of a distinctive voice in contemporary British fiction."

JOE MORAN

"May emerge as one of the great, eccentric London novels ." **TLS**

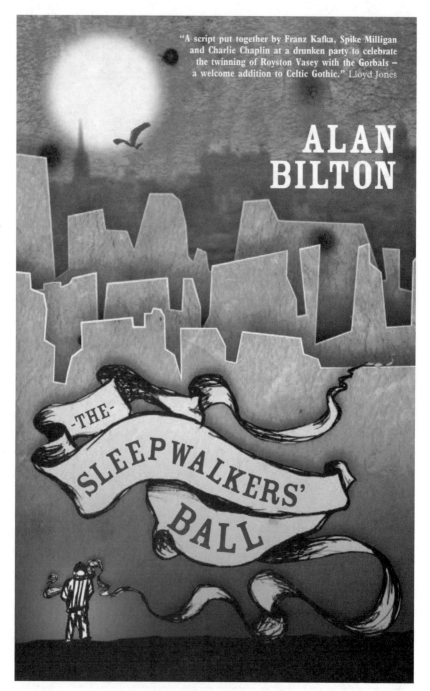

"A script put together by Franz Kafka, Spike Milligan and Charlie Chaplin at a drunken party to celebrate the twinning of Royston Vasey with the Gorbals – a welcome addition to Celtic Gothic." Lloyd Jones

ALAN BILTON

-THE-
SLEEPWALKERS'
BALL

[Uses] mythological structures mixed with street and shop talk… as enchanting as the ball to which the brothers Grimm sent their twelve dancers, wearing out their pretty shoes by morning… Bilton has the craft of an artist." **New Welsh Review**

THE BANQUET OF
ESTHER
ROSENBAUM
PENNY SIMPSON

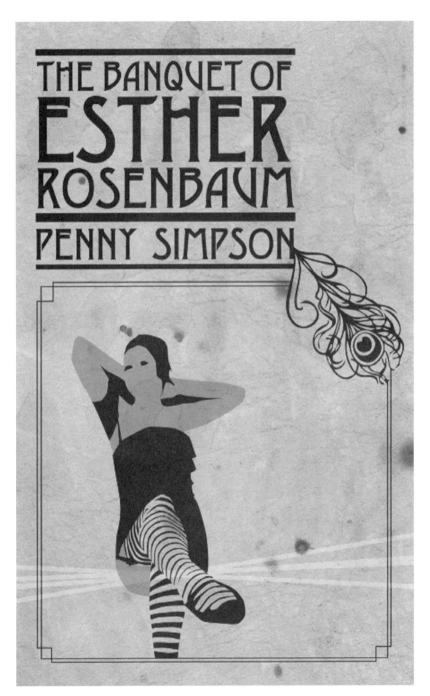

"An extravaganza where the real and the imagined take turn and turn about…
[marked by] humour, verve and hallucinatory strangeness." **TLS**

www.alcemi.eu

Talybont Ceredigion Cymru SY24 5HE
e-mail gwen@ylolfa.com
phone (01970) 832 304
fax 832 782

ALCEMI ⌔